FURBALL

Daniel C Tuck

ISBN-13: 978-1-8383106-0-8

To Cath and Robert.

1

1986.

Delicate fluffy snowflakes drift to the ground, their colour appearing more orange than white as they reflect the glow of the streetlights. They land softly, joining those that have already fallen to form a soft blanket on the roads, pavements and buildings.

A battered old silver Ford screeches down the road, tires squealing, the silence of the night broken, a violent interruption of an oh-so romantic scene.

The car swerves, skidding in the slippery snow.

The driver struggles to gain control of the vehicle, fighting with the road surface. It slides to a halt, right outside the police station.

Other than this car, the road is deserted. No signs of life.

The car door is flung open and Michael Swift steps out from behind the wheel. Twenty-one years old, dressed in a leather jacket and jeans, his face cut and scraped, he looks like he could be an action star, except for the unkempt hair and thick glasses adorning his face. An unlikely hero, perhaps. He looks up and down the street, taking in the sights before him.

Destruction. Everywhere.

The street is a scene of carnage. Cars bashed, huge dents in the sides, unrepairable. Street lamps bent double, having given up the fight against gravity. Round imprints in the metal poles as though they have been knocked into by something - something huge.

Occasional footprints are scattered throughout the snow. Some relatively recent, beginning to be coloured in by the fresh flakes, others older, almost gone.

Some appear to be from someone carefully stepping through the snow, others are spaced further apart; running, perhaps.

Some are human.

Some are not.

The passenger door to the car opens and Amy Wise steps out. Dressed in a similar way to Michael, they could be related, except the way that Michael looks at her isn't one of brotherly affection, but unfulfilled romantic aspirations. Amy brushes her long brown hair from her eyes, wipes flecks of snow from her eyelashes and takes in the scene before them.

She raises a hand to her mouth, shocked at the devastation. All of this destruction had happened within the past couple of hours; it wasn't that long ago since they were last there, in that exact spot, and at that time it looked nothing like this. It probably ended almost as fast as it began.

'Michael…' Amy whispers, unable to know what to say further than that.

As Amy surveys the street, something jumps out of the car to stand beside her. It's only small - little more than a foot high - covered in long, ginger fur. It has sharp claws for hands and flipper-like feet, a peculiar almost comical combination, like a cross between a gopher and a penguin. The strange appearance of the creature, alongside its wide, terrified eyes and its mouth, turned down as though it's upset, make it clear that this strange being is in no way a threat. This animal - this Furball *- appears to be friendly. It, too, inspects its surroundings, wrinkling its small black nose at everything it can see.*

There's nothing good here. Nothing but bad news.

The creature plods through the snow, its flippers making light work of the slippery surface, and heads around the car towards Michael. Amy follows. The three of them stand close to one another; protection against both the freezing temperature and the malicious destructive force that had only recently been at work there. They look around, wide-eyed and terrified, expecting something terrible but hoping it won't come.

'Get help,' Michael tells Amy, pointing towards the police station. 'I'll take a look around, see if there's any sign.'

They look at each other, gazing uncertainly into one another's eyes.

A moment's hesitation.

Michael makes his move: his puts his arm around Amy's waist, pulls her towards him and kisses her for the first time. Thoughts that it could also be the last time cross his mind and he finds himself kissing her more deeply, more passionately, more whole-heartedly, than he could have even imagined. Amy wraps her arms around him, fully envelopes herself in his embrace, sinking into the moment and forgetting about all that has happened so far and all that would be about to happen.

The creature gives them a look. It's almost as if it's embarrassed at the sight, like a child seeing their parents making out. It practically rolls its eyes in their direction.

Amy and Michael pull apart, but continue to stare at one another, the only regret either of them feel is that of not having got together sooner.

'Amy, I...' Michael begins, but can't bring himself to finish the sentence. Not now. It's not the right time. But if not now, when? There might not be another opportunity.

'I know,' Amy tells him.

She pulls Michael closer, kisses him again.

'Be careful,' Amy says.

'You too.'

Michael pulls a gun from the waistband of his jeans, previously concealed by his jacket. Perhaps he is the action hero, after all: he's got a gun, he's got the girl. It's like his whole life has been leading up to this one moment.

'Come on, Fuzz,' Michael says to the creature stood at his feet.

Michael reaches down, lifts up the Furball. Fuzz clambers up Michael, spins around and latches himself on to his shoulders, ready for a ride on Michael's back. It's not the first time he's performed such a manoeuvre.

Michael turns to Amy one more time.

'See you soon.'

'You'd better.'

Michael gives her a sad smile. Reluctantly, he turns and heads towards a dark alley to the side of the police station, the perfect place for something dark and dangerous to be hiding. Fuzz looks back to where Amy stands, watching them go. The creature gives her a small wave. Amy waves back as the distance between them grows longer.

She turns her attention towards the police station: dark and eerily deserted...

The destruction witnessed on the main road continues into the alleyway: bent, broken lamp posts; previously overflowing garbage cans crushed almost beyond recognition, flattened as though sat on by something huge and heavy, the contents left scattered and discarded across the street. A couple of destroyed cars, though it's hard to tell if they were decimated by whatever caused this destruction or if they were already in that state before this new turn of events; it's that kind of an alleyway that gives the impression of bad things happening all the time anyway, despite being in such close proximity to a police station.

Michael holds the gun out in front of himself, attempting to at least give the impression of being in control of the situation. His hand shakes so much that he probably wouldn't be able to hit anything on target anyway. He stays in the shadows, hoping not to be seen by anything that might be lurking in the area. Yet the

4

shadows themselves could contain any number of dangers. Nowhere is safe.

From where he sits on Michael's shoulder, Fuzz peers out, frightened but alert for any possible signs of danger that he needs to warn his friend about. He may be a peculiar creature himself, but he's no monster. Not like the thing they're looking for.

Nothing like that.

A movement within the shadows.

Something creeping.

A larger, darker, shadow emerges, stepping out of the darkness.

Fuzz lets out a fearful squeak, grabbing Michael's attention.

'What is it?'

The creature waves a trembling claw towards the black shape that shuffles towards them. Michael sees it immediately. He raises the gun, points it towards the featureless silhouette. The fear makes it impossible for him to aim straight. He clutches the weapon with both hands, trying in vain to steady himself.

The shadow gets bigger, looms towards them.

Hopeful he's pointing the gun in the right direction, Michael closes his eyes and squeezes the trigger. He flinches before the gun has even gone off, immediately angling his shot off course. It takes more effort to fire than he expects it to, but when it does, the crack of the gun echoes through the dark alley; a crack of thunder at violent odds with the gentle snow fall. The bullet hits a garbage can with a metallic thwack, the damage done by the gun lost amongst the existing carnage.

The shadow steps out of the darkness, holding its hands above its heads.

'Hey, hey, I didn't do nothing!' the shadow exclaims.

Michael squints into the black alley and realises the shadow isn't hostile. It's not the monster they're seeking, but an old man dressed in filthy clothes, skin black with grime, hair dark and greasy. A homeless man, living in the shadows of the alleyway.

Michael realises he's still pointing the gun at the man. He drops it to his side, embarrassed, but also relieved his aim was so terrible. The homeless man shuffles away as quickly as he can, glancing back every now and then to make sure he's not going to be shot at while his back is turned.

'Sorry!' Michael calls after him.

He breathes a sigh of relief, not only that he didn't do any damage to the poor man, but that the danger he had imagined in the shadows wasn't real. Not this time.

Amy ventures through the door to the police station and closes it behind her. She stands in the entrance, dark and empty: not as it should be. Even in a small town like this, there's always a police presence in the station. Always a drunk, or a shop-lifter, or someone who's come in to report their neighbour for being an extra-terrestrial or for practising witchcraft or some other such. But today there is nothing. No movement. No sound. Not even any lights, other than a pair of fluorescent strip lights hanging from the ceiling, partially torn down, flickering like sparks from a bonfire, casting long, dancing shadows one second, allowing the full weight of the darkness to return the next. It looks like the destruction outside had also found its way into this building.

Given the stillness of the place, Amy feels foolish for opening her mouth, but nonetheless she feels she has to try:

'Hello?'

The sound of her voice bounces back at her through the empty building, striking her full force and compelling an involuntary shudder.

Her feet feel like lead, unable or unwilling to move, but she forces them onward, one in front of the other, away from the empty reception desk and into the bull pen where the cops spent the majority of their time whilst in the station.

She squeezes a hand across her mouth before a scream can emerge:

Bodies of dead police officers litter the ground. Broken, bloody, torn apart by some unstoppable violent force of nature. Red streaks splashed across desks, walls and the floor. Some of the officers died with their guns in their hands, ineffective against whatever it was that caused this scene of carnage. It didn't stop at the cops, either: computer screens are smashed, filing cabinets torn apart, trays of donuts trampled and crushed.

A peculiar hissing sound comes from somewhere in the darkness; a rattle snake combined with a gas leak. Amy tries to adjust her eyes to the blackness in front of her as she steps forward, looking for the source of the sound. And in the blackness, something even blacker stirs, slithers, slides.

This time, there's no way Amy can stop the scream from breaking free.

Even from around the corner in the alleyway, Amy's scream is unmistakable, ringing out and piercing through the silence. Fuzz is first to react to the sound, letting out a worried yelp. Michael spins around and cries out her name. His fear is replaced by the need to protect the woman he loves, whatever the cost. He runs, sliding in the snow, to the end of the alley, skids around the corner towards the police station.

He only slows down once he reaches the building, a wave of fear hitting him as he approaches.

Something doesn't feel right.

Not that anything about this evening has felt "right".

He puts his hand on the door, bracing himself to enter the building, when the front window explodes outward. Something large flies out from within the building. Michael instinctively raises his arms in front of his face as shards of glass shower outward, a sharp horizontal blizzard coming from where the window was moments ago. Michael ducks, lands on the ground, sharp splinters falling from the sky around him, piercing the snow. Fuzz has fallen from his back. Michael moves to wrap his body around the creature, protecting him from the flying debris. Once he's sure that the violent shower has stopped, Michael lifts his head, looks around, first at the place where the police station window once had been, then across at whatever it was that had burst through the window with such force.

A crumpled form lays on the ground, the snow around it slowly changing from the purest of whites to a deep red.

Michael unsteadily gets to his feet. He picks shards of glass from his clothes, out of his skin. He's bleeding, but it's nothing that won't heal. His leg is hurt: he can walk on it, but it's painful and it's definitely going to slow him down.

He approaches the bleeding shape.

He knows what it is before he can even see it clearly for himself.

'No,' he whispers to himself and forces his legs to move faster.

'I'm so sorry,' he says as he crouches next to Amy's body.

He collapses beside her, lifts her head into his lap and strokes her hair. Tears fall from his eyes. He'd loved her from the day he first met her, all the way back in high school. There was no way he could have talked to her back then; he had even less confidence at that time than he did now, and even the thought of embarrassing himself was enough to paralyse him with fear. It was only the events of the past few days that had finally brought them together, finally brought Amy to notice him (or so he believed: secretly, Amy had always had something of a crush on him, despite - or perhaps because of - his goofy, awkward ways), and now it was too late. He should have taken the chance when he had it, all that time ago, and, perhaps, they could have had more than this short time together.

"Better to have loved and lost than to have never loved at all," so the saying goes. It doesn't feel that way when your heart is broken into a million pieces like shards of an exploding window.

'I'm so sorry,' Michael repeats.

Amy's eyes flutter open weakly.

'Amy!'

He gently rubs her cheeks, runs his hands up and down her arms, as though those physical motions might be the key to keeping *her alive.*

'Stay with me, Amy. Stay with me.'

'You have to kill it,' Amy tells him. 'You have to…'

Her eyes close again. Her head slumps.

She's gone.

Fuzz puts his tiny, furry claw in Amy's hand, but even the creature knows that it's too late. It wipes tears from its big brown eyes, looks to Michael for guidance. Michael, too, wipes tears away. His jaw sets, his eyes harden. He gets to his feet and looks down at Fuzz.

'Stay here,' he tells the creature.

Fuzz shakes his head firmly, lets out a sound of 'nuh-uh'.

No way.

'It's too dangerous.'

Fuzz crosses his arms, looks sternly at Michael. There's no time to argue. Michael sighs, picks up the furball and places him on his shoulders.

The two of them march across to the police station.

Michael picks up his gun, fallen in the snow beside the building when Amy was thrown through the window. There's no point in opening the door, with the whole of the front of the police station now laying scattered in the snow outside: a gaping hole through which they can easily climb without any additional effort.

It's as dark and still as it was when Amy went in there. No sound, no movement.

'Where are you?' Michael yells into the dark void in front of them, fear displaced by a thirst for revenge.

No response is forthcoming.

Michael's had enough. He lifts the gun, fires wildly into the darkness beyond, screams one long scream as the flash of the gun illuminates the scene for the briefest moment, time and time again, the recoil of the weapon a welcome reminder of the power he wields in his hand. He squeezes the trigger again and again and again, continuing to squeeze it as the gun replies with the click-click-

click *that indicates it has run out of ammunition. Michael keeps the gun held out as if the mere sight of it could provide some protection against the evil that lurks in the shadows.*

Still clinging to Michael's back, Fuzz lets out a sympathetic purr of sorts.

Michael looks back at his furry friend. They share a look of unspeakable sadness, the loss hitting both of them equally hard. Michael reaches around and pulls Fuzz from his back, cradles him in his arms. They slide down behind a large desk, the broken contents of which litter the floor. Out of sight, hopefully out of danger. Michael puts a hand to his face, winces as he touches a wound from the spraying glass. He looks at his fingers, his blood all too real on his fingertips. He can't help but think of Amy, laying there outside, dead, cold and alone. He feels bad for leaving her there, but if he gets out of this in one piece he'll go back to her and make sure she is properly taken care of.

Perhaps, given the circumstances, she got off lightly. Perhaps death is an easier option than whatever it is he's going to have to face in this dark building.

Or perhaps he should stop feeling sorry for himself, and do something about it so that Amy's death isn't for nothing.

He moves Fuzz, carefully placing the creature so that he's underneath the desk, hidden. He crawls to the end of the desk. He peers around the corner and immediately jumps back.

At the back of the room, lurching in their direction is a large, drooling monster. Long rubbery tentacles, a greyish shade of blue, extrude from the creature. They move independently of one another, feeling around the space, picking things up, crushing them, searching, investigating, looking for something. Or someone. The creature uses its tentacles to drag itself along the floor, one slimy suckered tentacle at a time.

Michael turns to look at Fuzz. The creature looks to him for support, but Michael can't summon any words of encouragement this time.

'I don't think we're getting out of this one, buddy,' he tells the Furball.

Fuzz climbs back up on to his lap, rests itself against him and allows itself to be petted.

The monster bellows in the darkness, a great, terrifying sound filled with hate and violence, in parts deep and guttural, but with a shrill, screaming sound layered over the top. Michael closes his eyes against the sound, as if that could possibly block it. The tears he had been trying to hold back can no longer be stopped. He's battered, exhausted and beaten.

Fuzz looks around, unsure what to do. He certainly doesn't want to sit there and wait to die.

There must be something they can do.

Something…

And there it is. A large fire axe mounted to the wall of the station, the glass case containing it already smashed open, presumably by the flailing tentacles of the monster, or perhaps by a police officer looking for something to defend themselves with moments before they were killed.

A foot high furball with an axe against a gigantic, tentacled, drooling beast. The odds aren't exactly in Fuzz's favour, but he has to try. He climbs down from Michael's lap, goes over to the axe. He has to jump to even be able to get hold of it, but he succeeds, hanging from the bottom of the handle as though he were swinging on a vine. It's a struggle, but he somehow manages to pull it loose from its support. The axe falls to the floor. Fuzz picks it up. It takes all his effort to hold it - the thing is twice, three times, as big as him. But the sheer tenacity of this creature is enough to overcome. Michael opens his eyes, notices Fuzz is gone. He looks around and sees him standing there holding the axe. He realises what Fuzz is going to do. It's too much for the little guy to take on on his own; he couldn't possibly do it alone.

Michael tries to push himself up to his feet, but immediately collapses back down again, trying desperately to hold in a cry of pain. He clutches his side. Blood seeps through his sweater. He's weak; more injured than he realised. He looks across again at Fuzz. The creature is more determined than ever; it's clear from his face that he means business.

Michael knows it's the only chance - however slim it might be - that they have.

'Give 'em hell, little guy,' he tells his friend.

The furball's eyes narrow as he steps backward, away from the desk they've been hiding behind: in full view of the monster.

The tentacled beast roars at the sight of its tiny opponent.

Fuzz isn't dissuaded: he roars back as best as he can, though it's little more than a squeak compared with the ferocity of the monster.

Fuzz lifts the fire axe as high as he is able.

He runs towards the monster.

The monster lurches on its tentacles towards Fuzz.

They move closer and closer.

Shortening the space between the two of them.

Fuzz lifts the axe that little bit higher.

And —

2

The movie paused, the screen freezing at that exact moment: the beginning of an epic battle between a foot high Furball wielding a fire axe twice its size and a snarling, drooling, multi-tentacled psychopathic beast. The convention hall audience knew exactly how it played out, most of them having seen *Furballs* several times over but there were still disappointed cries from the attendees when the film stopped. After a moment showing the now infamous image of the creatures launching themselves at one another - the one shot that sold the movie to audiences around the world when it was first released back in the 1980s - the *Furballs* logo appeared on the screen, superimposed on top of the image.

A smattering of applause came from the small collection of Fuzz devotees in attendance at Geek Fest. The popularity of the series was gradually dwindling, and there couldn't have been more than fifty people in the hall, all spread apart as if they were likely to catch something from one another, making the hall look emptier than it actually was. Even the recent wave of 80s nostalgia hadn't done much to bring the series back in any serious way.

Zach "Furball" Keary sat on the stage alongside the host for the panel - some kid in his twenties named Dalton of all things. Zach was now fifty-one years old, thirty years older, greyer, and not as lean as he was when he starred in the original *Furballs*. He hated the nickname he had been given. "Furball". How unoriginal. The tabloids had started calling him Furball Keary after the success of the movies, and during the albeit brief period in which the fame had gone to his head, and he had gone through the stereotypical drinking and drugs phase. He had quickly learned his lesson on that one, and had grown out of that time of his life. But, somehow, the nickname had stuck.

Over the intervening years, Zach had done more than his share of these panels. He could practically do them in his sleep these days. The same tired questions. The same exhausted answers. The same responses to the same answers to the same questions. Sure, the panel was dedicated to *Furballs*, but he wished once in awhile someone would ask him something about his *other* work. Work of which he was proud. Work for which the critics had proclaimed him as actually being (begin quote) "surprisingly good" (end quote). Admittedly, they were few and far between, but nevertheless it would be refreshing to talk about those for a change.

But, no: it always came back to *Furballs*. The movie that made him a household name, alongside the damned creature that he had a love/hate relationship with. Without Fuzz he probably wouldn't have a career. But without Fuzz he wouldn't have *this* career, known only as "that guy from those *Furballs* movies".

Zach glanced across at the seat beside him on the stage, between himself and Dalton. A chair reserved solely for the use of his Fuzz cuddly toy. Of course he had to bring it to each of these events: the fans wanted nothing more than to get their photo taken with Michael and Fuzz. Not just Michael; it *had* to be with Fuzz as well. If it was Michael alone, Zach could see the look of disappointment in their eyes. Hell, they'd probably even turn up to a Q&A with just the damn toy; at least they could imagine it giving the answers they wanted to hear, rather than the ones Zach provided.

Zach shifted in his seat, fixed a smile to his face, turned to look at the screen, taking in the still frame from the movie as though for the first time.

'That still gets me every time,' he told the audience.

Laughter from the crowd as he brushed a fake tear from his eye.

Same old. Same old.

Dalton laughed for a bit too long and brushed a (real? imaginary?) tear from his own eye.

'I'm sorry, Zach,' the interviewer said to his guest, voice oozing with fake regret, 'but I can't let you go without asking the inevitable question.'

Here we go, Zach thought. *Sequel talk.*

He fished the rehearsed answers to the questions from his memory bank, allowed himself to look interested, even puzzled about where the line of questioning could possibly be going.

'Oh? What's that?'

A titter of laughter from the audience. *They know what's coming, they know the answer I'm going to give, but they're hoping, hoping,* hoping *I'd choose this tiny little Geek Fest in the middle of God only knows what town I'm in today to announce the news they've been wanting to hear for twenty or so years. Gotta disappoint them once more.*

'This year is the 30th anniversary of the original *Furballs*,' Dalton continued.

'It is?' Zach feigned surprise. More cued laughter from the audience.

'It is,' Dalton continued. 'Can you tell us, once and for all, definitively: is *Furballs 3* ever going to happen? And if it does, what will your involvement be?'

Zach could feel the audience shifting in their seats, trying to close the gap between him and them, making it a more personal experience. *Let today be the day it's announced. Come on, come on, do it already.* He gave them a few seconds of anticipation as he pretended to think about his answers. *Perhaps he's working out what he's allowed to say? Perhaps he's building up to a huge announcement?*

'Yes, the movie will eventually happen,' Zach told the assembled crowd.

There was a collective intake of breath, smiles twitching at the edges of people's mouths.

'Yes, I'm sure I'll have to be a part of it,' he continued.

He's on the verge of announcing it...

'And, no, I don't know when it will be,' Zach finished.

The audience sighed, the inevitable sense of disappointment changing the whole atmosphere in the room. A few of them even got up and left at that point, as if Zach has personally, deliberately hurt or offended them in some way.

'But you're not handing over the *Furballs* reigns just yet?' Dalton asked him, clutching at something - anything - to keep the remainder of the audience interested.

'They couldn't really do it without me, could they? You think *Furballs*, you picture this face, right? Or, at least, a younger version of it. Even if I'm in it for half an hour only to be killed by a bolt of lightning, I'll do it. Like it or not.'

Dalton breathed a sigh of relief as he felt the room shifting back to being onboard. *Zach Keary says he'll do the next* Furballs *movie*: that was headline news as far as they were concerned, never mind the fact that Zach had been saying the same thing for the past twenty years or so. As far as they were concerned, it was a done deal; the cameras could officially start rolling tomorrow. Dalton smiled, relaxed a little.

'I think one more question from the audience, after which we can let you go.'

Zach glanced at his watch as half a dozen hands shot up in the audience. He frowned and leaned towards Dalton, covering his microphone.

'We were supposed to be done five minutes ago.'

'Last one. I promise.'

Dalton scanned the room, pointed to a woman towards the back wearing an original *Furballs* t-shirt a couple of sizes too small for her, way past its wear-by date, the colours faded and the print cracked from over-use. A technician trudged over to the woman, who eagerly snatched the microphone that was being handed to her straight out of his hands. Practically shivering with excitement, she stood up, gripping the microphone with two sweaty hands.

'Hi Zach,' she exhaled. 'Big fan. Me, I mean. I'm a big fan. Of yours.'

'Thank you,' Zach replied, looking down towards his lap, a shy smile on his face; practised timidity.

The woman wiggled her fingers in a peculiar, nervous wave towards the Fuzz cuddly toy.

'Hi, Fuzz,' she giggled, embarrassed but also thrilled to have the opportunity to speak to one of millions of stuffed toys that had been mass-produced over the past three decades. Zach's original got wrecked (perhaps deliberately, who can say?) some time ago, and had in fact been replaced many times over the intervening years.

'What's your question?' Dalton asked, trying to bring the woman's focus back.

'I was wondering,' she said, peeling her attention away from Fuzz and back to Zach. 'The way you're talking, would you *rather* be struck by lightning, like, in real life, than do *Furballs 3*?'

She fixed him with a glare. Almost daring him to give her the answer she was implying to be the truth. Zach had heard all the accusations before. He'd seen them in print before the Internet even existed, and since the Internet, there was barely a day that went by without him being vilified as the one person who has single-handedly halted the continuation of the *Furballs* franchise, denouncing it as something he wished to God he had never done, and - possibly - rumours of him burning *Furball* toys on an altar as a sacrifice to the gods of Hollywood that he should be given a second chance to do something *real*. Most of that was true, sure, but he'd never admitted it out loud, and certainly not to anyone who might make his feelings public.

He felt the whole room staring at him. Once again waiting with bated breath. The Twitter generation, looking for something, anything, to be angry about.

Not today, guys.

'No, no, I'd do it,' he told them, ever-professional smile spread on his face. 'Of course I'd do it. For one reason. You want to know why?'

The woman nodded her head so hard it could have rattled. 'Uh-huh.'

'Money. Plain and simple.'

The woman's mouth dropped open. An uncomfortable silence spread throughout the room. How could he - *the Michael Swift* - only be in it for the money? How could he not love this creation, this series, this fandom, he had helped bring to life? What right does he have to even be paid for doing something other people could only *dream* about doing? How could one man be so goddamned *selfish*?

Zach had only dropped the money comment as a half-joke, but he could immediately see it had back-fired. He glanced across at Dalton. Even the kid looked disappointed.

Zach held up his hands in mock surrender.

'I'm joking, I'm joking,' he laughed. 'Of *course* I would do it. And do you want to know the *real* reason why?'

The woman looked around at the rest of the audience as if looking for their encouragement, some support after she extracted such a disappointing answer from her idol. Eventually, she gave her head a small nod: yes, she would like to know.

'I would do it so that I could do more events like this, of course!'

The room erupted - as much as a one-sixth full room can erupt - in spontaneous applause. *Good save*, he congratulated himself. That could have been a disaster for the autograph table and photoshoot later in the day. These days, that was his only source of regular income, and the only reason he agreed to do events like this.

Other than meeting the fans.

Obviously.

'Well, all that's left to do is say a huge "thank you" to Zach "Furball" Keary,' (Zach glared at his host at that particular moment), 'and to thank all of you for coming.'

Even as Dalton wrapped up proceedings, Zach began unclipping his microphone. He smiled and waved to the audience, stood and skipped off the stage before they could mob him with requests for a "quick selfie" or "just one autograph, *pleeeeease*" without going through the officially sanctioned route of paying for it at his table.

If you can do something for money and people are willing to pay for it, why would anyone do it for free?

Having his photo taken with fans was always Zach Keary's least favourite part of an event like this one. But it also tended to be his most lucrative. At $30 a time for a photograph, and another $20 for an autograph, he was going to keep doing it for as long as there was the demand. People weren't exactly queuing around the block for him these days, not like they used to, but he could usually make an easy couple of thousand dollars in a day.

It would be easier if the actual fans didn't have to be there, though.

Zach waited in the photo booth, Fuzz cuddly toy held resting in his hands. He had learnt the hard way that he shouldn't hold it by its foot, dangling at his side, tapping it like a metronome against his leg; it might hurt the poor creature, apparently. A happy-to-be-here smile remained tattooed across his face until his cheeks hurt from the effort and it felt as though he would never be able to relax his facial muscles ever again.

A woman tiptoed into the photo booth, practically beside herself to be in his presence (or was it Fuzz's presence? Zach was never sure these days).

'Hi,' Zach greeted her.

'Hi,' she sighed with a joy Zach couldn't even begin to fathom.

'Closer,' the photographer instructed.

The woman inched closer to Zach, still leaving a gap, as if it was against protocol to approach such Hollywood royalty. Accidental touching of the celebrity would result in execution.

They held Fuzz between them, smiling at the camera, her with a genuine sunshine beam spread across her face; him forced, dead-eyed.

The flash went off, dazzling Zach. He'd better get used to those white spots clouding his vision; there was a queue outside.

The woman turned to him.

'Thank you so much,' she said.

'You're welcome.'

She hesitated for a moment, then decided it was now or

never: her one short - the opportunity of a lifetime! She flung herself at Zach, wrapping her arms around him, crushing him against her sweaty, nervous body. Zach could do nothing but allow it to happen. He patted her on the back.

'Next,' the photographer called, a clear sign to the woman that her intimate encounter with her favourite star was at an end.

'I'm sorry,' she said. 'Thank you. I'm sorry.'

She stumbled away, dazed, happy, almost forgetting to collect the photo on the way out.

As she left, a large man entered the booth, a good head and shoulders taller than Zach and almost twice as wide.

He extended a large hand, gripped Zach's in his own and shook it vigorously.

'Still one of my favourite movies, man,' he told Zach.

'Thank you.'

'You're awesome.'

'I appreciate that.'

The fan continued his firm grip on Zach even as the photograph was taken, shaking it over and over again until it was all done. Once released, Zach flexed his fingers, easing the blood flow through his hand back to normal.

The end of the day had rolled around. Zach went to the bathroom and scrubbed his hands thoroughly. Not that there was necessarily anything unclean or infectious about his fans, but after shaking so many hands in such a short space of time - many of them clammy and sticky from the excitement of meeting their hero - his own hands felt as though they were sorely in need of being disinfected.

As the hot water from the tap scalded his skin, he looked up at himself in the mirror above the sink. It was always so strange seeing himself in that film from thirty years ago - so young, so much hope and promise, so many future opportunities for doing great things - and then to see himself as he was now. Still the same in some ways, but very different in others. Older. Greyer. Less sparkle in his eyes, but more wrinkles underneath them. Where had those thirty years gone? What was going to be his legacy? He had never thought he would end up being best remembered as the star of a monster movie for kids.

He shook the water from his hands and sighed at his reflection in the mirror.

This was it. This was his life.

Nothing much he could do to change that.

Zach knocked on the office door backstage at the conference centre and let himself in without waiting for a reply. Inside, Dalton sat behind a desk, pouring over figures on a spreadsheet on the computer. He glanced up as Zach entered.

'Oh, hey,' he barely acknowledged Zach's presence before turning back to the screen.

'That's me done,' Zach told him.

'Cool.'

Zach stood in the doorway, waiting for more from the kid. Less than half Zach's age, Dalton seem to think he was in charge of everything. Just because he organised the event, that didn't mean he was in charge. It was the stars like Zach who were in charge. If they didn't turn up, there would be no event. They *made* the event. Dalton did the paperwork. The way he was making Zach wait, Dalton clearly didn't understand the true order of the world in which he was playing.

Eventually looking away from the computer, Dalton glanced back towards Zach. He looked confused for a second, as if he hadn't expected Zach to still be there.

'I need…' Zach began.

'Oh, yeah, sure,' Dalton jumped to his feet as if he had

genuinely forgotten about something.

Not likely, Zach thought.

Dalton rifled through a pile of envelopes on his desk and took one across to Zach. Zach peeled it open, pulled out the check from inside. He looked from the check to Dalton, back again. Dalton, meanwhile, looked anywhere other than directly at Zach.

'I think there's been a mistake,' Zach told him.

'Tell me about it; you're not cheap!' Dalton laughed. *Ha ha. Funny guy.*

'Come on, man,' Zach whined. 'What are you doing? This is less than last time.'

Dalton shrugged, headed back to the relative safety of behind his computer. He clicked around on the spreadsheet for a moment and turned the screen in Zach's direction, trying to indicate something on the screen Zach had no interest in looking at.

'Our payment policy reflects the anticipated audience response towards any of our guests.'

A well-rehearsed line. Corporate BS written out carefully by a law firm to try and sound like something that couldn't be contested.

'Which means?'

'Which means people give even less of a crap about you this year than they did last time. Ergo, you get less money than you did last time.'

The kid even had the audacity to finish the sentence with a smug smile. Like the show's investors were watching, listening, saying *you've done good, kid* into a hidden earpiece as they fed him his lines on how to calm the "talent" into taking less money.

'It's not what we agreed,' Zach tried to argue.

Dalton stood and came around from his side of the desk once again.

'I think you'll find, if you read the small print on your contract, it's *exactly* what we agreed.'

Dalton headed straight past Zach and held the door ajar for him. A clear indication that he was expected to leave.

'I want to thank you for giving up your valuable time to be here today and meet your fans,' he said, resuming his calm, robotic, well-rehearsed manner. 'I hope you'll join us again in the future.'

Zach stared at the kid for a long moment.

'Seriously?'

'Give the people what they want,' Dalton said to him, dangerously veering away from any scripted response. 'Make *Furballs 3*. Maybe then they'll care about you again.'

3

The bar was mercifully quiet for eight o'clock on a Saturday night. A few groups of friends scattered around the tables, a couple of lonely souls propping up the bar, a handful of kids trying their luck with the staff to buy alcohol. Zach found himself amongst the throngs of the solitary bar-proppers. He had taken an hour long cab ride away from the conference centre purely to make sure that none of those he had met throughout the day would be around. Somehow a handshake and a photo with Zach made some of them feel as though they were suddenly best friends, and entitled to having a drink with - or, preferably, bought by - him. Zach kept his head down, trying to delay the inevitable recognition for as long as possible, only showing his face when necessary to do so. Such as topping up his glass with another cold one.

Speaking to his manager on his cellphone at the same time as drinking was never a good idea. With some alcohol in his blood stream, Zach was inclined to be more forceful in his opinions about whatever new casting call he was about to be put forward for. To be fair, Richard Spengler was more than his manager; he was Zach's best, probably only, friend; his confidante, his conscience, his occasional drinking partner. Spengler was also, of course, always out for his fifteen percent of Zach's earnings, and the bigger that fifteen percent turned out to be, the better.

Zach felt himself become more agitated as their conversation progressed. The third beer working its magic.

'How is *Vampire Grannies 3* any different to *Vampire Grannies 2*?' he demanded from Spengler.

His manager made a wise-ass response.

'Other than the title,' Zach sighed. 'Other than the title, how are they different? I said no to the last one, I'm saying the same for this.'

Richard Spengler was sitting behind his desk in his office as he spoke to his client on the phone. He had it on speakerphone, leaving his hands free to fill in the day's crossword in the newspaper and toss the occasional salted peanut through the air and into his mouth. He tapped his pencil against the clue for four down: *No longer young, you forever leave work*. Ten letters.

'Budget, my friend,' he told Zach. 'That's how they're different. Did you hear me tell you what they're willing to pay for you to appear in this movie? Did you hear the sound of all of those zeroes?'

'It's not enough,' came Zach's response, tinny through the speakerphone, the voice sounding as distant to Spengler as the gap between his and Zach's ideas of what a good idea for Zach's career could be. 'It's not about the money. You know that.'

Spengler sighed. He ran his fingers through the little bit of dark hair that continued to cling for dear life to the sides of his head. He had known this was going to be the attitude he got for even suggesting this particular job. Sure, it was going to be a terrible film. *Terrible.* But there was a pre-made audience, poised and ready to buy their tickets as soon as they went on sale. There was a studio and distribution deal in place. The cameras were ready to roll, mere days away from beginning to shoot. One or two last minute casting decisions to be made and they would be set. The whole thing would be wrapped and in theatres by Christmas. The *Vampire Grannies* series had never been intended as anything serious; they were those self-consciously bad movies, intended to be watched with a group of drunken friends, something that would appeal to the midnight movie crowd who wanted little more than fun, gore and cheap thrills.

There was no way Zach was going to say yes. Spengler knew that. But what kind of a manager would he be if he didn't throw anything that came up in his client's direction?

'Come on, Zach,' he said, chewing the end of his pencil, staring down at the blank spaces in the crossword. 'You're going to have to take a new job soon. It may as well be this one.'

'I will,' came the reply. 'When something comes along that fits the plan.'

'The plan.'

Spengler sighed again. Zach hadn't worked in years. Still holding out for that "important" role that was going to re-shape his career as a serious actor. The kind of role that would win plaudits from the critics but never actually make any money because no one wants to go to the movies to be depressed. Spengler knew Zach's financial position only too well. He was essentially living off of the continued revenue from *Furballs*, and occasional appearances at conventions, all of which were slowing down year on year. Any time soon it would all dry up. Zach couldn't live off of it forever. Neither could Spengler. At sixty-four years young, Spengler was looking forward to the next chapter in his life and wanted to make sure the funds were in place to be able to make the most of it. If that meant being manager to the star of *Vampire Grannies 3* then so be it.

'I can't keep doing this low-budget horror crap.'

Spengler winced at Zach's choice of words. True horror fans never thought of his movies as *crap*. Some people liked them more than others, sure, and, yeah, there was the usual group who thought they were above them, and only admitted watching anything the studios branded as "elevated horror" because they wanted the critics not to immediately dismiss it. *True* horror fans would watch anything. They wouldn't immediately cast something aside as being "crap". They would find the merits in anything: "yeah, the plot's terrible, the acting's hammy, but did you *see* that kill?". Every movie was somebody's favourite. Sometimes it was hard to find that one person, or they were too embarrassed to admit it. But *every single movie* has its fans.

'*Can't* keep doing it or *won't* keep doing it?' Spengler asked.

'Pick one.'

'What you *can't* keep doing is not working.'

'You don't think what I've been doing today is work? Have you *seen* these people I have to deal with?'

Again with the contempt for his fans. Spengler sometimes wondered why he kept Zach on as a client. Zach turned down most work Spengler found for him. There was the constant threat that he would say something to upset a fan, which would make it in to the less reputable "news" outlets, causing even more of a rift between Zach and the public. The man was so damn stubborn. His financial situation steadily getting worse, Spengler would have thought Zach would bring himself to do at least one of these movies to pay the bills. It was all he had left to bargain with: money.

'When you do a low-budget horror, do you know where most of the budget goes?' Spengler asked his client over the telephone.

'Not on the script, that's for sure.'

Spengler stood up from behind his desk and headed across

to a small refrigerator in the corner of his office. He pulled out a cold bottle of Coke, knocked the lid off against the side of his desk and took a gulp.

'To you,' he told Zach. 'The bulk of the budget goes to the talent - that's you. And fifteen percent of that comes to me. Half the time the only way any of these movies gets made is if a name star is attached to the project.'

'Let Nic Cage do *Vampire Grannies 3* then.'

'He did the second one. They want fresh meat for the three-quel. Apparently they're willing to pay you more than they did Nic.'

'Why?'

'Beats me.'

Spengler could feel Zach thinking it through at the other end of the line. Perhaps if he kept pushing, this time he could actually be persuaded. Perhaps if -

'I feel like I need to do something more respectable,' Zach declared firmly.

Spengler sighed again. He'd heard that line so many times. What was "respectable" anyway? It was only certain critics and snobs who had decided horror movies weren't a "respectable" art form. The idea of one genre being more respectable than another was a completely irrational construct designed to make one group of people feel more important and high-brow than another.

'You know I have a plan too?' Spengler told Zach, staring down at the crossword clue that had been bugging him for the past half an hour. 'It involves getting my clients plenty of well-paid jobs so I can put my feet up one of these days.'

He hung up before Zach had a chance to respond, the answer to the clue staring him straight in the face: *No longer young, you forever leave work - RETIREMENT*. Wasn't that a cosmic kick in the crotch.

* * *

Zach threw his cellphone on to the bar top in frustration. He couldn't believe Spengler had hung up on him. Perhaps he *was* being stubborn, but it was *his* career, *his* reputation, *his* brand he was trying to protect, reshape and form into something more respectable than horror movie star. Zach glanced across the room and noticed someone at a table in the bar staring across at him. The guy, open-mouthed, half drunk, turned to his friends at the table, and jabbed an excited finger towards Zach. *Dammit.*

'Hey! Furball!' he yelled across the bar, drawing the attention of the rest of the patrons.

Zach grabbed his cellphone, put it against his ear and pretend to be engaged in a conversation.

'Okay, sure… Uh huh… Yeah.'

A tap on his shoulder. Zach looked around to find the guy from the table standing right beside him.

'I'm Steve,' he announced.

Zach smiled with all the politeness he could muster, turned away again.

Another tap on his shoulder.

'You're that guy, aren't you? You're Furball?'

Zach pointed to his cell phone and shrugged an apology, hoping half-drunk Steve would get the hint. One thing Zach had found over the years, though, was that fans - especially those who had had a few drinks - weren't easily dissuaded.

'Do the line,' Steve told him.

Zach looked around and noticed the rest of Steve's table creeping over to join their friend. Zach put his hand over his phone as if shielding the imaginary person on the other end of the line from hearing anything taking place in the bar.

'Sorry guys, I'm a little busy right now,' he told them.

'Come on, man - say it! Say the line!'

The rest of the table joined in with chants of "Say it! Say it! Say it!" By then half the bar was staring in their direction.

Some people were pointing, nodding their heads in Zach's direction, murmurs of recognition drifting around the room as they slowly recalled that movie they'd seen him in when they were kids. Cellphones were emerging from pockets. Cameras poised. Zach knew he was fighting a losing battle. He couldn't afford to have a disagreeable confrontation with a fan go viral. He was going to have to play along. Almost forgetting that he was pretending to be on a call, he went to put his cell phone down, but suddenly remembered:

'I'll call you back,' he said into the phone, then turned to give his full attention to the group. He sighed, took a breath.

'Give 'em hell, little guy,' he recited for the billionth time, with an emotionless delivery.

The crowd from Steve's table whooped and applauded, Steve slapping Zach on the back in appreciation, all of them acting as though it was the greatest thing they had ever heard. Cries of "Furball! Furball!" were chanted across the bar as though he were a wrestler winning a fight. Zach, meanwhile, could do little more but sit there with a half-smile on his face, feeling like little more than a performing monkey. He gave a mock bow.

'Thank you, thank you.'

He turned back to his drink, shifting his attention to the bar mat in front of him, trying not to prolong contact with these people any more than strictly necessary. Spengler would be proud: he gave the fans what they wanted and he wasn't rude about it. You can bet Nic Cage wouldn't have acted so professionally.

Much to Zach's dismay, Steve didn't go away. Instead, he pulled up a stool beside Zach at the bar, indicated for another beer, and pushed himself so close to this bona-fide movie star that Zach could feel the man's alcohol-filled breath on his face.

'You drinking alone, Furball?' Steve breathed, the slurred

words floating on a beery cloud towards Zach.

Zach glanced at his watch. Feigning surprise at the time it showed, he threw back the last couple of mouthfuls of his drink.

'I have to leave, actually,' he told his new best friend.

'Come on, man! Join us for a beer. We're all big fans.'

Steve's table watched him closely, waiting for his reply. Zach decided to have a little fun.

'If you're fans, name three of my movies.'

Steve's table of friends oooh-ed at the challenge he'd been set. Zach sat smiling, arms folded, waiting, practically able to hear Steve try to fish something - anything - out of the deep, dark recesses of his brain.

'Right, right, okay,' Steve said, fumbling around. 'There's that one with that fluffy thing. Then there's that other one, you know, with that woman, who could do the things. And there's that one that's the second part of that first one with the fluffy thing.'

Weirdly, Zach knew exactly what he meant. *Furballs*, obviously, even though he couldn't remember the title, despite previously addressing Zach as "Furball". Next was *The Witch's Sister* (a surprisingly deep-cut selection from Steve there, relatively unknown amongst Zach's lesser fans). The final movie, more likely than not, must have been *Furballs 2*. Steve's table cheered. Despite the lack of titles provided, in their minds he'd managed to "name" three films successfully. It was clear to Zach there wasn't going to be an easy way out of the situation. He sighed.

'Fine. I'll join you. But I have to use the bathroom first.'

Zach collected his things together, pulled his jacket on and headed towards the bathroom.

Steve followed.

'Alone, please?'

The man stopped, letting him go to urinate in peace.

* * *

The bathroom was pitch black, without a single light switched on and only the barest amount of illumination spilling in from the corridor outside, and the slightest orange glow from streetlamp coming from a small window in the far wall. Zach fumbled in the darkness, feeling against the wall for a switch, hoping and praying he wouldn't accidentally put his hand in anything unsanitary. He finally found the switch and flicked it. The bulbs in the bathroom staggered to life, casting a vomit yellow light around the room, showing off the discoloured, cracked tiles and grimy mirrors above stained sinks. It probably would have been a better place to visit in the dark, but nevertheless Zach waited in the half open doorway for the bulbs to warm up completely before closing the door behind him.

He had never been a particularly social person, so working in an industry which was very much about *who* you know rather than *what* you know had presented its own difficulties; it was little wonder he hadn't advanced as far in his career as he had hoped. In fact, it was kind of a miracle that he had reached the point he had at all, whatever he thought of that particular situation. The celebrity mixers with everyone moaning about the state of the industry, which director said what, which actor did that thing, and which actress they did it were all so *boring* to Zach. Not that he fared any better outside of Hollywood circles. He had been lucky enough to never have had to have a "proper" job, so the chances of him striking up a meaningful conversation with a "normal" was unlikely. As soon as they asked what he did for a living, he could either tell the truth and find the person he was speaking to turn into a fanboy or distance themselves from him, or he could lie and make up some profession or other. The second option had backfired once and he found himself having to blag his way through a conversation with "another" lawyer as he tried discussing with Zach the implications of the latest round of amendments being signed in to law by congress. By the end of the conversation he started to wonder if he would make a good lawyer after all; the lies were tripping off of his tongue with ease. On the other hand, that was often known as something called "acting".

Social situations, essentially, terrified him.

So when Zach noticed the small, wooden window, half open to set at least some of the stench contained within the bathroom free, a plan formed in his mind. He locked the door from the inside and went over to inspect the window. The catch was old and rusty. It looked like it had probably been perched in a half-open position for countless months or even years, the contaminated air in the bathroom corroding its metal, leaving it with strange growths and a sticky coating.

Zach jabbed at the catch from underneath with his palm, trying to get it to shift. After a few hits it came free, covering his hand in a light coating of powdered rust. But the window itself wouldn't open any further, the hinges being in a similar state to the catch. Zach shoved it, banging against the peeling paint of the frame, trying to persuade it to open further. After some great effort, it gave way, opening a few more inches. Possibly enough for him to climb through.

He could either give it a shot or he could go back in the bar and talk to those people.

Zach pulled himself up on to the window ledge and pushed his head and shoulders through the opening, breathing in the outside air. The alley at the back of the bar also stank of alcohol and urine, despite the close proximity to an actual bathroom; some people must have literally waited until they left the bar to piss *against the bathroom wall*. And there were those who wondered why he didn't get on with people.

He inched himself forward, further towards the freedom of

the outside world.

His cellphone rang, all the way down in his pants pocket. He wasn't in the best position to be taking calls, but it could be something important; it could be about that life-changing role he had been waiting for. He didn't want to lose that opportunity because he happened to be hanging out of a bathroom window at the time the call came.

He twisted an arm around, trying to reach his cellphone. But the angle didn't help. The shape his body was in jammed him in place. Wedged in the window frame, the top third of him outside, the rest dangling inside, his cellphone still ringing with no way to answer it.

He writhed, wiggled, twisted, struggled. But to no avail. He was stuck.

The cellphone stopped ringing.

That was it. His dream could be over. Perhaps he should have stayed in the bar and -

BANG - BANG - BANG.

Someone pounded at the bathroom door from outside. Zach wasn't sure how long he'd been in there, but it couldn't have been that long, surely.

'There's someone in here,' he called out, trying to not sound panicked.

He had to get free. He tried twisting again, struggling hard to break from the window's grip.

BANG - BANG - BANG.

Louder this time. Either someone was worried about him, or they were particularly desperate to pee.

He wondered if he could shift his position to reach the frame itself: if he couldn't get through, perhaps he could pull out some of the woodwork surrounding the window. It was in such a bad condition, surely it would break easily enough.

He twisted his head to take a look at what he was dealing with.

He noticed something strange:

A stall door was slowly opening outward.

Like someone inside it was pushing it open.

It burst open.

The door crashed against the side wall.

Zach turned his attention back to getting outside.

The lights switched off, plunging the room once more into darkness.

Zach struggled, wriggled, pushing with all his might.

Someone grabbed him, hard, trying to pull him back inside, with a tight grip around his ankles.

The force being used made it clear they weren't trying to help.

He lashed out with his feet, trying to kick at his mystery assailant, unable to see who or what was attacking him.

He struck out, hard, managed to land a blow.

The grip on his ankles freed up for the briefest of moments, but grasped him again and pulled harder.

'Help! Help!' Zach screamed, all hope of leaving this situation with any trace of dignity going out the window, metaphorically speaking.

The bathroom door flew open with a massive crash and blessed light filled the place once more. Half-drunk Steve barrelled into the room, the door having been on the receiving end of his large shoulder. Taken by surprise, he pressed himself against the bathroom wall as a figure dressed all in black rushed from the room, disappearing around the corner and out of sight.

Steve blinked as if unsure whether he had seen something real or if it had been a figment of his beer clouded brain. He looked into the bathroom and saw Zach hanging from the window. He smiled, laughed even.

'I've been there, man,' he told Zach. 'Need a hand?'

Zach slumps against the window ledge, humiliated,

pained, defeated.

'Please.'

Steve lifted the window with ease. He held it up to let Zach free from its grip. Zach slid down the wall and collapsed back into the bathroom.

'Thanks.'

'Hope I wasn't interrupting anything,' Steve replied with a grin.

4

The cab pulled away, leaving Zach alone in the night at the tall iron gates of his home. The realtor sign at the front of the property smiled down at him, a constant reminder that something was going to change, one way or another, and also that his status within Hollywood was slipping. His home wasn't cheap enough for a regular person to buy, but it also wasn't anything an A-list star would have any interest in. He himself had dropped to B-list, at best. The house had been on the market for months, with the only interest being from people who had discovered it was Zach who was selling the place and making an appointment to view it out of curiosity, leaving disappointed when they realised Zach himself wouldn't be there to show them around.

He headed away from the gates, around the side of the fence. These large gates were purely for show. He hadn't opened them for a long time. To the side was a smaller, relatively hidden gate, tucked away in the foliage. Zach unlocked it and stepped through. Motion sensors activated lights illuminated the path towards the door to his house. He looked around, checking the shadows for movement, examining the darker spots for signs of life.

He locked the gate behind himself. Not that there was

much need for the illuminated pathway: the actual house was lit from top to bottom, lights on in every room. Partly it was for security, giving the impression of a house full of people, but mostly (though he wouldn't admit it to anyone) it was because Zach Keary had nyctophobia.

For as long as he could remember he was terrified of the dark. Anything could be hiding there. For someone who had spent most of his adult life starring in horror movies, it would have surprised a lot of people, since many of the movies involved things that went bump in the night. A lot of the action also took place in darkness. But that side of things had never bothered Zach: there was always far more light on movie sets than it was made to appear, and more often than not, he was surrounded by dozens of people during those shots where he was apparently "alone in the dark". The movies didn't scare him. He'd worked behind the scenes enough to know all of that was make believe. What *did* scare him was the evil that existed in the real world.

Zach's guiding principle for getting through life had become: no darkness means there's nowhere to hide. Simple as that. There was no childhood trauma that had caused it, unless he had suppressed the memory, which was possible but unlikely. It was something he had grown up with. He'd never admitted it to anyone but himself; he'd never shared a house with anyone, so there was no need for it to be anyone else's business. It was part of who he was and he'd learnt to accept it, and deal with it in his own way.

Zach unlocked his front door and stepped inside. He keyed in his four digit code for the alarm and locked the door again. He breathed a long, deep breath, glad to back in the sanctuary of his home. Somewhere safe. Somewhere he knew. He unzipped his bag and pulled out his Fuzz soft toy. He looked at it for a long moment. Love/hate. He sat it down beside his keys on a small table inside the front door, sitting upright as if on sentry duty.

Taking out his cellphone, he glanced at the screen: no notifications.

He looked again, double-checking.

Nothing.

Fuzz sits on a cluttered desk in Michael's bedroom. Its large, round eyes stare up at Michael and Amy, looking for reassurance from Michael that it's safe. Michael smiles as Amy watches the creature in astonishment. It's the first time she's seen the Furball; the first time she's seen anything like it. Fuzz sees the way Michael looks at Amy and realises she can be trusted; she's not going to hurt him. The creature gives Amy a smile and her heart practically melts.

'Can I?' she asks Michael as she extends her hands tentatively towards Fuzz.

'Sure.'

He's glad she likes Fuzz. Some people probably would have been freaked out by the sight of the creature, but Michael knows Amy is different. He knows he can trust her. He knows she won't tell anyone about this. It's their secret; something they can share together, something no one can take away from them. Something that will finally bring them closer?

Amy slowly reaches out her hand and places it gently on Fuzz's head. The fur is soft against her fingertips, the warmth from the creature emanating through the fur, warming her hand. She carefully moves her hand, stroking Fuzz. The creature leans in to the stroke, closes its eyes, enjoying the contact with this beautiful, gentle woman.

Amy smiles at Michael, her face alight with joy and wonder. Michael smiles back, his heart soaring, knowing life will never be the same again for either of them, and he's more than happy with that.

The doorbell to Michael's house rings. It startles Fuzz, who jumps down from the desk, trying to land on the floor, but instead toppling in to the trash basket. Amy can't help but laugh at the creature's antics, but is overcome with sympathy for it. She crouches down and carefully pulls it out of the basket.

'Don't worry,' she tells Fuzz. 'It's the doorbell - nothing to be scared of.'

The creature is still trembling, terrified, but Amy's words and presence bring it some relief.

The doorbell rings again. Fuzz's eyes widen, but being held by Amy helps it feel calmer than the first time.

'Who could that be?' Michael asks and goes to -

Zach muted the movie as his cellphone rang. He'd gone up to his bedroom, collapsed on the bed and switched on the TV to try and find something to watch to help him unwind. Ironically, he came across *Furballs*. What were the chances. It was quite near the beginning - the parts he enjoyed the most, where he had more dramatic, down-to-earth scenes, before all of the monster mayhem and carnage of the second half, where things were far less realistic. Before all the big set pieces and scenes everyone remembered.

He put down his bag of chips, brushed crumbs from his lap and reached across to pick up his cellphone from his bedside table.

This could be it. The Call. It was late - the only calls he should be getting at that time of night were going to either be good news or bad news, nothing in-between. He didn't know enough people to be called at night with bad news, so that could only mean one thing...

He cleared his throat, prepared himself.

'Zach Keary speaking,' he said into the phone, professionalism sounding through every syllable.

A brief moment before the voice at the other end of the line began to speak:

'Good evening, sir,' the voice said. 'I'm calling to ask if

you've recently considered switching your cellphone provider?'

Zach punched the red icon on his cellphone screen to end the call.

He threw the phone back on to the side table and switched off the TV.

Maybe tomorrow.

5

Zach woke with a start at the sound of the school fire alarm going off. He had been standing at the front of the class, reading a short story he had written for his homework. When the class started to laugh at him he thought it was due to his lack of talent. Humiliated, he raged at his classmates, telling them they hadn't done any better (even though he knew they had; their stories were far superior to his). The laughter grew louder, and they started to point at him. He looked down and realised he was naked.

That's when the fire alarm went off. He felt relief as the class evacuated. He didn't care if he burnt to death with the school collapsing around him; he was glad the ordeal at the front of the class was over.

The dream was familiar, but it had never ended with a fire alarm going off before.

Stumbling from sleep, it took Zach a moment to realise the fire alarm wasn't a fire alarm at all, but rather the sound of his cellphone ringing beside his bed. He flung his arm to the side and grasped around until he made contact with the device. Blinking to see the screen clearly, he saw it was Spengler calling.

'What?' he growled into the phone.

'And a good morning to you too,' Spengler replied.

'What time is it?'

'Early. Ish. Get over to my office. Now.'

'What's going on?'

'Just come.'

A *beep-beep-beep* through the cellphone told Zach that Spengler had hung up. He looked at his phone dumfounded, as if hoping the device itself could provide some sort of a reason for the mysterious phone call, yet no answer was forthcoming.

He sighed, scratched, and climbed out of bed.

The call from Spengler had put him on edge. He didn't like surprises, as well Spengler knew. But there was something in his voice on the phone which made it sound important. If it hadn't been for that particular tone of voice, Zach probably would have told Spengler to leave him alone so he could go back to sleep. He wondered if it was anything to do with what happened at the bar the previous evening - the mysterious attack in the bathroom. Zach hadn't told Spengler - or anyone - about it. The last thing he needed was bizarre headlines in the news about a B-list (at best) horror movie star who claimed to have been attacked while climbing out of a bathroom window in a rundown bar because he was trying to avoid - *gasp* - socialising.

Dressed in suit and tie (because without knowing what situation he was about to walk into, he thought it best to be overdressed than under), Zach stopped by the front door and looked in the mirror above the side table. He looked old and tired. He also thought he looked like someone on his way to court with no clue as to which way the jury was going to side.

A single hair stuck up from his head, completely out of place. Zach tried to press it down, but it bounced straight back up. He tried again, even tried wetting his fingers and smooshing it down with moisture. Nothing. He gripped the offending hair between his thumb and forefinger, yanked it hard, and pulled it from his scalp. There. All better. He adjusted his tie, making sure the knot was aligned squarely in the centre of his shirt collar.

He almost looked presentable.

As he grabbed his keys from by the front door, he noticed the Fuzz cuddly toy on the side table was laying on its front, face to the table. He frowned, sure that wasn't how he had left it the previous evening. It must have toppled over during the night. Zach picked it back up, planted it in a seated position and watched it for a few seconds. It stayed in place.

One last look in the mirror.

Deep breath.

He unlocked the front door, switched off the house lights.

He switched them back on again.

Off once more.

He looked around.

He couldn't chance it - he had no idea what time he would be back later in the day. It could be dark on his return.

He switched the lights back on.

Thirty minutes later, Zach arrived outside Spengler's office, the words RICHARD SPENGLER - TALENT MANAGEMENT etched on a small glass window embedded within the door frame. The office block in which Spengler's offices were located was a relatively modern building, with some beautiful, high-tech office spaces inside. Glass and chrome everywhere, huge screens for video calls, multi-directional microphones so many people could argue over the top of one another from anywhere in the world at the exact same time. Spengler, though, was old school. None of the glass and chrome in his space, it was all natural, wooden, furniture. Comfortable chairs. Windows that could actually open if it got to warm inside - none of this fancy air conditioning nonsense. He still used *filing cabinets*, for crying out loud. He came from old-Hollywood, liking to do everything in person, making deals and signing contracts over liquor and cigars, rather than by email or - God forbid - through a text message.

Zach took a deep breath, braced himself to give Spengler a piece of his mind for getting him out there for no real reason. For not telling him what it was all about. For any other tiny reason he could think of in the spur of the moment, because, frankly, Zach was already in a bad mood after his abrupt awakening, and he wanted to take it out on someone.

He opened the office door to find Spengler sat on the edge of his desk, watching and waiting for Zach. When he saw his client enter, a huge grin spread across his face. Any thoughts of yelling at Spengler disappeared as confusion reigned in Zach's mind.

'What's going on?' he asked.

'Come on in,' Spengler told him.

Zach closed the door and took a step further into Spengler's office.

'Are you going to tell me why I'm here?'

'All will be revealed.'

That grin again. On second thoughts, Zach *did* want to yell at him. He wasn't in the right frame of mind for games, and Spengler was in an annoyingly good mood, which made Zach feel even worse.

'Follow me.'

Spengler jumped down from his desk, headed across to the door that led to what was officially known as the conference room, though it was little bigger than the outer office; it just had more chairs and a larger table to sit around.

'Are you ready?' he asked Zach.

'For what?'

Spengler pushed the door open, grinning once more. He

stepped aside to let Zach through. Confused, Zach looked through the door and stopped.

Sat at the conference table was what could only be a hallucination: a man Zach had dreamt of meeting for so many years. A man whose work Zach had followed, analysed, obsessed over. A man revered, critically acclaimed, but still nothing short of an enigma. A man named Francis Romanelli. Sitting there, in Spengler's conference room, not twelve feet away from Zach. His face obscured behind a cloud of cigarette smoke, Romanelli's features were nonetheless unmistakable. At seventy-one years old, his face was set with craggy, deep lines from a lifetime of coffee and cigarettes, his hair large and wild, yet somehow also stylishly ruffled. And his eyes: his eyes were deep, endlessly kind, but you could be sure they were taking in every little detail. At that very moment they were taking in everything about Zach. The man - the legend - Francis Romanelli sucked on the remnants of a cigarette in his hand, set it down in an ashtray situated directly in front of him and twisted it, stubbing it out alongside the other half a dozen that were already in there. Eyes never leaving Zach, he pulled a packet of cigarettes from his pocket, tapped one into his hand, lit it and inhaled until his lungs were ready to burst, a look on his face like it was the greatest pleasure of his life.

Mesmerised by the sight before him, Zach failed to realise he had been stood there, unmoving, for longer than was necessarily deemed normal or polite.

'Are we going in?' Spengler tried to usher him forward.

'Could I have one moment of your time?' Zach asked him.

Spengler smiled an apology at Romanelli, held a finger out, *one moment*, pulled the door closed and turned on Zach.

'What the hell are you playing it?' he half-whispered, half-hissed.

'That's Francis Romanelli,' Zach told him.

'I'm aware of that. And that's why we need to get back in there. Right now.'

'But it's Francis Romanelli.'

'And he's here to see *you*. So get back in there.'

Zach thought back to all of the films in Romanelli's filmography - *films*, not *movies*; there was a difference. So many great pictures, so many great performances from his cast. According to interviews and reports, Romanelli was an absolute pleasure to work with, allowing each actor to fully immerse themselves in their roles and make suggestions he would actually *take on board*. His calm, quiet demeanour betrayed the analytical mind, always working away, always watching, always calculating, but not in a bad way; rather the best way to get the best possible performance from his cast to make the best possible film. Across the mere six films he had made over the span of several decades, Romanelli's cast had accrued a total of fifteen Academy Award nominations, of which there had been nine wins; the odds of a win were relatively good, should you become a part of Romanelli's working family. Ridiculously, the man himself had yet to win anything at the Oscars. He'd been nominated for Best Original Screenplay and Best Director for three of his films, but (and this was just Zach's theory) because his films made you *think*, without spoon feeding you the emotions you were supposed to be feeling at the time, because you had to *work some stuff out for yourself*, the nominations felt as though they were there by default, but the Academy members always failed to vote for Romanelli once it came down to the wire. They preferred saccharine tales of redemption or triumph over illness / race / gender to anything with a more subtly implied meaning.

Zach couldn't help but fantasise about his chance in the spotlight, his place on the stage collecting that little naked golden man. This could be his one shot. This could be his final chance at doing something *great*. This could be the only way of breaking out of the cycle of horror sequels.

This was… too much. Even before he had the chance to talk to Romanelli, he could feel the pressure mounting. What if he wasn't good enough for the director? He'd never heard of someone being fired and recast from a Romanelli picture before - could he live with having the stigma of being the first? What if the picture came out and was universally beloved, but his performance was singled out for being the one weak part of the whole thing? What if it was the only Francis Romanelli film to be released which the critics hated, purely because of him?

A tension headache brewed in his temples. He could feel beads of sweat starting to pop out across his forehead. He rubbed the moisture away with the back of his hand, loosened his tie a little, trying to make his breathing work a little more easily.

'Why?' Zach asked.

'Why what?' It had been so long since they had last spoken that Spengler had forgotten the last thing he said.

Zach perched on a chair, held on to the armrests as if they were the only things stopping him from floating off into the dark, endless void of space.

'Why's he here to see me?'

Spengler's face reddened with exasperation. He had arguably the greatest living director sat in his conference room, waiting to meet with his client. But his client was in the middle of a crisis of confidence, despite this being the exact scenario that said client had dreamt of and wished for for years, even going so far as to turn down lucrative projects in case a call came in and he couldn't do it due to scheduling clashes.

He tried to control himself.

It didn't work.

'He's a director, you're an actor!' Spengler exploded. 'Gee, I wonder what possible reason he could have for being here?! Why do you *think* he's here, Zach? Why are you doing this to me?'

'Why am I doing this to *you*? You can't spring something like this on me! I'm not prepared.'

Zach stood and advanced towards the conference room door. He looked through the frosted glass window. He could make out the outline of Romanelli's hair, unmistakable even in silhouette form.

'Not prepared? This is the *exact moment* you've been preparing for over the past however many years.'

Zach paced the office, chewing on his fingernails, casting occasional glances back over to the conference room door, as if checking whether he could still see the hallucination sitting at the table, waiting to speak with him.

Spengler took him by the elbow, led him back to a chair, sat him down. He crouched in front of Zach like a parent in front of a child, trying to soothe them after a raging tantrum because their carrot was slightly the wrong shape.

'Listen. He turned up this morning out of the blue. No warning, no call, nothing. It surprised me as much as you, I can assure you. Do you know when the last time was that I had an Oscar nominated director - an Oscar nominated *anything* for that matter - in my office?'

Zach looked up at him, eyes wide, scared, child-like.

'Never?' he ventured.

'Exactly. Never. And it may never happen again if we - if you - blow this.'

Zach looked across at the door again, chewed on his fingernail a little more, thinking things over.

'What's the plan?' he asked.

'The "plan" is to get you a role in his movie so I can get paid. Now get your ass back in that conference room and make me proud.'

Zach nodded, though his expression was still unsure.

Spengler helped him to his feet, led him towards the door.

'Ready?' he asked his client.

Zach nodded again.

6

Spengler opened the door to the conference room for a second time and half-shoved Zach inside. Romanelli was still there - still sitting at the table, within touching distance of Zach. He was sure he would wake up at any time soon. He looked down to double-check: he was still wearing his clothes, so maybe it was real? But it couldn't possibly be. Spengler led him to a chair, pushed him down into it. Zach's eyes never left Romanelli, taking in every crevice, line, feature on the great man's face. Romanelli in turn watched Zach, eyes narrowing as he sucked on his cigarette, the ashtray in front of him more full than it had been a few minutes previously.

Reasonably confident Zach wasn't going to get up and run from the room, Spengler took a seat beside him. At least from there he could grab Zach if he tried to make a run for it.

'So sorry about that,' Spengler addressed the director. 'I had just remembered something important I needed to discuss with Mr Keary.'

Romanelli sucked on his cigarette, the faint glow from the tip illuminating an orange spark in his eyes. He held in the smoke for a moment, savouring the flavour, the feeling of it filling his mouth. He let it out with great patience, a mesmerising smoke trail emanating from his lips, drifting towards the ceiling.

Spengler turned to Zach.

'So, Zach, to fill you in on where Francis and I - sorry, may I call you Francis?' Romanelli didn't move his eyes from Zach, didn't even acknowledge the fact that Spengler was talking. Spengler continued, taking the silence as permission. 'To fill you in on where Francis and I got to in our discussions. Francis - ' (he was already starting to feel like he was overusing the name *Francis*, but to switch back to calling him Mr Romanelli would be equally as awkward, if not more so, than continuing the way he was already going) ' - is putting together a cast for his new movie and was very excited to meet with you to discuss it.'

Spengler stopped talking and stared at Zach for long enough that Zach's attention was drawn away from Romanelli. He realised Spengler was waiting for him to make some sort of response. He opened his mouth to speak, but nothing came out. He tried again, and eventually some semblance of words emerged:

'It's a pleasure to meet you, Mr Romanelli, sir.'

Romanelli responded by stubbing out his cigarette and straight away lighting another from his pack. Realising no words were forthcoming, Spengler continued speaking.

'The film Mr Romanelli - Francis - is working on is called *A Penchant for Sorrow*.' Spengler held his hands out in front of his face as he announced the title, as though he was reading it from a marquee on the outside of a cinema. 'It's a serious, hard-hitting drama, about - and feel free to jump in at any point here, Francis, if I should get anything wrong - it's about a family so full of pride, so sure they know it all, that they refuse any sort of help over anything. Have I got that right?' He looked to Romanelli for validation, but the director still hadn't averted his gaze away from Zach, like he was taking him in, studying him, trying to work him out. 'Uh, so, this family. Their pride sends them spiralling towards mutually assured destruction. That's how you described it to me, right?'

Having reached the end of the brief pitch, Spengler was sure the director would have something to say for himself, but still nothing. Even Zach was beginning to emerge from his trance. He was starting to feel uncomfortable in the man's presence, and not because of his genius.

'Is there a specific character you have in mind for me?' Zach asked.

Spengler decided to chime in, knowing he wasn't likely to get an answer from the director, who was *supposed* to be there to talk to Zach, but had apparently delegated that particular responsibility to Spengler himself. Romanelli had been talkative enough when it had been him and Spengler alone in the office; the silent treatment had only begun once Zach had arrived.

'You'd play, uh - ' he checked his notes in his small black notebook he carried with him everywhere, just in case, '- Fred. The eldest son in the family. He sounds like the worst of the bunch.'

Spengler smiled, laughed a little. *Worst of the bunch*, Zach repeated to himself. It sounded like the opportunity of doing something properly dramatic.

'How does it end? For my character? For Fred, I mean,' Zach corrected himself, in case he came across as being presumptuous about being given the role.

Spengler closed his book, grinned at his client.

'Tragically,' he told Zach.

'It sounds perfect,' Zach beamed.

There was nothing the Academy liked more than a tragic figure. Pair that with a director like Francis Romanelli, and he could practically hear his name being announced at the ceremony already.

Zach and Spengler turned in unison to face Romanelli, smiling from ear to ear.

Romanelli stubbed out his cigarette, likely the twentieth he had exhausted since landing in Spengler's office. But instead of lighting another, he surprised them both by standing up from his seat. He fastened a single button of his jacket. Zach and Spengler held their collective breaths, certain the director was about to speak, to say something of great importance that was going to change their lives forever.

Without a word, without a glance, Romanelli left the room and closed the door behind him.

Zach and Spengler stared after him, waiting for him to come back in. After thirty seconds or so of watching, it became apparent that he wasn't returning any time soon.

'What's wrong with him?' Zach blurted out.

'The man's a creative genius,' Spengler tried arguing with a shrug, perhaps to convince himself as much as Zach. It didn't work for either of them.

'I don't know why he's even here,' Zach protested. 'He's clearly not interested in talking with me.'

'He wouldn't have come here if he wasn't interested.'

'He hasn't opened his mouth once, except to shove another cigarette in it.'

'All geniuses have eccentricities.'

'Genii,' Zach corrected, regretting it the second he did. He was always being accused of being pedantic about things like grammar. He hated himself for it, but somehow couldn't stop.

'What?' Spengler asked.

Zach sighed. Too late now. 'It's "genii".'

'What is?'

'The plural for "genius".'

'And that's what's important to you right now?'

It wasn't the most important thing in the world, sure, especially not at that point, but somehow focussing on a grammatical issue, where Zach actually had the answers, helped take his mind off the whole Romanelli situation. He didn't want to keep arguing about it, but, on the other hand, he also did. It was a sense of control; ever since he'd walked in to Spengler's office that morning, he'd had no control of the situation. Everything had been thrust upon him with no room to plan or even breathe. Grammar was something controllable. Something with rules that could and should be stuck to.

'All I'm saying is: if you're going to be talking about geniuses, you ought to talk a bit smarter.'

'Genii,' Spengler grinned.

'What?'

'You said "geniuses",' he informed Zach with infuriating smugness.

Zach opened his mouth to speak, but at that very moment the door to the conference room opened and Romanelli wandered back in clutching a cup of hot coffee in a disposable cup. Spengler couldn't think where he'd got it from - the nearest coffee shop was ten minutes away, and there was certainly no machine on the premises that Spengler knew of. They both watched as Romanelli crossed the room back to his seat, not speaking, not acknowledging his absence, or indeed their presence in the room at that moment.

He sat down, examined the cup, took a long, slow sip.

He winced.

'That is terrible coffee,' he told them, the very first words Zach had heard him speak.

It may have been terrible, yet he continued sipping on his hot beverage as Zach and Spengler sat and watched.

7

It was dark by the time Zach reached home. The meeting ended after Romanelli went out for coffee for the fourth time and failed to come back after two hours. Spengler was ready to call it after forty-five minutes, but Zach was convinced Romanelli would return the second they left the building if they did that, so insisted they hang around for longer, just in case. Deep down he knew they were done, but he didn't want to risk throwing what little chance he had at the role by being gone on Romanelli's return.

The whole day had been a complete waste of time. It was true what they said about never meeting your heroes: Romanelli had been a big part of Zach's life, from a distance, for as long as he could remember, and now he had met him he didn't know what to make of him. "Reclusive, eccentric genius" were words often used to describe him in the media. Some of that was certainly true, but Zach had come away doubting himself in his hero worship. Eccentric? Sure. Genius? Hard to know, when he had barely said a word, other than to express dissatisfaction with the coffee.

Zach spoke on his cellphone with Spengler as he headed up the path towards his front door, repeating, again, the things they had spoken about for a couple of hours after giving up on Romanelli returning.

'Are you telling me that if you're offered the role, you'd turn it down?' Spengler asked him.

'He's not going to offer me the role.'

'But if he did?'

'I don't know. Of course I want it. But... he really didn't seem interested in me.'

Surely if the director had even the slightest interest in recruiting Zach for his film, he would have engaged in some form of conversation, spoken to him about what the role required, had him read some lines, get to know him a little better... Something. Anything. All he did was sit there, drinking apparently terrible coffee, smoking his cigarettes and studying Zach. Romanelli had acted nothing short of bored and disinterested.

Zach could vaguely hear Spengler chuckling at the other end of the line, but he had become distracted. Something wasn't quite right at home. Something had caught his eye. A shadow, perhaps, in a downstairs window. Maybe it was tiredness; it had been a long day.

'You would turn down a chance to work with Francis Romanelli?' Spengler mocked.

'No. Yes. Maybe.'

'Yeah. Sure you would.'

There it was again: he definitely saw it that time, through the living room window. A definite shadow drifting across the room inside: a supposedly empty room in his supposedly empty house. Fear gripped him. He was frozen. This was the first time anything like this had happened to him; he had no idea what to do or even how to react.

'There's someone in my house,' he found himself saying to Spengler over the phone.

'What are you talking about?'

He could picture Spengler sitting behind his desk with his

feet up, flicking those salted peanuts into his mouth, rolling his eyes at his stupid, paranoid client.

'In my house. Right now. Someone's there.'

'Are you sure?' Spengler's voice had changed, more serious, almost as though he believed Zach. Perhaps he even sat up straight in his chair, planted his feet on the ground at the gravity of the situation.

'I'm pretty sure,' Zach told him.

'"Pretty sure" doesn't sound that definite.'

'Alright, I'm absolutely sure. Happy? There is someone in my house. Right now. I saw their shadow through he window.'

'It's not the maid, or a cleaner? Long-lost relative dropping in for a visit?'

'You know I can't afford a maid, and if it was a long-lost relative, how would I know, and why the hell would they let themselves into my house without warning?'

'Alright, alright. Calm down. I'm trying to rule out any possibilities.'

'Except the one that's actually happening, right now, as I'm wasting time talking to you.'

'Oh, well, if this is a waste of time, I may as well hang up.'

'No, no! Don't do that,' Zach begged. He needed that comforting, though sarcastic, voice at the other end of the line to talk him through things. 'What should I do? I should call the police, right?'

'You call the cops and there's no one in your house, tomorrow morning the papers will be full of more headlines about paranoid has-been celebrities seeing things and wasting police time.'

There was an urgency in Spengler's voice Zach couldn't ignore, but at the same time, that wasn't what his brain decided he should focus on: Spengler's choice of words jarred, stabbing him like an electric current zapped out of his cellphone and into his ear.

'As my manager, should I be worried that you're referring to me as a "has-been"?' he asked.

There was nothing but silence from Spengler's end of the line in response to his question.

'Hello?!' Zach cried. Then, because he was worried that he was talking far too loudly and might draw the attention of whoever was in his property, he whispered, but with what he believed to be an edge to his voice. 'Spengler? Are you there?'

After another couple of seconds of stress-filled silence, Spengler returned.

'I've got a call coming in,' he told Zach. 'I'd better go.'

'Wait! But - '

Too late. Spengler had hung up on him. The one time he needed his help, and the guy had hung up. Zach called him back but it went straight through to his voicemail. He was on his own. He couldn't go in the house - who knew what kind of dangerous individual was waiting inside for him. A crazed fan, perhaps ("fan" was an abbreviation of "fanatic", after all); a drug-addict, desperate, looking for money or somewhere to sleep; the modern-day equivalent of the Manson family. That whole situation had played out not a million miles from where Zach lived, after all; who knew what was in the water? It could happen again.

On the other hand, Spengler had told him not to call the police. Zach could understand why. A couple of negative, mocking headlines and he would be finished. His career, such as it was, was in a precarious enough position without being made the laughing stock of Hollywood for his lack of courage.

It came down to one simple question: would he rather risk death or humiliation?

8

Zach took so long deciding on the best course of action to take that the decision ended up being taken out of his hands. As he stood frozen by the front door, phone in one hand, door key in the other, blue and red lights flashed in front of his property. Car doors slammed as two police officers stepped out from their vehicle. They found their way to the side gate and went up the path towards Zach, guns drawn, aimed towards him.

Officer Brian Davies stood a short distance behind his partner, allowing Officer Helen Cole to take the lead. It was a small detail she never failed to notice.

'Sir,' Cole called out to Zach, who was still staring at the front door, oblivious to their presence. 'Sir, I need you to put your hands above your head.'

Zach continued staring at the door, lost in his own fears.

'Sir,' Cole called out louder.

Zach turned and noticed the officers standing there. Confusion swept over his face.

'Did I call you?' he asked.

'Can I ask what you're doing here, sir?'

'This is my house. There's someone inside.'

'This is *your* house?'

'Yes - isn't that why you're here?'

'Can your prove this is your property, sir?'

'I can, but - '

'Hey, aren't you that Furball guy?' Officer Davies spoke out for the first time.

'Davies,' Cole said, a warning in her voice.

'No, it's fine,' Davies put his gun away. 'He's that actor from those movies.'

He stepped forward, making a move like he wanted to shake Zach's hand, rather than put him in handcuffs.

'Davies,' Cole snapped again.

It wasn't the first time she'd had to remind Davies that just because someone was a celebrity it didn't mean they couldn't also be a criminal. In Davies' book, if someone had ever appeared on TV or in a movie they were clearly incapable of committing a crime. In Cole's experience, the opposite was true; it was just harder to prove.

'If this is your home, could you open the door for us, please, sir?' Cole asked Zach, gun still unholstered, more cautious than Davies.

'There's someone in there,' Zach told her.

'Who?'

'I don't know.'

'Are you *sure* this is your house?'

'Yes - it's my house! I got back and saw someone in there.'

'Why didn't you call us?'

'You're here now, aren't you?'

Cole rolled her eyes.

'We received a report of someone acting suspiciously outside this property. And here you are.'

She had been on this beat in Hollywood for long enough to have dealt with her fair share of celebrities who thought they could talk to whoever they wanted in any way they wanted. Officers like Davies didn't help the situation, treating them in the way they believed they should be treated: as if they were better than everyone else. It wasn't necessarily Davies' fault, though. Having recently transferred to Los Angeles from a small, rural community, he had grown up only seeing these people from a distance, on a thirty-foot high screen. It was hardly surprising that he considered them to be above regular, real-life people.

'Let me deal with this,' Davies brushed past her, demonstrating the exact problem she kept coming up against.

Davies approached Zach, playing the friendly cop.

'Have you been inside the property, sir?' he asked.

'No - why would I?'

'You didn't even take a look?'

'I thought they might still be in there,' Zach explained.

'There are lights on inside,' Davies pointed out to obvious.

'I left them on before I went out.'

Davies glanced at Cole. He saw her face harden and knew exactly what was coming.

'Cole, don't…' he began, but too late. She was in that zone already.

'Don't you care about our planet, sir?'

'Excuse me?'

'I'm sorry, sir - ' Davies tried to interject.

But Cole strode towards Zach, her gun still drawn, waving it in front of his face.

'Wasting our precious resources.'

'Is that really… is that a crime?' Zach stammered, taken completely aback. An eco-warrior with a cop badge and a gun could never end well.

'It should be,' Cole declared.

Davies took hold of Cole's arm, eased it backwards slightly, placing the gun back into her holster as Cole continued to glare at Zach. Wanting to divert their attention back to the actual possible crime occurring, Davies tried

Zach's front door. It was locked, no sign of any sort of damage.

'No sign of forced entry,' Davies told Zach. 'If I could borrow your key please, sir.'

Realising he was still holding the front door key in his hand, Zach handed it to the officer. Davies carefully placed the key in the lock and twisted it. He flinched at the slight click it made as the door unlocked, as if half expecting the whole place to explode. He pulled his gun back out from his holster, stood to the side of the doorway and tapped the door open with his fingertips. Another sign that he'd grown up watching movies, Cole thought, recognising the typical Hollywood moves for entering a property without getting your head blown off.

Davies nodded his head towards her. Cole pulled her weapon back out and joined Davies beside the door, making sure to take her turn at being at the back of the line for a change. She didn't go in for gender politics, but she went first the last time, and clearly Davies was playing up the macho bravado in front of this actor, so, whatever: let him have his moment, if it would make him feel better. While he was willing to put himself in the line of fire rather than her, she would gratefully accept the opportunity to be second.

The door creaked open. They stood for a moment, listening.

No sounds came from inside.

Davies peered around the doorway, looked in the building. No sign of life, other than the lights blazing throughout the property. No deep, dark shadows in which anyone could be hiding.

'This is the police,' he called out, perhaps to no one. 'If anyone's in here, please come forward with your hands above your head.'

Davies was almost disappointed no one came out. Saving a

celebrity from a possible home invasion would no doubt have looked good for him. Perhaps he could go into private security work for the stars.

The two officers stepped through the doorway and glanced around the room.

Everything was still, normal.

No sign of anyone having been there, nothing damaged, no slogans written in blood on the walls.

Davies turned to look at Zach, who stood outside his home, watching the officers.

'Does anything look out of place?' the officer asked.

Zach took a tentative step inside, watching his feet cross the threshold as though he was stepping over a barrier of salt, used to protect him from oncoming evil.

'No, it all looks - '

Something on the floor caught his eye. He trod over to it and picked it up, frowning. He turned it over in his hands, felt it, unsure exactly what it was he was touching. It was soft, springy, white. A ball of fluff, like stuffing from a soft toy.

'What's that?' Davies asked.

He pulled a rubber glove from his pocket and snapped it into place over his hand. He took the fluff from Zach, handling it as a CSI technician would handle a solitary strand of hair found at a murder scene, the vital piece of evidence that would crack the years long case that had haunted them all of their career.

Zach looked around and noticed another ball across the room. And another. And another.

Zach followed the trail, picking up the fluff balls as he came across them; breadcrumbs, leading to -

He stopped.

There was incontrovertible proof someone had been in his house, that he wasn't going crazy. He would have been happy, except for what it could actually mean.

A decapitated head lay on the floor.

But instead of blood spilling out of it, there was fluff.

Fuzz's head, staring up at him, white stuffing protruding from its neck where its head had been removed from its body. Ripped apart, destroyed. Zach picked up the head, cradled it in his hands. The body was nowhere nearby; perhaps taken.

'What is that?' Davies asked him.

Davies and Cole stepped closer to Zach to take a look at the peculiar object for which he held so much affection. Recognition dawned on Davies.

'Hey, it's Fuzz!' he cried out, delighted.

Zach's cellphone rang, a harsh chirruping sound breaking the quiet of the building, causing the three of them to jump. Zach pulled the phone from his pocket, looked at the screen. It was Spengler calling. Zach answered the phone.

'I'm going to have to call you back,' he told Spengler and hung up before Spengler had a chance to reply.

Davies took the Fuzz head from Zach, looked it over.

'I used to have one of these when I was a kid,' he told Cole, a warm, nostalgic smile spread across his face.

He suddenly looked serious, and turned to Zach: 'Is this the real one from the movie?'

'Of course not.'

Disappointment flooded across Davies' face.

'Probably as well,' he said, perhaps trying to cheer himself up. 'Wouldn't want this to happen to the real thing.'

Davies passed the head to Cole, who also examined it.

'Looks like you've got yourself a rodent problem,' Cole declared grimly, handing the toy back to Zach.

'Rodents?'

'Rats. raccoons. Something like that.'

'I don't think so.'

'They do this kind of thing. They're like cats - they find something soft and chewable and they'll rip it apart, play with the stuffing. I'll bet if you took a good look around, you'll find droppings all over the house.'

Zach wasn't buying it. He'd never had problems with that sort of thing, not once. Come to think of it, he'd never seen any wildlife around his neighbourhood at all. Maybe that was because all of the creatures were living in people's homes, hidden, ready and waiting to destroy their personal effects. A shudder ran through Zach's spine as he thought about what could be there, in his house, living in the walls, under the floorboards, crawling over his pillows when he wasn't around.

'It's climate change alright,' Cole tried explaining. 'Drives the rodents and critters inside when the weather turns unseasonable.'

It kind of made sense to Zach, except for one, pretty important thing everyone seemed to have forgotten about.

'But what about the shadow I saw through the window? There's no way that could have been a rat, unless it was six feet tall and walking on its back legs.'

'Didn't you make a movie about that?' Davies asked.

'No.'

Yes, but he wasn't going to admit it at this point. He wasn't going to give them more ammunition for their "you imagined the whole thing" theory. Spengler was no doubt right about not getting the cops involved. He could imagine the headlines already: FORGOTTEN MOVIE STAR CALLS COPS OVER SIX-FOOT RAT IN HIS HOUSE.

'You probably *thought* you saw a shadow,' Davies told him, his voice changed from admiration to one he would use when talking to a dear old lady who had lost her cat. 'Probably a trick of the light.'

'There's no sign of forced entry, no damage - except to this stuffed creature,' Cole said, waving a hand vaguely towards the Fuzz head Zach was holding. 'Nothing missing. I don't think anyone's been here.'

'So you're not going to do anything?'

'What can we do? There's no one here, there's no sign of anyone having been here. We have nothing to go on. I'm sorry, sir, but we have thousands of cases like this every single day, and we don't have the resource to investigate every one of them. Especially when there's no sign of a crime having taken place.'

'Thousands?'

'Thousands.'

'That's... not very reassuring.'

'I'll tell you what,' Cole said with a smile. 'You let us know if any more of your toys get broken, and we'll be sure to drop everything and come over right away.'

Davies turned away from Zach to hide his smile, trying to stifle a laugh from becoming audible. Usually Cole was serious and by-the-books; he'd never heard her speak to someone like that before. He kind of liked it.

Zach, on the other hand, couldn't believe what he was hearing. He stared at Davies, open mouthed.

'You... you can't talk to me like that,' he stammered.

'What, because you're a "movie star",' (the air quotes she made as she spoke hurt more than the inflection in her voice), 'we have to treat you as though you're special?'

That's exactly what Zach had been thinking: it was what he was used to from most other people but of course he wasn't going to let Officer Cole know that. It worked in most situations, he kind of got used to getting things he wanted, or jumping queues; people would be happy enough to feed off of the story that they let Zach Keary get coffee in front of them because he was on his way to the studio and couldn't be late for filming. They wouldn't care if they had to wait that little bit longer.

But he had never tried the "look at me, I'm a movie star"

routine with cops before. In hindsight, it was probably a mistake.

'I meant,' Zach said, though it wasn't what he'd meant at all, 'what do I do if the intruders come back?'

'*If* there's an intruder…' Cole said with a smirk; she may as well have been winking at Davies, '*you give 'em hell, little guy.*'

She quoted the *Furballs* line in a mock "action hero" voice.

She tipped her hat towards Zach and made her way towards the front door.

'Goodnight, Furball,' she said as she passed him by.

Davies couldn't believe it: Cole knew the movie. She had known who Zach was all along, but she'd played it cool. And then she delivered the killer blow right at the last second. The woman was unbelievable. Davies made a mental note of what she had done; he knew he'd want to try it out for himself sooner or later - if only he could learn to stay chilled in front of a celebrity for once, he might have a chance.

Cole called out to him from where she stood outside.

'Are you coming?'

'Sure.'

Davies turned to leave, but at the last second stopped and turned back to Zach.

He took his notebook from his pocket, held it out along with a pencil.

'Can I get your autograph?' he asked.

Playing it cool could wait at least one more day.

9

After the police left, Zach couldn't bring himself to stay inside the house. Whether it was large rodents, or a more human intruder who had invaded his house, he didn't feel comfortable in there right at that moment. He sat outside on his doorstep, the severed head of Fuzz on the cold concrete beside him. Despite the chill in the air and the encroaching darkness, it somehow felt safer. Zach had argued with himself for some time about whether to leave the front door open behind him to provide an easy escape route should someone try and attack him from the front, or to close it to make sure that, if someone was lurking in his house, they couldn't sneak up on him and garrotte him from behind. In the end he decided he would rather see someone coming and have the chance to get away than risk the sneak attack, so the door was firmly shut. He had switched on the outside lights to reveal as much of his property as possible, but, unable to control much of the land in front of his house, there were still hidden corners and shadows.

The building wasn't that large, relatively speaking when compared with some of his neighbours' properties. He had four bedrooms, three bathrooms, a small pool at the back and a stunning kitchen. Most of it was wasted space, though.

Being only him living there, he rarely ventured out of his bedroom with en suite and the kitchen, which had a seating area to the side of it. There was little point going anywhere else in the house, and it was very rare anyone came to visit. The real estate agent and Spengler had convinced him to buy the place: he would have been happy enough with an apartment, but to be taken seriously as a movie star, you apparently had to have a large house, with a large gate, far enough away from the front door to make it look as though you needed to protect yourself from potential invasion of privacy. If you look as though you're doing well, you *must* be doing well. Appearances - in this town even more so than most others - were everything.

Zach looked down at the Fuzz head on the step beside him.

Who could have done such a thing? He refused to believe it was any sort of animal. This was done by a person, and the Fuzz toy was deliberately targeted. He just didn't know by who, or why. In some ways he hoped never to find out, but it still bothered him that someone clearly had enough of a problem with him to somehow make their way into his house and destroy one of his possessions. In the grand scheme of things, sure, ripping apart a soft toy was hardly the worst thing that could have happened; it was more the thought of someone unknown being in his house without his knowledge and apparently holding some sort of grudge against him that was horrible. Would they come back? And if they found him home next time they were there, would they do to him what they'd done to Fuzz? Would someone have to come in and pick up pieces of Zach the same way that he had had to pick up pieces of the Furball?

Zach watched from his doorstep as a car drove down his street. It slowed as it approached his gates.

The car stopped right outside.

The engine switched off, then the lights dimmed away, leaving silence in the night again.

The click of the driver's door opening.

The slam of it closing again.

Footsteps coming closer.

The unmistakable creak of the side gate of his property opening.

Someone was coming his way.

Zach stood up, but he couldn't move from the spot, his legs feeling as though they were going to give way at any second.

A figure headed towards him, little more than a shapeless silhouette as the brightness of the outdoor lights shone in Zach's eyes, stopping him from being able to see anything clearly.

Zach opened the front door, stumbled inside, and shut the door behind him, fumbling with the lock, desperately trying to secure it.

The latch in place, he leaned against the door and slid to the floor, beads of sweat forming along his brow.

With fumbling fingers he pulled his cellphone from his pocket.

BANG-BANG-BANG.

A fist pounded on the outside of the front door.

Zach dialled 911, waited to be connected.

BANG-BANG-BANG.

'911. What is your emergency?' the operator asked at the other end of the line.

'Police. I need the police,' Zach hissed.

'One moment.'

BANG-BANG-BANG.

'Are you going to make me wait out here all night?' a voice called from the other side of the door.

Spengler.

Zach breathed a sigh of relief and hung up his phone. He

opened the front door. Spengler took in his appearance - sweaty, dishevelled, eyes wide, scared and tired.

'I got here as quickly as I could,' Spengler told him.

Zach ushered him inside, closed and locked the door behind them.

'Thanks, but there's nothing you could have done.'

Spengler looked puzzled.

'About what?'

'The intruder,' Zach told him.

Realisation dawned on Spengler's face. The intruder. He'd completely forgotten Zach mentioning about someone perhaps being in his home when they had spoken earlier. Lots had happened since. Spengler glanced around. Everything looked normal. Other than Zach, of course, but he never knew what sort of a state his client was going to be in when he saw him. There was always something he was worried or anxious about, and somehow it always came down to Spengler to fix it.

'Oh, sure. The intruder,' Spengler said. 'Have they gone?'

'The police - '

'You called the police? What did I tell you about that?'

'I didn't call them. Someone thought I was breaking in to my own house. I had to - '

'Yeah, yeah, yeah, I'm glad it's all over. Hopefully you haven't done too much damage. That's not why I'm here anyway. I tried calling you, but you hung up on me.'

'I was a little busy.'

'Yeah? Well I've been busy too, that's why I was calling. I came here because I need to get an answer from you.'

'About what?'

'"About what", he asks. About what. Romanelli. He wants you for the part.'

'What are you talking about?'

Spengler wondered if he should be worried; Zach looked

genuinely confused by what he was saying. Perhaps he should have waited until the morning to go over this, but there wasn't the time.

'Geez, did this intruder guy clonk you over the head or something?'

Spengler headed down the hallway through to the kitchen. He yanked open the fridge and pulled out two beers, Zach trailing behind him like a lost little puppy. Handing a bottle to his client, Spengler tried to spell out the situation:

'The. Part,' he said slowly. 'Romanelli. The movie. Remember?'

'He wants me?'

Some sense was gradually starting to creep back; Zach's cognitive abilities were on the verge of reigniting, and he was close to understanding what was being said to him.

'What did I just say?' Spengler asked sarcastically as he rummaged through Zach's cupboards looking for something to snack on.

'He really wants me?'

Spengler opened a bag of nachos and shoved a handful into his mouth.

'Uh-huh,' he grunted, crumbs spraying from his mouth.

Zach sat down. He rubbed his cheeks, the back of his neck, brushed his hands through his hair.

'Well, I don't know,' he told his manager. 'I need to think about it.'

Spengler sighed. He'd seen this act from Zach far too many times already. The self-doubt, the second-guessing, the goddamn frustrating part where he talks himself out of a role and *Spengler doesn't get paid*.

'What's to think about?' Spengler asked, perching in a chair beside Zach. 'This is the plan, isn't it? Exactly what you've been waiting for.'

That was the way to do it: remind Zach of his goals, his

ambitions, how this role fit in to the Master Plan, which, so far, had done nothing but hold him back and prevent him from taking on any sort of work whatsoever.

'Sure,' Zach replied doubtfully. 'But…'

'Quit thinking and give me an answer.'

'What's the rush?'

'Rehearsals begin tomorrow.'

Spengler took another long swig of beer, watched Zach out of the corner of his eye as the news sunk in. He would have laughed at the reaction if he hadn't been thinking about the money he could be about to loose should he fail to get Zach fully, one-hundred percent on board right now.

Zach launched out of his chair, the fastest Spengler had ever seen him move.

'Tomorrow?!' he exploded. 'There's no way I can do it. I'm not prepared. I couldn't possibly be ready. No way.'

Spengler took hold of Zach's shoulders and eased him back down into his seat.

'Take it easy, take it easy,' he told Zach, miming taking in and letting out deep breaths. Meditation, relaxation. That was the thing in Hollywood these days. The more you relaxed the calmer you would be when you were ready to blow your freaking top at someone for no particular reason other than a sense of entitlement. All the stars were doing it.

'You want me to tell him no, I'll tell him no,' Spengler said with a sigh that made it clear this was not a route he wanted to go down.

Spengler pulled the beer bottle from Zach's hand, lifted it to his lips and fed him the delicious cold liquid as if he was feeding his own grandchild some milk.

'I mean,' he continued, 'it will probably mean neither of us ever get any work again, but whatever. I'm only a few years off retirement. I can cut back. Make some major lifestyle changes. If you say "no" to Romanelli, you're essentially saying no to everyone in the film industry. After all, if you're above working with him, who is there left? Only God himself, and no matter what the rest of those guys out there will tell you, God doesn't work in the movies.'

'It's just - ' Zach tried explaining.

'I know, I know. You need to plan. You need room to breathe. Blah blah blah. But you know, you've turned down a lot of lucrative roles waiting for The One. This movie has awards season written all over it. Sounds like it fits with the grand plan to me.'

Zach's head turned, ever so slightly, in Spengler's direction. Spengler smiled to himself; he was starting to get through. Spengler knew how Zach's mind worked; it's not like he hadn't already thought about the prospect of winning awards for this film, but for someone else to speak Zach's own thoughts out loud - that was essentially validation of what he had been thinking all along. Spengler had worked with, and for, him long enough to know one or two psychological tricks to use on his client. They didn't always work, but they were always good things to try.

'Alright,' Zach said slowly, thoughtfully. 'Alright. I'll do it.'

'I mean, if you're too scared...'

'I said I'll do it.'

More firmly that time. Spengler could tell he was actually, completely, decided. His work was done.

'Good man,' he said and headed towards the kitchen door.

'On one condition.'

Spengler stopped in his tracks. A condition for taking on work? That was a new one.

'What's that?'

Zach looked around at his large kitchen, the empty hallway stretching out past the kitchen all the way to the front door. Large and empty, ominous now, with all he believed had come before, despite being lit with hundreds of watts of electrically generated light.

'Stay here tonight,' he told Spengler. 'Help me prep for the morning.'

'Stay over?' Spengler laughed. 'What are we, twelve year old girls? Can we put on PJs and talk about boys?'

'Please,' Zach begged. 'I need to be ready.'

Spengler could see Zach was serious. And they were both seriously in need of a pay check. Spengler couldn't afford to have him chicken out now, not for the price of a night sleeping on Zach's couch and listening to him whine all evening about not being ready. He could do it, if he had to. He had to keep reminding himself about the end goal of living out his last days as a recluse by the sea. He simply had to live long enough and bring in enough money to make that happen.

And Zach wasn't going to be the one to spoil it for him.

'Fine,' he sighed. 'But we're not top and tailing.'

'Of course not. You can have my bed, I'll take the couch.'

'And you need to do something for me in return.'

'Okay…?' Zach cautiously replied.

Spengler looked around the house, bright as daylight despite it being practically the middle of the night already.

'Switch some damn lights off so I'll be able to actually get some sleep.'

10

Regardless of best intentions, there wasn't much sleep to be had at Zach's house that night. Without so much as a scene from the script available to them, there was little that could be done by way of preparation. Yet, somehow, Zach kept coming up with questions, thoughts, ideas, general worries. Eventually Spengler suggested Zach sit and watch a couple of Romanelli's films and study the performances from his actors, if only to shut the guy up for a few hours. Zach agreed it was a good idea, leaving Spengler to believe he was going to get the chance to sleep. It didn't work out that way, of course, as Zach disturbed him every five minutes or so with another random worry that had jumped into his head as he watched the films.

The following morning, a bleary eyed Spengler put on a pot of coffee and slumped at Zach's breakfast table, sipping the life-saving liquid. A pizza box sat on the counter, a couple of slices remaining of their order from the previous night, staring at Spengler and begging to be eaten. Normally he would, but that morning he couldn't bring himself to eat any of it. The newspaper had recently been delivered, and a headline in the less serious section had put him off food:

FUR BRAINED FURBALLS STAR CALLS COPS OVER

BROKEN TOY.

He turned the paper over so it wouldn't stare at him oh so mockingly.

Zach entered the room, showered, shaved, dressed, smelling like a perfumery. He was distracted, fiddling with his tie, adjusting his shirt cuffs and not paying attention to anything or anyone in the room except himself.

Spengler turned the newspaper back over, making a point of ensuring the headline was visible.

He slid it in Zach's direction. Zach glanced towards the paper, but failed to notice anything that should cause him to divert his attention from what was truly important. Spengler coughed, tapped a finger against the headline.

'I don't have time,' Zach told him.

He grabbed the coffee pot, poured himself a cupful. He took a single sip then absentmindedly poured the rest straight down the sink.

'Sit down and have some breakfast,' Spengler told him.

Zach sat beside him as instructed, and immediately jumped back up again.

'I can't eat.'

'Most important meal of the day.'

He slid the pizza box across to Zach and opened the lid. The scent of the pepperoni and cheese on the cold pizza wafted out of the box and hit Zach square in the face. Spengler could have sworn he saw Zach's skin turn green.

'I feel sick,' Zach told him.

'Relax. You'll be fine.'

Watching Zach in this state was enough to make Spengler feel uneasy himself. He was laid back and easy going about pretty much everything. But seeing someone so aggravated over nothing - particularly when that someone was the key to him receiving a nice juicy pay check in the near future - was enough to turn his own stomach. He had to maintain an air of restfulness and calm, rather than validate Zach's irrational behaviour. He pulled the pizza box back towards himself, braced his stomach and chewed down on a slice. It wasn't that bad after all; sure, the cheese had turned to rubber, and the base was more like thick cardboard, but he'd eaten worse.

'Could you do me a favour while I'm gone?' Zach asked him.

'What's that?'

'Keep an eye on the house for me, would you?'

Spengler grinned, grabbed the newspaper.

'Is that in case the, uh - what was it?' he consulted the story in the paper. ' - raccoons - come back, do you mean?'

'Do this one thing for me. Please.'

Spengler refolded the newspaper with a sigh.

'The twenty percent I earn from this movie had better be worth it.'

Zach shot him a look.

'It's fifteen.'

'After last night, I deserve an extra five percent.'

'How much you get is down to you and your contract negotiation skills.'

'I could have gotten a much better fifteen percent if you'd taken *Vampire Grannies 3*,' Spengler grumbled.

He was still trying to work out ways to get Zach to take that part. The script was bad - *terrible*, in fact - but in a hilarious way. Spengler was sure it was destined to become a cult classic. In the right kind of cinema, it could run once a month every month for the foreseeable future and they could keep reaping in a percentage for years to come. It was certainly going to have more of a repeat viewing appeal than Romanelli's film, even though there was no doubt that would be the better picture. Whatever "better" meant, anyway. For someone, somewhere, *Vampire Grannies 3* would be their *Citizen Kane* (which, quite honestly, Spengler considered to be over-long and over-rated).

He could see he'd already rankled his client with the mere mention of that particular project. Probably not the best idea to wind him up even more than he'd already managed to do to himself; not on today of all days.

'See how good I am to my clients?' Spengler reminded him. 'I'm looking out for you. Putting you up for the roles *you* want to get, rather than the roles my *accountant* wants you to get.'

'You're a regular saint,' Zach told him.

Spengler grinned, pulled another slice of pizza from the box. He'd already lined his stomach with the first slice, so a second shouldn't do any further damage.

'You remember that,' he aimed the pointed end of the slice at Zach.

'Think of what a fitting end to your career it will be, as I stand on that red carpet and acknowledge your existence in my awards acceptance speech, telling the whole world how much you've helped me get to where I am today.'

'Couldn't you have won it twenty years ago so I could get more clients - clients who actually took jobs?'

'You'd be lost if it wasn't for me.'

'I'd be on a beach sipping margaritas with Amy Adams if it wasn't for you.'

'So it's my fault you're old and unattractive?' Zach retorted.

Spengler grinned despite himself. There was the old Zach rearing his head. For the briefest of moments he had forgotten about everything that was about to happen, stopped worrying and acted as himself instead of putting on the mask he always wore when things got difficult or stressful. Typical actor: everything was a show. It was as if they spent so long making believe as someone else that they forgot who they really were themselves, finding it hard or even impossible to get back "into character". In that regard, Zach was about as good an actor as they came: he had managed to convince pretty much everyone he was a well-adjusted, sane human being.

'Well, I wouldn't go writing your acceptance speech yet. By the time this film's released, I could be six feet under.'

'You're not escaping me that easily.'

Zach picked a slice of pizza from the box and lifted it to his mouth. About to take a bite, the smell got to him. He threw the slice back down again and rushed from the room, hand over his mouth.

Spengler switched on the TV and turned the volume up enough to cover the sound of Zach throwing up in the bathroom. He could only hope and pray to whichever god might listen to him that Zach would make it through the day.

11

Zach hadn't realised he lived a mere fifteen minute cab ride away from Francis Romanelli. If he had known, he would likely have been round to meet him before; but that was probably why these people didn't announce where they lived, in case random weirdos turned up on their doorstep begging for a role in their latest movie. The cab arrived at the gates way too early for the time he was supposed to get there, so he asked the driver to go around the block a few times. As it dawned on him that what should have been a fifteen minute journey was starting to cost him a small fortune, Zach asked the cab driver to pull in to the property. The driver pressed the intercom beside the tall wrought iron gates. No one spoke, but the gates opened and allowed them inside.

A long driveway swept up between the gates, alongside a large lawn, up to a turning circle right outside the front door. The grounds had certainly been well taken care of, with the grass trimmed and expertly maintained, and the hedgerows looking in perfect condition throughout. The property was huge; certainly putting Zach's "humble" home to shame: a large building, old-fashioned in some ways, but with a modern aesthetic, with plenty of windows. Each of those windows had electronic shutters on the outside: perfect for anyone too rich or lazy to go around the whole property closing drapes. A single press of a button was all it took to seal the house off from the outside world. For now, those shutters were wide open, allowing the morning light to flow unfiltered through the windows and into the house.

Zach looked up at the large white front door, took a deep breath and knocked. There was no bell or intercom, so knocking had to suffice.

He waited for what felt like a polite amount of time. When no one came to let him in he knocked again.

Still no response.

He tried the door handle. It turned: unlocked.

He pushed the door open and peered inside.

'Hello?' he called out, loud enough to be heard, but not so loud as to seem aggressive.

He stepped inside and closed the door behind him.

The entrance hall was vast; more like the lobby of a luxury hotel than someone's home, with a huge, modern crystal chandelier hanging in the centre of its high ceiling. A red carpet drew a line from the front door, across the lobby, to the foot of a massive staircase which led up a flight of stairs before splitting in two separate directions. The red carpet followed the split, trailing forever upwards. Other than the carpet, the lobby itself was almost empty; a pair of simple seats on either side of the space and some low-maintenance house plants (practically the size of trees) the only furnishings that Zach could see. The decor was very plain - minimalist, if you wanted it to sound as if putting nothing in a room was a style choice. The walls were beige, save for a couple of small pieces of abstract art hanging, perfectly positioned to compliment the empty space. A dash of yellow, blue and green in deliberately random shapes provided a much needed dash of colour, preventing it from being a completely white room save for the arterial stream of red carpet that splashed across the floor.

Doors opened out to other rooms, and long hallways led off to further areas of the house from either side of the lobby.

'Hello?' Zach called again.

He stood and listened. Muffled voices broke through from somewhere to his left, presumably from a room off of the hallway. It sounded like there were a few people there already, talking amongst themselves. Zach followed the sound of the voices, down the hallway and to an open door.

He stopped and peered inside, not wanting to intrude.

It was the dining room. In any other circumstances it could easily have been described as a banquet hall. It was vast, with a huge wooden table in the middle of the room, a fully stocked drinks cabinet to the side.

At the far end of the table, Zach caught sight of Romanelli, sitting with a full ashtray in front of him, a half-smoked cigarette hanging from his lips.

As if seeing Romanelli in his home environment wasn't enough for Zach, beside him was another sight to behold: the unmistakable figure of Alice Blake. In her late fifties, she was still very much the glamorous actress she had always been. Beautiful, imposing, fiercely intelligent; and by all accounts apparently plain fierce. She was an incredible actress, but had been known to make life difficult for cast and crew of her movies. Every inch the diva, she was nevertheless frequently rewarded for her efforts by way of multiple award nominations as well as the occasional win.

At that precise moment, Alice was giving a good demonstration of exactly that infamous attitude. She paced back and forth behind Romanelli, hands on hips, face red with annoyance.

'Where is he?' she demanded of anyone who might be listening. 'Goddamn useless producers. He should have been here an hour ago.'

She snatched her cellphone from the table in front of Romanelli, punched the screen to redial the last number she had called, and waited for a reply.

As a connection was made with the other line, her face settled into a smile, but the hardness of her eyes remained, and a sickly sweet tone of voice betrayed her true feelings.

'Good morning,' she purred into the phone. 'This is Alice Blake, again, calling on behalf of Francis Romanelli. Again. Could I ask that you please *get your ass over here immediately?* Thank you so much.'

Alice jabbed a finger at the disconnect button and flung her cellphone back on the table.

'Is everything okay?' Zach ventured, aware he had been standing in the doorway for an impolite amount of time and was starting to feel uncomfortable about it.

Alice whirled around at the sound of his voice. Her lips tightened as she marched towards him. Zach put out a hand ready to greet the actress as she approached.

'Hi, I'm - '

But Alice passed straight by him, letting out an aggressive growl as she went, leaving the room and disappearing from sight. Unsure exactly what had just happened, Zach clenched his fist, looking at his hand and rubbing it, as if that had been his intention all along.

Romanelli watched Zach from the other end of the table as he took a final drag from his current cigarette, stubbed it out and lit another.

'What's going on?' Zach asked. The tension weighed heavy in the room, even after Alice's abrupt exit.

'They can't get hold of Sid,' a woman's voice said from behind him.

Zach turned and saw Jennifer Hughes and Tim Astin approaching the room from the lobby.

'Excuse us,' Jennifer said with a smile, and slid past Zach

into the dining room. Tim followed close behind.

In their mid-twenties, they both looked like the young actor he had once been, back in the days of the first *Furballs* movie. So full of ambition, joy, love for the movie industry and their craft. They were still full of something he had once known as *hope*. Jennifer with her pixie haircut and wide, innocent eyes, and Tim sporting a tiny goatee on his chin, only because it was the most facial hair he was as yet able to grow, and it made him look a little older than the teenager for which he kept being mistaken.

So young. So much to learn.

'Sid?' Zach asked.

'Cosgrove. The producer,' Jennifer clarified.

'He was supposed to have been here ages ago, but there's no sign of him,' Tim explained.

Sid Cosgrove. That was a blast from Zach's past. Cosgrove had been instrumental in getting the *Furballs* movies up and running, and - so legend had it - was a major influence in getting Zach the part of Michael Swift. If that was true (and Zach had no reason to suspect otherwise), Cosgrove was responsible for Zach's career up until that point. Zach wasn't sure whether he wanted to thank him or blame him. Either way, it sounded as though he was going to have the opportunity to express his feelings in person very soon.

'Sid Cosgrove is part of this project?' Zach asked, surprised. He thought Cosgrove only ever worked on genre movies.

'He does, like, a *lot* of movies,' Jennifer explained. 'I'm Jennifer, by the way. This is Tim.'

Tim half-heartedly waved at Zach as the pair of them headed towards the drinks cabinet. Zach saw Romanelli watching, but he couldn't work out whether the man was amused by them or if it was a look of disdain.

Jennifer slammed back a vodka and nodded towards the

doorway behind Zach.

'And that's Dave,' she told him.

Zach turned again to find Dave Curtis standing silently behind him. Zach realised the doorway probably wasn't the best place to remain standing, so edged his way in to the room; not too far - far enough to be out of the way, but close enough to the exit should he need it. In his early sixties, medium build and fairly ordinary looking, Dave looked out of place in the whole situation, but as Zach shook his hand there was something familiar about his appearance.

'What have I seen you in?' Zach asked. 'I know you face from somewhere.'

'I doubt that,' Jennifer scoffed. 'This is his first acting job.'

'Your first job and you're working with Francis Romanelli?'

'I got lucky,' Dave replied with a shrug as if it was no big deal to be working with one of the greatest film directors of all time.

'Damn right you got lucky,' Tim piped in. 'Have you seen the crap I had to do to get noticed by someone like Francis Romanelli?'

Zach couldn't help but feel uncomfortable that they were all talking about Romanelli right in front of the director himself, as if he wasn't there. But there was a twinkle in Romanelli's eye; he was enjoying the show playing out in front of him. Zach was sure he didn't need a boost to his ego, so it wasn't a confidence boost making him happy. Perhaps Romanelli found it to be an amusing scene to sit and watch. If he had made comedies rather than more serious fare, this could well have ended up being a scene in one of his films. Not to say that Romanelli's films were *completely* devoid of humour - you sometimes had to be a particular type of person to get the humour in the situations his films presented. Zach got it, and he thought he understood why this current scene being played out was funny to the director.

'*No one* has seen the crap you've done,' Jennifer told Tim after downing another vodka.

'Hey!' he snapped back.

'I mean, seriously. They've all tanked.'

'I suppose *The Sorority Slaughters* was high art,' Tim sneered.

'At least people saw it.'

'Yeah, perverts and weirdos.'

'Those perverts and weirdos made me a lot of money.'

'You know who else makes a lot of money from perverts and weirdos?' Tim quizzed her

Before he had a chance to elaborate further, Alice swept back in to the room, armed with a large glass of chilled white wine. Ignoring everyone else there, she glided to the far end of the table and draped her arms around Romanelli's neck, latching on to him from behind like some giant crab. The director himself continued his detached surveyance of the scene unfolding around him through a haze of cigarette smoke, unfazed by Alice's reappearance. Zach had no idea they were together; even seeing them there, right before his own two eyes, to an outsider it was an unlikely pairing. Zach wondered if perhaps Alice had told Romanelli they were in a relationship and Romanelli hadn't dared to say anything to the contrary.

'I'm sure Ms Alice Blake needs no introduction,' Jennifer hissed, some real spite obvious in the way she spoke.

Zach left the sanctuary of the doorway and ventured across to the opposite end of the room. He stood beside Alice and extended his hand once again.

'It's a genuine pleasure, and a real honour, to be working alongside you, Ms Blake,' he told her. 'I'm - '

'I know exactly who you are, Mr Keary,' she told him, giving his outstretched hand a sneer as though it were infected.

'Oh, really?'

Zach was surprised she knew his name. It was possible that Romanelli had told her about him, of course, but there was something about the way she said his name through gritted teeth that made him think there was some other reason for her to know about him, and it wasn't necessarily something that had put him on her good side, by any stretch of the imagination.

Alice marched across to the drinks cabinet. She pulled out a chilled bottle of wine and topped up her already three-quarters full glass. She took a long sip from it as she looked Zach up and down, a look of disgust permanently etched on her face as though there was some bad smell nearby and she couldn't quite work out what it was, but she knew it was something that shouldn't be there.

'There are no UFOs for you to blow up in this particular movie, Mr Keary. You know?'

Zach hadn't been sure what he had expected Alice to come out with, but it certainly hadn't been anything to do with UFOs. Perhaps she had got him confused with someone else, though that was highly unlikely.

'UFOs?' Zach prodded.

'That's what you do, isn't it?' she asked. 'Aren't all your so-called movies about aliens or spaceships or other such ridiculous nonsense?'

Nope. Zach had been in a lot of movies, mostly genre movies, but never once had he been in anything to do with UFOs, aliens, space or anything similar. It became apparent to Zach that this woman had heard of him, and knew he tended to make low budget horror films, but was also the type of person to make sweeping assumptions about them without ever actually having watched one. This, somehow, had led her to believe they were all about aliens. Zach had seen plenty of prejudice about horror movies in the past, generally based on what people *think* they know about them, rather than anything they actually *do* know, but this was a new one, even for him.

'I don't recall making a movie with aliens I'm afraid, no,' Zach told her.

'Well, whatever,' Alice replied, brushing his response off with a wave of her hand as she would a fly crawling up her arm. 'You still don't get to do that here.'

'Point taken,' Zach forced a smile in an attempt to remain amicable.

Alice picked up a newspaper from the table and flung it in Zach's direction.

'Try not to embarrass us all, will you,' she told him.

Zach caught the paper and saw it was open at the story about what happened at his house the previous evening. *That* was why she was mad at him. Not that the story had anything to do with UFOs or aliens - he hadn't accused any extra-terrestrials of breaking into his house, after all - but Alice was the sort of person who was always right, even when she wasn't.

'Ignore her,' Tim said, sidling up to Zach and passing him a drink. 'She's still pissed after last night.'

Alice glared at him, rubbing her temples as though trying to massage away a headache.

'Goddamn Meryl Streep,' she muttered under her breath.

'What did Meryl Streep do?' Zach was dumbfounded.

'She beat Alice at the Golden Globes. Again,' Jennifer explained.

She plucked the newspaper from Zach's hand, turned the pages until she found what she was looking for and handed it back, circling the pertinent information for him with one perfectly manicured fingernail, a barely concealed smirk on her face.

The list of winners and other nominees (otherwise known

as "losers") from the previous night's awards show. Zach hadn't felt the need to pay any attention to them for a long time. Without working on anything that was likely to earn him so much as a nomination, there didn't seem much point in following the events. He used to watch them religiously, but it all became depressing, watching the same people win over and over again, for the most predictable movies. Certain people, if they made an appearance in a film at all - even the briefest of cameos - they were going to receive a nomination. It was almost like a participation award: "let's give them a trophy because they've survived in the industry for another year without blowing their brains out".

Alice glared at Jennifer, not needing to be reminded about what Meryl goddamned Streep did this time. She swept back out of the room, head held high, as though posture was enough to maintain one's dignity.

'How many times is that now?' Jennifer called out after her. 'Seven? Eight?'

There was no response from Alice as she drifted away and out of sight. Jennifer and Tim laughed and exchanged a high five.

Zach couldn't help but feel that this shoot was going to be a particular interesting experience.

But not necessarily for the right reasons.

12

There was no real reason for Spengler to stay at Zach's house: if someone broke in, what was he going to do about it anyway? Leave to make sure he didn't get hurt, most likely. There was nothing in the contract with his client that put Spengler in charge of security. The little money he received from Zach certainly didn't warrant putting himself in any sort of physical danger. And if a raccoon or some other vermin crawled out of its hiding place, he was likely to have a more than similar response to the situation. Again, nothing in the contract about being pest control or exterminator.

Though there was, in his opinion, no need for him to be there, Spengler felt no real urge to rush off either. Zach's house was more spacious than his own; Zach's television was larger than his by a good few inches; and Zach's refrigerator was far more well-stocked than his.

Zach's bathrobe was, of course, also far more luxurious than his, since he was keeping score, made from one hundred percent pure Egyptian cotton. Zach hadn't allowed himself a great many luxuries, but this particular one was worth the money as far as Spengler was concerned. Spengler wandered through the kitchen wearing the robe, enjoying the feel of the fabric against the skin of his neck. He browsed through the cupboards and shelves, seeing what there was available to him. He pulled open the refrigerator, plucked out a bottle of beer and examined the label. He shrugged.

Good enough.

'May as well relieve you of fifteen percent of your alcohol, too,' he muttered and went to close the fridge door.

Changing his mind at the latest minute, he pulled out a few more bottles, tucking them under his arms and in the robe's pockets.

A box of iced ring donuts sat on the side, begging to be eaten. They were a couple of days old and on the verge of hardening. As someone who was very much of the opinion that good food should never be wasted, Spengler grabbed one and, holding it clenched between his teeth, lifted the rest of the box with his free hand. He carried the donuts and beer out of the kitchen and planted himself in front of the TV in the living room.

Sticky frosting from the donuts coated his fingers. He licked the worst of it off and ran his fingertips across the robe so as not to put fingerprints all over Zach's stuff. He grabbed the TV remote control and fired it at the screen. Spengler settled back into the deep, plump sofa as the TV sprang to life and the seventy-five inch images blasted themselves in his direction.

He was ready for a long, hard day guarding his client's property.

13

Even a full hour after Zach was required to be at Romanelli's house, they were still waiting to begin rehearsals. Despite the continued absence of the producer, Cosgrove, Zach could see no reason why they couldn't at least begin without him being present; he didn't think he'd ever been to a rehearsal with a producer in attendance. They usually waited until production was in progress before geting in the way, trying to put their own stamp on proceedings. Much as he admired Cosgrove, Zach didn't need extra suits in the building when he was trying to make a more respectable mark in the film world.

Zach sat with Tim, Dave and Jennifer on a large, modern sofa to one side of the dining room, all of them huddled together waiting for things to start. It reminded Zach of Physical Education lessons at school: groups of sweaty kids sat too close to each other, waiting to be picked for the team (or not, in Zach's case).

Across the other side of the room, Alice remained close by Romanelli, whispering like Wormtongue into his ear and casting occasional glances in their direction. Zach was sure he wasn't being paranoid when he believed that Alice was talking about him, probably trying to persuade Romanelli to fire him even before they began the whole process. Romanelli, as ever, remained still, save for occasionally placing his cigarette in his mouth and pulling it back out again, unmoved by whatever it was Alice was saying to him.

Zach watched Alice's lips, trying to make out what she was saying to the director, but she was an expert at concealing her mouth behind a hand, or her hair, or Romanelli's cloud of smoke. The first couple of times Alice caught him watching them, Zach quickly looked away. But he decided that if she was talking about him, he wanted to let her know he knew what she was doing, so he maintained eye contact for an uncomfortably long time, even as she slithered her way into Romanelli's brain.

'You're coming tonight, right?' Zach heard Jennifer ask.

It took him a moment to realise he was the one being addressed. He peeled his eyes away from the conspiratorial one-sided conversation happening on the other side of the room.

'What's that?' he asked.

'To the party, duh! Here, tonight.'

Her tone implied that it was obvious what she was talking about, and no explanation should have been necessary. It was the first Zach had heard about any sort of party, but he'd only been there for an hour and had barely been spoken to in all that time. Not even by Romanelli, and certainly not about any party.

'I don't think I'm invited,' he admitted.

'So what? Just come,' Tim chipped in. 'You're coming, right, Dave?'

Dave, wedged in between Tim and Jennifer, shifted his head back and forth as the pair spoke to and around each other.

'I don't know yet. We'll see how today goes,' Dave replied.

A fair, honest answer. He wasn't going to last long in the movie business, being so truthful, Zach thought.

'You *have* to come,' Jennifer insisted, a childish whine in her voice. 'Everyone's going to be there.'

'Everyone?' Zach asked.

'Except maybe Dave, apparently. Not, like, only us, but *everyone*.'

'Give me your cellphone,' Jennifer told him. 'I'll put my number in there for you, so you can text me if you're coming.'

Zach obligingly handed over his phone.

'It's going to be the who's who of Hollywood,' Tim told him. 'You *have* to be there.'

Zach wondered what they meant by that. After all, the "who's who of Hollywood" to these guys probably meant a bunch of YouTube stars or Instagram influencers rather than important people in the movie business. But, if the party was being held at Romanelli's place, Zach was pretty sure Romanelli would have invited some *real* Hollywood figures; assuming it was Romanelli who had organised the party in the first place. It was possible he knew nothing of it, or had somehow agreed to it happening without caring about what was happening or who was turning up.

Yet, despite loathing social events, it could turn out to be an important one for Zach. If the right people were there, it could be the *next* step on his quest for a more fulfilling career. If the right people saw him getting along with Romanelli, and if Romanelli had a good word or two to put forward about him, Zach could be set for proper, high quality work for the next few years of his life. It could be a party that he might actually have to make an effort to attend.

But he was getting ahead of himself. Alice was still speaking at Romanelli, so Zach could only hope he even made it through this, the first day, without anything terrible happening.

'Have any of you guys seen a script yet?' he asked, trying to change the subject and get back to business, as Jennifer gave his cellphone back.

Look professional. Always.

Before anyone could respond, Alice jumped up from beside Romanelli, clapped her hands together loudly three times as if there was a whole crowd in the room she needed to address.

'All right,' she called out. 'Let's get started.'

Zach sat up straight, listening attentively. Whatever it was Alice wanted, even if she was trying to get rid of him - *especially* if she was trying to get rid of him - he needed to make sure to stay on her good side, one way or another, however painful for him that might be.

'As I'm sure you all know,' Alice continued, 'the film we're about to begin creating is entitled *A Penchant for Sorrow*, and I'm sure you've all been given an idea of what it's about.'

Vague murmurings of agreement arose from the group.

'Well,' Alice smiled, rubbing her hands together with glee, 'the exciting thing is, for this film that's *all* there is so far: there's no script. There's an *idea*. A seed of a thought that Francis wants us to water, to nurture and to grow to become something magnificent - '

Zach felt some strange pains swelling in his stomach. Was it actually possible to physically feel stomach ulcers forming? His throat closed up and his mouth went dry. He could practically feel the colour draining from his face. He felt numb all over. He wanted to run away and hide somewhere, though he didn't think any part of his body was currently working well enough to allow him to do that.

No script.

How was that going to work?

He lifted his hand with trepidation, like a child wanting to be allowed to go to the toilet during a school lesson.

Alice had seen him, but was ignoring the raised hand.

She continued:

' - creating moments of artistry which Francis can choose to put in the final film - or not - ' (here she made a point of deliberately lingering her gaze on Zach. There was no doubt about it. The narrowed eyes and tight smile as she turned to look at him gave it away completely) ' - as his particular whim would have it.'

Alice finished speaking and looked across the group, carefully monitoring their reactions. The two kids were excited by the prospect. Fresh from acting classes, they were probably used to improvisation, *becoming the moment*, centering their character or whatever the hell it was they were being taught that was of no practical use whatsoever in the real industry. At least, it was of no practical use until this exact point in time, when it just so happened that the great Francis Romanelli had decided to improvise *an entire film*. Why him? Why now? If Zach had known this was going to be the case, he would never have agreed to be a part of the film - or he at least would have giving it *serious* consideration. He wondered if Spengler knew about the situation. If he did, he had deliberately - and very shrewdly - kept it to himself.

Zach lifted his hand higher, waved it in the air. The others in the group looked at him, and Jennifer even pointed in his direction, until Alice had no choice but to address him.

'What is it?' she snapped.

'To be clear,' Zach said, licking his suddenly ridiculously dry lips and forcing the words out. 'There's *no* script. Right?'

Alice stepped closer to him. She smiled again and Zach felt a shiver run down his body. It wasn't a pleasant smile by any stretch of the imagination. She crouched down in front of him, took his hands in hers. Her fingers were icy cold as her eyes and, Zach believed, her heart.

'Is that a problem for you?' she asked, pouting in mock concern.

Zach swallowed, ran his tongue over his lips again.

'No,' he whispered, then coughed to clear his throat. 'Not at all.'

Though unconvinced, Alice's smile flashed momentarily to a scowl. She stood up straight again, peered down at him.

'Good,' she said. 'Let's take five to grab a coffee and we'll make a start.'

14

Zach rushed from the room, not for want of another shot of caffeine, but to speak to his manager / therapist / friend / life-coach, Richard Spengler. He found a quiet corner in the house and hid behind a doorway, peering around on occasion to ensure he hadn't been followed and wasn't going to be overheard. The others drifted around with cups of coffee and glasses of various harder refreshments, but no one ventured in his direction.

'I have a problem,' Zach declared the second that Spengler answered his phone.

Spengler had hoped he was going to have a quiet day. He had, perhaps foolishly, thought Zach would be too busy fan-boying over Romanelli to need him for anything. He should have known Zach couldn't be trusted to look after himself for a whole day; not that it had been anything *close* to a whole day - barely two hours had gone by, and Spengler was still sitting in front of the TV in Zach's bathrobe, the only signs of time passing were the donut box having been completely emptied, and the sugary evidence of their demise spread around Spengler's mouth. His feet up on a footstool, half empty bottle of beer in one hand, Spengler muted the TV with his free hand. Seeing donut sugar fingerprints on the remote control buttons, he sucked the excess sugar from his fingers as he spoke with Zach.

'What's going on?' he asked.

'There's no script,' Zach told him. 'Did you know there's no script?'

'Sure,' Spengler admitted, without the slightest trace of guilt in his voice.

'Why didn't you tell me?'

'I knew you'd freak out.'

Just as he was doing now.

By not telling Zach, Spengler hadn't prevented the inevitable panic attack, he'd merely delayed it. He had assumed - again, foolishly - that if he was at Romanelli's place when he found out the news, Zach wouldn't have the opportunity to direct his fall-out in Spengler's direction. Work and life in general had been so much easier before the invention of the cellphone: back then, if someone wanted to have a go at you they had to either find a landline, or wait until they saw you in person, by which time you had the opportunity to board a plane to another country. Nowadays you were expected to be there at the end of the line at anyone's beck and call twenty-four hours a day.

'I would have preferred to have freaked out in my own house rather than in Francis Romanelli's,' Zach told him.

'You didn't have a full meltdown in front of everyone did you?' Spengler asked, suddenly concerned.

So concerned, in fact, that he stood up for the first time since Zach had left the house. He didn't like the way this day was going after all.

'Of course not. I found a quiet place to have a meltdown in private.'

'Good,' Spengler breathed a sigh of relief. 'You want to play with the big boys, you've got to play the game their way.'

'Meaning what?'

'If you want to win the awards, you're going to have to work differently from before. You can't dial it in based off of a third rate script hacked together by a committee of executives who Googled the current highest grossing movies.'

Spengler could hear Zach thinking about it. The silence on the other end of the line was almost painful.

'I can't work like this,' Zach announced. 'I need something concrete to work with. I can't do it. Even the thought of it is giving me the sweats.'

'You want me to call Romanelli and tell him you're doing *Vampire Grannies 3* instead?' Spengler asked.

It was unfair, but sometimes the possibility of abject humiliation was the only thing Zach would respond to; at least in the way Spengler wanted him to respond.

'No, I - ' Zach stammered.

'Because I could do that, if that's what you want.'

There was a brief moment of silence as Zach weighed up the pros and cons. An easy life with no respect and an empty cabinet where the awards should be (and that particular cabinet actually did exist; Spengler was looking directly at it, right there in Zach's living room, as he spoke) or pushing through a potentially stressful, difficult situation and coming out the other side with plaudits, laurels and perhaps even that coveted naked golden man.

'Is that what you want?' Spengler asked again.

'No,' Zach admitted.

'Then suck it up.'

Spengler could hear Zach exhale heavily on the other end of the line, and could imagine him standing there with his forehead pressed against the wall, eyes closed, wondering if he was making the right decision.

'How're things there anyway?' Zach asked.

'Oh, fine,' Spengler told him, dropping back down on to

the sofa and putting his feet up now that the latest imminent threat was contained. 'I'm patrolling the perimeter as we speak.'

He turned his head and looked behind the sofa, craned his neck to peer through the living room door and out into the hallway beyond.

'No sign of any intruders as of yet,' he reported.

'Good. Thanks.'

The fear and despair could still be heard in Zach's voice. Spengler almost felt sorry for the guy. Almost. But he remembered that if Zach quit, he wouldn't get paid. He had to keep him there, working on that movie, regardless of what he felt about it. It was time for him to grow up and push himself.

'Listen,' Spengler said, putting on a kindly, fatherly voice, 'you'll be fine.'

'Are you sure?'

Sure I'm sure, son. Gee, thanks Dad.

'I'm sure,' he said aloud. 'Besides, it could be worse.'

'How?'

'They could be making you bond with the others through ice-breaker games.'

Spengler grinned. He couldn't help himself. Sarcasm and mind-games came to him far more easily than compassion and kind words. They were a lot more fun to dish out as well.

'Ugh,' Zach groaned.

Zach continued speaking over the telephone, but Spengler was no longer paying attention.

He picked up the TV remote control and turned up the volume slightly, loud enough to make out what was being said whilst simultaneously not letting Zach know that he wasn't listening. A news report was on the air, a picture of a bald, seventy year old man covering the majority of the screen as the news anchor made their report:

Movie producer Sid Cosgrove was found dead in his home in the early hours of this morning. Police are appealing for witnesses to what has been described as a brutal murder. Cosgrove, who made his name by launching the hugely successful Furballs *franchise, was found by a concerned neighbour.*

'Uh, Zach - ' Spengler tried getting his client's attention on the phone, but Zach was going on about something or other that Spengler had missed the beginning of and had no intention of picking up the thread now. Zach was on a roll, not stopping to listen to anyone.

Strangely, the news report continued, *the decapitated body of a* Furball *soft toy was found at the scene.*

Cosgrove was dead. Spengler couldn't believe it. He'd worked with the man on and off for years, ever since that first, fateful, *Furballs* movie. Spengler had become Zach's manager almost immediately after he had been cast, so between them he and Cosgrove were responsible for Zach's career. They had crossed paths many, many times since, more often than not with Spengler having to turn down Cosgrove as he offered Zach another starring role in another potential blockbuster franchise. It had got to the point where Cosgrove would precede his telephone calls by saying 'I know he's going to say "no", but...' Zach had turned into something of a running joke between the two of them, but that didn't stop them from becoming pals. They enjoyed frequenting the same bars and relished a greasy burger or two when they had the chance to get together. He was going to be sorely missed, not only by Spengler, but by the movie industry as a whole.

And to have been murdered as well.

Cosgrove was one of the rare cases in Hollywood of an executive who got on with everyone. Literally everyone. There wasn't a single person who had a bad word to say about him, and that wasn't because he had a non-disclosure agreement signed by them, or some sort of career or marriage ending dirt on them should they say a word out of line. He was genuinely loved and respected within the industry.

Genuinely loved and respected within the industry, the report continued, *Mr Cosgrove's death is sure to be felt deeply throughout Hollywood and beyond.*

'Zach,' Spengler tried again.

'Hold on,' Zach told him. 'I think someone's coming.'

Jennifer poked her head around the corner in Romanelli's house, finding Zach lurking there facing the wall, speaking to Spengler on his cellphone.

'There you are,' she said, breathing a sigh of relief. She shouted out to the others: 'I've found him.'

'One second,' Zach told her, indicating to the cellphone pressed to his ear.

'We're ready to get going,' she said. 'We're doing ice-breakers!'

She clapped her hands excitedly, jumping up and down and squealing like she'd made it to the cheerleading squad at her high school.

'Great!' Zach replied, a fake grin spread across his face so hard it hurt. 'I'll be right there!'

Jennifer clapped her hands again and galloped away to join the others.

Zach closed his eyes once more.

'I've got to go,' he told Spengler. 'We're doing ice-breakers.'

Normally, Spengler would have relished this moment. He would have revelled in it, teasing Zach endlessly, mercilessly. Somehow, now didn't seem the right time to be doing that, though. Cosgrove's death felt important. The decapitated *Furball* soft toy being left at the scene - that had to mean something, surely. A message, perhaps. But what?

It was then that he remembered the dismembered head of the soft toy Zach had found the previous evening. A head here, a body at Cosgrove's place. That sounded like too bizarre a similarity to possibly be a coincidence. Was the possible break in at Zach's house connected to Cosgrove's murder? Perhaps Zach had been right, and someone actually had been inside. Perhaps Zach had been lucky to get away with his life; he could have been intended as a victim.

'Zach, wait - ' Spengler said into the phone, wanting to warn his client of a potential coming danger.

But Zach had hung up.

'Dammit,' Spengler cried out to no one in particular.

He jumped from the sofa and switched off the TV, shrugging out of Zach's bathrobe and letting it drop to the floor. He rushed to the door, but changed his mind at the last second. He went back into the living room and picked up the half finished beer. Guzzled it down, put the bottle back on the table and headed back out again.

In the hallway, Spengler called Zach on his cellphone again, but Zach wasn't picking up. The *one* time he needed to speak with him and he was actually unavailable. He reached for the front door, about to leave the house, when he stopped again.

Perhaps Spengler had been working in the movies for too long. No one would want to hurt Zach; he wasn't that important.This was like the plot from one of Zach's movies, and not a particularly good one at that. But as he looked at the dismembered Fuzz head perched but the front door, Spengler still had the uneasy feeling that something was very, very wrong.

He looked around at the lights in the house, blazing despite the sunlight flowing in from outside. Zach would kill him, but he couldn't leave them on.

He switched off all of the lights and left the house, grabbing the Furball head to take with him on his way out through the door.

15

The atmosphere in Romanelli's dining room was thick with tension. You could practically feel the heavy, bulbous clouds of anxiety forming overhead, black with threat and ready to unleash some sort of hell upon anyone who might be unfortunate enough to be standing underneath.

Or maybe that was just Zach.

Jennifer and Tim sat together on the edge of the sofa, looking excited at the prospect of playing ice-breaker games. Judging by everyone else's expressions, it must have been their idea: Dave sat separate from the others, head in hands, perhaps regretting his first foray into acting. Alice continued to gulp down white wine next to Romanelli, eyes narrowed, watching, always watching, particularly Zach, of course.

Now Zach had decided to commit himself to the project, regardless of what might happen, he was anxious to actually get on with some proper acting; developing his character, helping to shape and evolve the story. It was going to be challenging, most likely frustrating, and certainly terrifying. But he kept thinking about the press junkets he would have to attend when the film was released:

'Why, yes, that part *was* my idea. Francis loved it, and insisted we develop it further. I had *no idea* it would become the very soul of the picture.'

But for now he had to sit through *ice-breaker games*. Spengler had been right: that was worse. Like his two young co-stars, Zach, too, sat on the edge of his seat, but with abject terror rather than excitement, wringing his hands together, dreading what they were going to decide to play.

Jennifer snapped him out of his reverie by clapping her hands together with excitement.

'I know! I know!' she cried out, jumping from her seat. 'Let's play *Truth or Dare!*'

Dave groaned, Alice rolled her eyes, and Zach's fear returned with a vengeance.

Truth or Dare. Spengler's words from the previous evening came back to Zach, from when Spengler had accused him of wanting a sleep-over. Between this and the idea of ice-breaker games being brought up by Spengler, Zach was beginning to wonder if his manager's words were actually prophetic.

It was clear that, for whatever reason, Alice had allowed Jennifer to be in charge of this part of their day. Perhaps she knew Jennifer would make life even more of a hell for Zach. Despite her initial reaction to the game suggestion, Alice said nothing and allowed them to proceed. Only Jennifer and Tim, the two people in the room under the age of thirty (or even fifty), were happy about the prospect.

'I'll go first!' Jennifer declared, as if anyone else would have been fighting her for the opportunity. 'Tim: truth or dare?'

'Ooooh,' he said with a loud exhale, finger to his lips as if it was the hardest decision of his young life. 'Truth!'

'Okay,' Jennifer smiled. 'Who is the worst movie star you've had to deal with?'

'Present company excluded?'

Alice rolled her eyes again.

'Not… necessarily…' Jennifer replied with caution.

'In that case…' Tim grinned.

But he didn't get the chance to finish as Alice rose from her place beside Romanelli and marched over to them.

'Oh, Jesus,' she snapped. 'That's not how you play it. At least ask something vaguely interesting.'

She turned her sights to Zach and smiled that malicious smile he had already grown accustomed to having thrown in his direction.

'Zach,' she purred in his face. 'Tell us your most embarrassing secret.'

Zach could already feel his face redden as everyone turned their focus towards him. He thought he even saw Romanelli straighten up a little in his chair, and for the briefest of moments he could have *sworn* the director stopped smoking. Alice wore a look that had Zach convinced she already had a "correct" answer in mind for her question. So, if Zach didn't come out with whatever it was she was thinking, she would say it anyway, and, therefore, if he said something embarrassing that *wasn't* what she was thinking of, he would have inadvertently revealed *two* embarrassing secrets about himself within the space of a couple of minutes.

There were plenty of things it could be, he just wasn't sure which would be considered the *most* embarrassing. And what did Alice actually know about him anyway? Was it a bluff? A double bluff? Perhaps she didn't know anything at all, and was goading him into revealing something that she could use against him going forward.

Jennifer and Tim were forever fiddling with their cellphones - would whatever Zach said in the next few moments go straight on Twitter for their multitude of followers to revel in?

Zach opened his mouth to speak, but something was preventing him from putting together a coherent sentence:

'I… what?… there's nothing…' he stammered.

Alice rolled her eyes once more.

'Well,' she said, 'I think this ice is officially broken. As apparently is Zach's brain. Can we get back to being grown-ups now, please?'

16

Alice stood with her face so ridiculously, uncomfortably close to Zach that when she moved, even involuntarily, Zach could feel the tip of her nose rub against his. A scent combination of white wine and peppermint flowed from her mouth whenever she spoke; a sweet and strangely appealing mix. Though he didn't mind the aroma too much, Zach didn't particularly appreciate this invasion of his personal space. He'd tried backing away at first, but she kept closing the gap between them; it wasn't worth even trying, otherwise he'd have ended up pinned against a wall with nowhere to escape.

The tension between them was palpable. The rest of the room watched in silence as they stood there, sizing each other up. Two warriors about to engage in mortal combat. The winner was all but guaranteed, and no one was betting on Zach.

The audience perched on the edge of their seats, waiting for... something...

A high-pitched melody rang out, breaking the silence, jerking everyone from the spell that had been cast upon the room.

Zach fumbled his cellphone from his pocket, jabbed at the call dismiss button and put it away again. He looked back into Alice's hard, glaring eyes, his own face red with embarrassment and annoyance at himself for such an amateur mistake.

'Sorry,' he told her and resumed his position.

Alice closed her eyes and took a deep breath.

'You're a fool if you think I'll let you get away with it,' she told him, her whole voice and posture changed, somehow larger and stronger than she was before. A nothing less than intimidating presence.

'I...' Zach began.

'Did you really think I'd sit back and let it happen? Did you really think you wouldn't get found out?'

Zach couldn't think of the words to say. The whole situation was too much and he was in over his head. Without knowing exactly *what* he had hoped not to be found out about, it was very difficult to come up with a suitable response for her.

Improvisation had never been one of Zach's skills, and now here his was, having to improvise a scene with one of the world's greatest actresses. This was not an unfounded boast on Alice's part; she had actually been voted as such by multiple popular film magazines, journals and websites - a point she was always more than happy to point out should the situation arise which would allow her to mention it. Of course, if the situation *didn't* arise naturally, Alice was more than capable of forcing the topic. She even had scans of the articles on her cellphone, pinned to the top of her photos for easy, swift access.

If Zach only had some sort of context for the scene, he might stand a better chance against Alice, but she had launched straight into it without any sort of a plan as to what they were doing.

She had called it a "warm-up exercise".

It was certainly working, because already Zach could feel

drips of sweat running down his neck, across his spine and down into his pants. It he hadn't felt uncomfortable before, he certainly did now. The thought of the dark, damp patches forming under his armpits, staining his shirt, only made him sweat all the more.

Alice stared at him, eyes wide, lips quivering with rage.

She was good.

'I don't…' Zach tried. 'I can't…'

Alice slapped him across the face.

Hard.

A genuine, rage-fuelled slap. He thought he might have blacked out for a second, but he couldn't have done because he was consciously aware of the rest of the room gasping in shock at what had just happened.

'Alice, you can't - ' Jennifer began to protest.

But Zach held up his hand, stopping her from speaking. He didn't want to give Alice the satisfaction.

If he stopped the scene now because of a little slap, he may as well give up and go home. She would have won. He rubbed his cheek, circled his jaw around, trying to ease the tension in his face. It clicked as it moved from side to side, but that was his age. Nothing was broken, though it was likely to leave a mark. He could imagine having Alice Blake's palm print permanently etched on his cheek like a war scar. A physical memento of this wonderful day they had spent with one another. He looked at Alice and within a second she went from looking at him with cold, hard, malicious eyes to tears flowing down her cheeks, eyes bulging with hurt, a broken wreck of a woman.

She was *very* good.

'How could you?' she whispered, but the words themselves couldn't have sounded any louder. 'How could you.'

'I think… I mean…'

Zach still couldn't get any sort of response out. He needed to join in properly, otherwise she was going to stand there slapping him for the rest of the day, and he wasn't sure his face could take it. She had put a lot of force into that first one; if he annoyed her even more he could well end up with a black eye or two. Yet part of him was secretly enjoying this acting masterclass she was putting on, and he had a front row seat for it.

It was *supposed* to be interactive, though.

'You never thought about anybody but yourself,' Alice continued. 'Not once. It's only ever been about you, hasn't it? Even now, all you can think about is yourself. After all that's happened, after all you've done, after all you've put me through. It's all about you.'

She looked at him with expectation, waiting for him to say something, anything, that could move the scene along, but *still* Zach couldn't figure out where to take it. Multiple scenarios ran through his head, things he *could* say, things he probably *should* say; but what if he said something and she subsequently said something so far removed from what he was expecting that he no longer had any idea of what to say after that. When you play a game of chess, you don't plan one move ahead; you have a whole list of moves prepared: a strategy to help you win. You don't make it up as you go along. But Alice wasn't playing chess. Or, if she was, she had a whole strategy in mind that Zach had never previously seen played out.

This was why people spent weeks, months, sometimes years, writing a script. Because you *can't make it up on the spot*.

At least, Zach certainly couldn't. Alice, on the other hand, was in her element and enjoying the whole experience.

It probably helped that she was able to hit him and get away with it: she wasn't likely to get too many chances like that, and she intended to make the absolute most of it.

Realising Zach wasn't going to make any sort of worthwhile contribution, Alice sank to her knees and put her head in her hands, her whole body convulsing in silent sobs. She whispered, and everyone leaned forward in their seats, making sure they didn't miss a single word of what was being said.

'His death should have meant something to you. You should be feeling something right now. But there's nothing left in you, is there? Nothing. You're empty. Hollow. You're like that shell we found on our honeymoon - do you remember? Of course you don't. Why would you? You — '

Zach's cellphone screamed to life again.

Alice jerked a rage filled face towards him.

'For the love of God,' she snapped.

Zach took his phone out of his pocket. A quick glance at the screen showed him it was Spengler calling. Again.

The man should know better than to keep ringing when he was trying to rehearse. Highly unprofessional. Zach switched the phone to vibrate mode.

'Sorry. Again,' he smiled sheepishly at Alice. 'Please, carry on.'

Alice got to her feet, trembling with anger. She stood tall, right in Zach's face as they had been before.

'Carry on?' she asked.

'Sure.'

'I can't turn it on and off, you know.'

'Okay, but — '

'I'm taking five,' she announced.

Remembering she wasn't officially in charge, she turned to face Romanelli, who continued to lurk in the background, smoking, and told him:

'We're taking five.'

She stormed from the room, leaving Zach standing there, frustrated, embarrassed and afraid of what might happen when she came back.

17

The day hadn't begun well, and the face Zach saw reflected in the bathroom mirror face was showing it. He had to get it together and make sure no one - especially Alice Blake - saw that it was getting to him. She would use any excuse to get Zach kicked off the production. Zach put his cellphone beside the sink and ran water through the faucet until it was as cold as possible and splashed it over his face. He could feel his skin tighten as the cold water hit, the over used sweat glands closing in on themselves. He watched in the mirror as the drips ran down, cooling his skin, before falling into the sink in front of him.

'I can't turn it on and off, you know,' he quoted Alice in the mirror, quite impressed by his own imitation.

He almost laughed, but he suddenly felt self-conscious and childish and hoped no one had seen him.

He grabbed a towel from beside the sink and wiped the excess water from his face.

A shadow moved across the mirrored reflection of the bathroom doorway.

But, with the towel covering his eyes, Zach didn't notice.

He hung the towel back up again, straightened it out, trying to ensure he left it exactly as he had found it.

BZZZZZZZZ.

Zach jumped at the sudden sound.

It took him a second to realise that it was his cellphone, vibrating against the marble surface by the sink. It skittered along the top as it vibrated. Zach grabbed it before it got too far and leapt to its death on the floor.

The display showed that it was Spengler calling. *Again.*

The man was starting to annoy him now. He had never been this pushy before. He must be desperate for this latest pay check, checking up on his client every few minutes.

'You're going to get me in trouble,' Zach told the unanswered cellphone, and pressed the call reject button.

He took one last look at his tired, stressed, ageing face in this mirror.

'You've got this,' he said to his reflection, trying to motivate himself. But then, more realistically: 'Who are you kidding? You'll be lucky to survive the day.'

He sighed and left the bathroom. He took a couple of steps down the hallway before he realised he had left the light on - force of habit. He trotted back, reached around for the switch and flicked it off.

He started to go back down the hallway: a long row of doors on one side, railings on the other guarding against a fall to the ground below. Several abstract pictures (originals, not prints, Zach was sure) and a couple of mirrors hung on the wall. It was as minimally furnished as the rest of the house that he had seen so far.

It was in one of those mirrors that a flicker of movement caught his eye. Nothing major, but enough to draw his attention. He stopped and looked around.

There was no one there.

Probably his mind playing tricks on him, as usual.

He continued down the corridor.

But there it was again. There was definitely something or

someone moving around up there with him. Probably Alice, trying to catch him doing something that she could use against him, the thought. He stopped beside a mirror and watched the reflection out of the corner of his eye, as if looking directly at it would scare whatever it was away.

Still nothing.

Yet he had the peculiar feeling of being watched. A shiver ran down his spine. Zach decided it was probably time to rejoin the rest of the group.

He picked up his pace.

But the hallway appeared longer than it was before, somehow. He didn't feel like he was making much progress. *Mind tricks*, he told himself. *The adrenaline is causing everything to seem like it's moving in slow motion.* He had learned that through the screenplay for *Ghost Dinosaurs* (the sequel to *Ghost Dinosaur*; the bigger budget for the sequel meant they could afford to pluralise). He hadn't bothered checking if it was true of not, but it made sense in the context of the movie, and gave the filmmakers the opportunity to try out some cool camera tricks.

Despite his half-hearted reassurances to himself, Zach was still convinced there was someone there. That's the trouble with lying to yourself: you know you're doing it, so it can never be especially convincing.

Zach faltered in his efforts to appear fearless, and glanced over his shoulder as he headed down the hallway. There was no one behind him. It was completely empty, other than him.

He turned back to face the way he was going.

Someone was there.

Right in front of him.

'Sorry,' Zach apologised, out of habit, after nearly colliding with them.

He stepped back and looked at the person in front of him. A man dressed entirely in black: black trousers, black hooded top, black gloves, black mask covering his face, black handled knife with a wicked steel blade that shone with a vicious glint in the lights.

Zach took what felt like far too long processing what he saw before him.

But when he realised what he was looking at, he stepped back. Fast.

The figure took a step forward, matching him.

Zach stepped back further.

The figure advanced.

Zach turned on his heels and sprinted down the hallway, back the way he had come. He rushed past the closed doors lining the hallway, aware of the figure close behind.

He grabbed a door handle as he passed by, yanked at it, desperate for it to open. But it was locked.

And another: also locked.

He glanced over his shoulder.

The figure was close behind, almost on top of him, the knife outstretched, ready to do its work.

Zach didn't have time to try all of the handles; if he slowed down much more he was going to be caught.

He turned right, around a corner at the end of the hallway, heading towards the back of the house.

A dead-end.

He almost stopped and turned back, but he knew if he did that, it would be his end.

Several doors led off of this part of the hallway, too. Zach wondered how many rooms this house actually had; there were doors everywhere. But they were all locked. Every single one of them. Zach didn't know if Romanelli was hiding something, or if he was just very protective of his privacy.

He had no time to try multiple doors.

And he had no escape at the end of this passage.

Zach chose a door at random and tried the handle, just in

case. It was locked, of course. He took a step back, then launched himself at the door.

The lock broke on impact, sending Zach tumbling through the suddenly open doorway and into a pitch black room.

18

The darkness of the room engulfed Zach as he closed the door and leaned against it, forcing himself to stay there, despite the overwhelming instinct to flee from the black void he had entered. The room wasn't merely dark, but rather, completely, absolutely, black. He fumbled in the darkness, twisting his body as he tried to angle himself towards a light switch whilst keeping pressure against the broken door. When he couldn't find a switch almost immediately, he realised he was wasting valuable time, and this darkness which had once been his enemy could be the only protection he had. He took out his cellphone and switched on the screen. The brightness glared in his eyes, causing white spots to float around in his vision, like snow caught in headlights.

He pressed the icon on the screen to activate the flashlight function and cast the garish white beam around in front of him.

The handle to the door rattled, grabbed by someone from outside the room.

Zach's beam flashed across a large unit close by. He dashed across the room, following the beam, and crouched behind the unit. He switched off the flashlight as the door creaked open a fraction, no more than a couple of inches or so, spilling light from outside the room into the place Zach hid. Enough of an opening to let a black-gloved hand slide through the gap and grope at the wall on the inside of the room, searching for the elusive light switch. The mystery hand, too, couldn't find it. It slid back out, into the hallway where the rest of the mystery figure presumably remained. The door pulled shut, plunging the room once more into blackness.

Zach waited where he crouched for what felt like an hour, but was actually little more than ten seconds. With no sign of the masked intruder returning, Zach let out the breath he hadn't realised he had been holding until that moment. He switched the cellphone light back on and stood up, daring to emerge from his hiding place.

He shone the beam slowly across the room. It illuminated a pair of heavy-duty black curtains at the far side; thick enough to block out any light that might try to seep in through the windows of the room - assuming there even were windows behind the curtains. It was so dark it was impossible to tell if there was anything there other than a void. Zach considered ripping the curtains open, letting blessed daylight flood in to the room. But part of him was terrified of what he might find back there: another masked attacker, perhaps, or maybe an endless chasm, blacker than the room, waiting to suck his very soul from his body, forever lost.

It was more likely that there would be windows behind the curtains, rather than a soul-destroying void, but the darkness was already starting to get to Zach. He was used to constant illumination, nowhere to hide, everything and everyone around him lit up like Christmas and perfectly visible at all times. How he longed to be back downstairs where the only things he had to worry about were being slapped by Alice Blake, and being mocked for his inability to conceive of an entire plot in his head within the space of thirty seconds.

Absolute bliss compared with what he was currently having to go through.

He vowed to himself that he wouldn't complain about it again if he got out of there safely, though part of him knew that wasn't a promise he was likely to be able to successfully keep.

He continued to scan the room with the cellphone torch. The beam caught something, causing Zach to backtrack. His mouth fell to the floor in disbelief at what he was seeing. He tiptoed across the room, eyes fixed on what the flashlight had found:

Posters, props, toys and figures.

Hundreds - perhaps even thousands - of items. All different shapes, sizes, materials, colours. The room was a museum of movie memorabilia. It wasn't so much the things Zach had found that surprised him, it was the movies all of these things were from - the last types of movies he had expected to find commemorated (albeit in a somewhat secretive way) in Francis Romanelli's house:

Every single poster, figure, toy, prop, costume, weapon was from a trashy, low-budget, B-movie genre movie. There was the original UFO prop from *Alien Bounty Hunters 3*. A battery operated toy version of one of *Hell Dogs* satanic canines. A full size poster for *Dracula's Monster*. The actual, screen-used, animatronic of a lycanthrope dressed in a shawl taken directly from the set of *Grandma Werewolf*. Multiple display pieces from *Waxwork*. Hundreds upon hundreds of other assorted items, mostly well organised and displayed as though they were placed in a permanent exhibition, but there were also several large boxes filled with miscellaneous odds and ends.

Zach wandered around the pieces, wondering why Romanelli had them all. He could only assume the director was so offended by these movies that he hoarded the items in a dark room away from prying eyes to make sure that they couldn't be celebrated. It was unlikely, though. As far as Zach could make out in the beam of his cellphone, they were all arranged as if they were there for display. Most pieces weren't under glass, and none of the toys were in boxes, so they weren't stored for financial purposes. They looked like they must have been there for Romanelli's personal enjoyment.

And then Zach found it: the display stand that took his breath away simply at the sheer, staggering, incomprehensible sight of it being there, in Francis Romanelli's house.

A whole section of the room was devoted to Zach's very own movie, *Furballs*. There was the leather jacket Zach had worn during the first movie's finale. Beside it stood a prop fire axe, identical in every way to the one Fuzz had picked up in his attempts to destroy the drooling, tentacled beast. Zach reached out and ran his fingertip across the very tip of the axe blade. It was sharp. Memories came flooding back from the production:

Already over budget and over running, only halfway through the shoot, they had run out of money for production of props and costumes. A production assistant was sent to a local hardware store to purchase the cheapest possible axe for use in that scene. A real, honest to God, wood and steel axe. Cheaper than the safe rubber versions they would generally have used, but there were none of those available at that particular time, and they couldn't afford to have one constructed especially for the production. They could - and probably should - have been shut down for it, but somehow they were never found out. Yet here it was: the actual axe they had used, still sharp after all this time. Zach pulled the axe down from where it was hooked on to the display stand and felt the weight of it in his hands.

'You could do serious damage with that,' he said to himself.

He returned the axe to where it had been hanging, making sure it was securely in place.

Despite how he felt about a lot of his filmography, those early days working on *Furballs* had been happy ones. He had enjoyed the whole shoot, learnt so much, and made a lot of friends. Zach smiled at the memories and curved the flashlight around.

It fell upon a glass case. Inside that glass case was the original animatronic puppet of Fuzz. A little worse for wear now, with patches of fur missing, some of the electronics showing through the fake skin, but it was unmistakably the genuine artefact. The puppet had been a stressful piece of work for everyone involved, with frequent malfunctions, days when it wouldn't work at all, and even the occasional minor explosion. By the end, once they had ironed out the majority of the kinks in its mechanisms, it had almost come to feel like a true member of the cast.

Zach placed his hand on the glass case, staring at the creature stood there in front of him.

Incredible.

'Hey, buddy,' he whispered, feeling simultaneously nostalgic and kind of embarrassed.

'Impressive, isn't he?' a voice spoke behind Zach.

He whirled around, ready to run but wishing he'd kept hold of the axe for that bit longer.

The flashlight beam skittered through to darkness to the source of the voice.

Romanelli.

Zach hardly recognised him without his trademark cigarette wedged in his mouth, and it was little wonder that he didn't immediately recognise the sound of the man's voice: he had barely heard him speak since he'd first met him the previous day. Romanelli stood looking past Zach, straight at the *Furballs* collection Zach had been admiring.

'You scared me,' Zach told the director as he stepped forward, brushing past Zach, straight towards the Furball animatronic.

He looked over the piece, at the surrounding items. He cast a slight frown at the fire axe and shifted it on its stand by an imperceptible degree. Rearranging the prop to be aligned to within a degree of perfection satisfied him, and his frown lifted as he turned to look at Zach.

'What are you doing in here?' he asked.

'Did you see anyone out there?'

'Like who?'

'A man in black. With a knife.'

As soon as the words spilled from his mouth, Zach knew that they sounded foolish, like an exchange two characters from one of his previous movies might have had before one of them was gratuitously murdered. His insides tightened, waiting for Romanelli to laugh at him, mock him for making up such foolishness: of course there was no knife-wielding black-clad man prowling the premises.

Yet Romanelli took what Zach had said in his stride, replying with no real change of tone in his voice:

'I can't say that I did. Why?'

'Someone tried to attack me,' Zach replied, flustered by the lack of questioning over his current mental state of mind.

'Attack you?' Romanelli repeated.

'They chased me with a knife. I came in here to hide.'

'You're not very good at hiding,' Romanelli told him, his eyes crinkling into a small smile, apparently amused by the whole situation. 'I found you very easily.'

'You didn't see *anyone* out there?'

'Not a living soul. No dead ones either, in case you were worried.'

'That doesn't make sense.'

'You're under a lot of pressure - ' Romanelli began.

'I didn't imagine it, if that's what you're implying.'

'I wouldn't dream of it.'

Zach couldn't understand it. The figure in black had been right outside the door not long ago. Zach was sure he hadn't been in the museum type room for particularly long; anyone trying to break down the door couldn't have miraculously disappeared in such a short space of time. Unless... He shone his flashlight over Romanelli, trying to remain inconspicuous, sweeping the beam over the director's clothes. He was wearing tan pants and a navy sweater with white shirt underneath. Getting changed out of the black clothes and into those that Romanelli was currently wearing was almost as impossible as completely disappearing from the scene. And Romanelli's hair was immaculately wild - somehow both haphazard and perfectly, delicately styled: there was no possible way he had been wearing a mask and hood moments before.

Romanelli was an unlikely suspect, despite being the first person to appear after the incident had taken place, and for some reason appearing in the middle of the dark room, without switching on any lights, practically sneaking up on Zach. But if he had wanted to kill him, he would have had the perfect opportunity: rather than announcing his presence there, right behind Zach, Romanelli could have easily slid a knife between Zach's vertebrae, and he would have been dead before he had even realised something had happened.

Zach thought it best to move on from the subject, at least for the time being. If Romanelli *was* the attacker, Zach didn't want to arouse his suspicions that he was on to him; and if he *wasn't* the attacker, should he survive the day, Zach didn't want to get fired for making baseless accusations against his favourite film director of all time and the man who currently had the power to make or break Zach's career.

A cautious silence was, for now, the best option.

Instead, Zach waved the flashlight around the room, illuminating the artefacts that surrounded them.

'What is all of this stuff?' he asked.

Romanelli smiled.

'I knew that if *anyone* would appreciate my collection, it would be you. You *do* like it, don't you?'

Romanelli seemed to want Zach's approval; his voice had changed in that last sentence, like a child asking if his parents liked the latest artwork they had created of a dog that looked like little more than a swirl, a rectangle and a couple of ovals on a piece of paper.

'I can't believe someone like you would be even remotely interested in movies like these,' Zach replied, dodging having to answer Romanelli's question directly.

'Someone like me?'

Romanelli sounded genuinely hurt.

'You know - a world-renowned, award winning director.'

Even to Zach's ears, he sounded like he was coming on a bit too strong. The man knew he'd won awards, he didn't need to be reminded of that fact.

'Just because I make serious films, it doesn't mean I don't know how to enjoy myself,' Romanelli snapped.

'Sure. But these movies are…'

Zach trailed off. He wasn't sure how to finish that sentence without betraying his thoughts on his own work and his own career. He was sure it was common knowledge that he wasn't the biggest fan of the movies he made, but on the other hand he didn't want Romanelli thinking that once he'd finished making this particular film he'd go off and trash it to anyone who would listen.

Yet Zach couldn't bring himself to lie. No lie was going to convincingly finish his sentence anyway.

'These movies are what?' Romanelli prompted.

'Crap,' Zach told him with a sigh. 'Utter crap. Why would you waste time on stuff like this?'

He had frequently asked himself the same question throughout the process of making many of those movies. It generally came down to two things: money and desperation. Or, one thing: desperation for money.

'They're entertaining in their own way,' Romanelli told him, straightening the clothing on *Grandma Werewolf*. 'Not all movies have to be profound. They don't have to have deep insights into race, gender, identity, politics. They don't really have to be about *anything*.'

And that's why they don't win any awards either, Zach thought.

'I'm done with this stuff,' he told the director with a dismissive wave across the vast collection. 'All these cheap monster movies. I want to make movies about life. About the human condition. What it is to live.'

'With respect,' Romanelli said to him, placing a gentle hand on Zach's shoulder. 'That's bull crap.'

'Sorry?'

'You want to see what kind of a person someone is? Watch how they act when they're chased by a hideous, blood-thirsty creature. How someone faces imminent death, how they cope with that situation, how they react when others around them are dying, what kind of sacrifice they make: *that's* how you see the *true* nature of a man.'

Enthralled by the man and his argument in favour of those movies, Zach was broken out of his trance by his cellphone vibrating. Spengler, yet again.

He pressed the call reject button.

'Let me show you something,' Romanelli told him.

19

Spengler tossed his cellphone on the passenger seat of his car. He had been trying to get in touch with Zach ever since he saw the news about Cosgrove, but Zach was still blocking his calls.

It was only a short ride to Romanelli's property, and Spengler would normally have been there within a few minutes. But already the Los Angeles traffic was building up, and it was taking far longer than it should have done to get there.

He cast the occasional glance across to the cellphone laying on the seat, sure Zach would call him back at any second. The man practically lived on his phone and was usually on the line with Spengler every five minutes. Yet this time - this *one time* - that Spengler urgently needed to get in touch, there was no response.

In a way, that worried Spengler more than Cosgrove's murder.

He glanced across again at the screen.

Still nothing.

A bump in the road caused the cellphone to slide across the seat. Spengler lunged across and grabbed it before it could fall between the chair and the door. He breathed a sigh of relief at the narrow escape and looked back up.

The traffic in front was at a complete stop.

Spengler slammed his foot on the brake. The tyres screeched against the road, complaining at the sudden violent action. The car slid to a halt, the fender with less than an inch gap between it and the rear end of the vehicle in front.

Spengler pried his fingers from their tight grip on the wheel. With hands shaking from the adrenaline rush of the moment, he grabbed the cellphone from the seat and tried Zach one final time.

20

Romanelli rolled up the left sleeve of his sweater, revealing his bare skin underneath, inch by careful inch.

'Look,' he told Zach.

Zach cast the beam of the cellphone flashlight across Romanelli's arm. He tracked the light up and down, illuminating a long, ragged, raised scar that extended from Romanelli's wrist halfway up to his elbow. It was an old scar, healed over the course of many years, but the raised flesh remained as a permanent reminder of whatever event it was that had caused it.

'What happened?' Zach asked.

'You want serious drama?' Romanelli asked. 'The truth about the human condition? Here it is. Real life.'

Romanelli waited for the truth to sink in with Zach. His eyes widened as it slowly dawned on him. Despite everything he had seen and read about Romanelli over the years, it was the first time Zach had heard anything about this.

'You did this to yourself?'

'Thirty-five years ago.'

Thirty-five years. The man had worked in the film industry for longer than that, and yet somehow he had managed to keep his suicide attempt a secret all this time. Zach couldn't imagine what he must have gone through to bring himself to do something like that, and what he must have continued to go through to keep it hidden. In the back of his mind, Zach wondered if he was the only person to know about it, and if he was, what did that mean about his relationship - such as it was - with Romanelli?

'Why did you do it?' Zach asked.

'It doesn't matter. I've got this scar as a permanent reminder to myself. I don't need to talk to anyone else about it: I know what happened and why it happened, and that's enough for me.'

'You never told anyone?'

Romanelli brushed his question aside.

'The point is, I didn't succeed in ending things. I was found in time, stitched up, my life saved.'

'Thank God.'

Romanelli smiled a slight smile, as if the very mention of God amused him for some reason.

'After that,' he continued, 'I took some time out and re-evaluated my life: the path I had so far taken, the path I was currently on, and the path I *wanted* to take. It wasn't all conscious decision making, it was more stepping back, away from everything, looking at the world from a new perspective. I spent a lot of time alone, just me and my thoughts, taking time out to heal both physically and emotionally.'

Zach nodded his head; he didn't know how to respond any better than to agree that Romanelli took the best course of action for him at that time. He did wonder what he himself would have done in that situation, but he was pretty sure he wouldn't have sat in a room by himself contemplating his existence. He could barely stand to be alone with himself as it was.

'You know what I did during that time of recovery?' Romanelli asked him.

'What?'

Romanelli smiled.

'I watched as many of those movies you so unflatteringly describe as "crap" as I could get my hands on. One after another. Obsessively.'

Zach laughed.

'Seriously?' he asked, scanning the flashlight over the props and posters in the room.

He lingered on the poster for *Demon College*. One of his own movies, and one he regretted the most, yet there he was, front and centre on the poster, acting scared as a possessed squad of half naked cheer-leaders advanced towards him from the background. The cheer-leaders were never actually a part of the movie; they were added to the poster to try and entice more teenage boys to attend. Rigorous marketing analysis indicated they were the least likely demographic to go to the movie, but showing a mock-up of the poster with additional cheer-leaders did wonders to their pre-conceived notions of what they were going to watch. There was backlash after, of course, but that was before the days of social media, so it was relatively well-contained. These days the backlash about anything was far more vocal, and usually began with someone who hadn't even seen the particular movie with which they had a problem.

'There's something about them,' Romanelli explained. 'There's fun. Joy. A weird kind of spirit.'

'Spirit?'

'People fighting for survival against overwhelming odds. The characters in these movies endured far more than I had to - *real* fears, *real* danger, *real* issues. I thought if *they* could do it, surely I could do it too.'

'Sure, but you know they're just movies, right? And I don't

know what it was you went through, but I'm sure you weren't fighting against psychotic penguins.'

His flashlight had found an action figure for the movie entitled *Killer Psycho Penguins*. They had hoped to launch an entire franchise based on that one movie, but audiences didn't buy the characters not being able to escape creatures that could only waddle. Admittedly they did it at a faster speed than regular penguins, but they were still waddling nevertheless.

'It's all a metaphor, though, isn't it?' Romanelli asked, more of a statement than a question that demanded any sort of an answer.

'If you say so,' Zach scoffed.

'Well, believe me or don't, that's how it is. And I'm here as testament to that fact. These movies, quite literally, saved my life.'

Zach cast his beam around the room, taking it all in again. With Romanelli's words fresh in his head, he tried to look at everything with an open mind, tried to see what Romanelli saw in the movies. Perhaps the director had been on particularly strong painkillers at the time, making it feel like a far more important, transcendent experience than it actually was.

Or perhaps there was some truth in what Romanelli was saying.

Perhaps a viewing of *Grandma Werewolf* could have life-changing effects on a person.

You just had to be in a really, *really*, dark place in your own life to be able to see it.

The flashlight fell at last on the Fuzz display case.

'Beautiful, isn't it?' Romanelli said.

That movie had changed Zach's life; not in the way Romanelli was talking about, but certainly in multiple other ways. It had given him everything he had - a degree of success and financial freedom; some sort of a career; fame. Maybe it hadn't all worked out exactly the way he had wanted, but that was through choices he himself had made after his career had launched.

It wasn't the fault of *Furballs* that things turned out the way they had.

The movie had made him, and given him a new life.

Perhaps there was some truth in what Romanelli was saying, ridiculous as it sounded.

21

Zach and Romanelli left the dark room filled with the director's collection, returning to the brightness of the hallway outside. Romanelli pulled the door to as Zach blinked, getting used to the light after being in the blackness for what felt like a particularly long time. The door frame was splintered from where Zach had forced it open: the only physical evidence that what Zach claimed had happened actually had happened, but not necessarily proof enough of any sort of attack having taken place.

'Sorry about the door,' he told Romanelli. 'I'll pay for the damages.'

'I'll talk to your manager,' Romanelli replied, but with a smile.

That jogged Zach's memory. Spengler had been trying to contact him for the past few minutes. He should probably take the opportunity to call him back to find out what was so urgent.

'Do you mind if I make a quick call,' he asked.

'Fine,' Romanelli replied. 'I'll join you downstairs shortly.'

They went their separate ways, Zach heading for the staircase to find a private space to make a call, and Romanelli wandering off along the hallway towards another room.

Romanelli stopped, turned back and called to Zach.

'Do me a favour.'

'Sure.'

'Don't tell anyone else about the room.'

'Sure.'

'Most people wouldn't understand; but I knew you would.'

'Whatever you say.'

Romanelli was right about one thing: most people *wouldn't* understand. But he was under the impression that Zach *did* understand. That wasn't entirely true: Zach could see and appreciate Romanelli's point of view; his arguments were well thought out and explained, but he still couldn't understand how anyone could find a deeper meaning within those movies, something to latch on to as a lifeline in dark times. It was true that horror movies were always more popular during times of unrest, whatever the cause might be, perhaps as a form of escapism from the horrors of the real world. *This economic crash isn't so bad - I may have lost my job and my home, but it could be worse: I could be being pursued through dark woods by a seven foot tall maniac wielding a razor wire net;* or: *there's a viral pandemic spreading throughout the entire world, but - hey! - at least it's not a killer clown luring children to their doom.*

But surely, Zach thought, that's all there was to it: escapism. Nothing life-changing about them.

On the other hand, Romanelli's testimony to their power was compelling and, apparently, very real. All things considered, he knew he would respect Romanelli's wishes and not tell anyone. After all, who would even believe him? World-renowned, universally acclaimed, multi-award winning director Francis Romanelli is a closet horror movie fan, who hoards memorabilia in a secret museum in his home.

No. He wouldn't tell anyone.

Well, maybe Spengler.

Zach took his cellphone from his pocket and trod down the staircase towards the lobby.

Halfway down, finger primed to dial the number:

BANG-BANG-BANG.

Someone was pounding on the front door.

Zach looked around, but there was no one else there, and nobody was coming. It felt weird to answer someone else's front door on their behalf, but:

BANG-BANG-BANG.

He couldn't leave them outside pounding on the door. Was it ruder to answer the door to someone else's house, or to ignore it and pretend he never heard anything? He had a call to make anyway.

He continued down the stairs and rang Spengler.

His manager picked up after the first ring.

'Open the goddamn door,' he told Zach immediately.

'That's you?' Zach asked.

'No, I'm pretending.'

Spengler's sarcasm shone through all the more when he was annoyed about something.

'What are you doing here?'

'How about you open the door and let me in, and *then* we can talk.'

'Okay, sure. I'm coming. But what - '

Spengler had already hung up, sure his message had got through.

Something felt wrong: Spengler had sounded out of breath on the phone, like he'd been rushing around. That wasn't like him at all. The only time Zach had ever seen Spengler rush was when he realised he only had ten minutes to get to an early-morning meeting but hadn't yet had a chance to get his first coffee of the day. Caffeine was supposed to give you energy, but in Spengler's case the thought of *no* caffeine was enough to produce that extra boost.

Zach unlocked the front door and pulled it open a fraction.

He peered around the opening.

'Spengler?'

'Who were you expecting?'

'Are you okay?'

He was out of breath, his face red, beads of sweat on his brow, stooped like a man thirty or so years older than him and trying to draw oxygen in to his lungs.

'I got here as fast as I could,' he told Zach as quickly as his lungs allowed.

'Why? What's going on?'

Zach pulled the door open a little wider now he could see Spengler, but something still didn't feel right, and he'd rather have the opportunity to slam the door shut again if he needed to.

BUMP-BUMP-BUMP.

A strange sound came from the staircase behind him.

He turned around as the *bumps* continued.

Something was rolling down the stairs, tumbling down one step at a time, bouncing as it hit each one. It was small, but quite heavy. As it reached the ground at the bottom of the stairs it continued to roll, all the way across the lobby, coming to rest at Zach's feet.

He picked it up, his back turned to Spengler and the front door.

'What is that?' Spengler asked, unable to see what Zach had picked up.

Zach stared at the object in fascination, but also mounting dread:

It was the head of the Furball animatronic prop he had been looking at two minutes previously in the prop room. Though he was sure at the time it was still attached to the rest of the model, it was now missing everything below the neck. It had been removed with some force, from the look of the jagged tears in the wires protruding from it.

This was the second Furball head that had been detached from its body Zach had held in his hands over the course of the past twenty-four hours.

Suddenly it dawned on him that Spengler actually did have a very good reason for rushing over there.

Suddenly he wished he hadn't dodged Spengler's calls all morning.

Zach turned around to face Spengler and apologise.

But the man in black was there.

Outside the front door.

Right behind Spengler.

'Watch out!' Zach tried to shout, but fear constricted his windpipe and he garbled an incoherent squeal.

Spengler got the gist of what was being said.

But too late.

Before he could move, or even see who was behind him, the figure wrapped his arm around Spengler's neck. A firm hold. Crushing his neck and cutting off his breath.

Spengler writhed around in the grip, tried to grab his assailant's arm, make some space between his attacker and his throat in a desperate attempt at gasping for air. But the attacker was too strong, and Spengler was too old and unfit. He had no chance of breaking free.

'Help me!' he gasped at Zach, wasting the little oxygen remaining in his lungs.

Zach hadn't moved.

He couldn't move.

He was literally frozen with fear at the sight of his manager and friend being strangled to death right in front of him.

'Help!' Spengler repeated, his face red, eyes bulging.

The figure continued to tighten his grip, unfazed by Zach's

presence, or, perhaps, performing this act directly in front of him for a reason.

Like he wanted Zach in the audience.

The grip of fear released Zach just enough to allow him to move.

He looked around, but there was no one there to help him.

He was on his own, with no idea what to do.

The figure released his grip on Spengler.

Spengler tumbled forward a couple of steps, gasping for air, his lungs struggling to function through rasping coughs.

If Spengler would only stumble inside, Zach could close the door and they could call the police.

The figure took a step forward.

The knife flashed its wicked steel in his hand.

He slammed it into Spengler's back, twisted it, pulled it out, slammed it back in, twisted it once more.

Spengler let out a brief cry of agony before collapsing to the floor.

The attacker, knife in hand, looked from Spengler's fallen body over to Zach.

Zach slammed the front door shut.

Survival instinct comes more easily when it's your own life on the line.

He pulled out his cellphone and dialled 911.

911. What is your emergency? he heard the operator say at the other end of the line.

'Someone's been killed.'

The briefest of pauses, then: *Could you repeat that please, sir?*

'Someone has been killed. Murdered.'

Okay, sir. What is your name and location?

'My name is Zach Keary,' he told the operator. 'I don't know my exact address. I came here in a cab, and they knew where they were going, because I told them the house I needed to go to, and they knew exactly where it was, but I don't know the address, because I didn't have to come here myself.'

He could hear himself babbling.

The adrenaline kicking in, he thought, again retrieving insights gained through working in the movie industry, where every scriptwriter had great insight into the mental and physical workings of a human being. He hoped he was right, and it was adrenaline, because the alternative was that he was having some sort of breakdown. Which, given the circumstances, wasn't an unlikely scenario.

Okay, sir. What can you tell me about your location, if not the address?

'It's Francis Romanelli's house,' he said.

There was silence on the other end of the line. A pause that went on for too long. He looked at the screen of his cellphone to check he hadn't been disconnected. Everything looked okay there; he was still on the call as far as he could tell.

'Hello?' he asked into the phone.

Sir, the operator responded, slow and cautious, probably waving for a supervisor to listen in on the conversation. *You're telling me that you're Zach Keary and you're at Francis Romanelli's house.*

'That's what I said, isn't it?'

The actor Zach Keary, at director Francis Romanelli's house.

Time was being wasted. Why did he have to keep repeating himself? He thought 911 operators would have been trained better to listen to what was being said to them the first time around. It was a life or death situation, after all.

'Yes! That's exactly it.'

Zach Keary from Furballs?

Zach rolled his eyes.

'That's me.'

Another pause.

Sir, this number is for emergencies only -

'That's why I'm calling!'
- *wasting police time is a criminal offence.*
'So is murder!'

22

The squad car was parked in a side street, hidden between buildings where it couldn't easily be spotted. Not because Officers Cole and Davies were on a stakeout, or anything like that: Davies was eating a double egg and sausage McMuffin they had picked up from McDonald's, and Cole wanted to make sure no civilians saw cops eating their breakfast while on duty. Sure, breaks were allowed, and indeed encouraged, but to watch an officer of the law chow down a McMuffin, grease dribbling down his chin, rubbery cheese being ripped apart between his teeth… that was no way to gain the respect of anyone. It was bad enough that Cole had insisted they go through the drive thru in the squad car to order, rather than standing in a queue with other civilians. The look of panic on the face of the kid who served them when he saw a police car pull up was something to behold, though, and almost made up for it. They probably could have got their order for free, their server was so anxious to see them go. But Cole had told Davies not to even try it.

Davies licked cheese and grease from his fingers. With fingers still wet from being in his mouth, he picked up his vanilla milkshake container and slurped up the last dregs. Milkshake with a McMuffin for breakfast. Cole hoped they didn't have to pursue anyone by foot any time soon; Davies was sure to suffer from indigestion after that. She watched as he crumpled all of his wrappings together into one giant ball and let out a belch from the very depths of his belly, filling the car with a sickly sweet aroma.

Cole rolled down a window and glared at him.

He felt the glare before he saw it.

'What?' Davies asked.

Cole stared with meaning at the pile of trash Davies had collected together.

Davies didn't get the hint.

'What?' he asked again.

'Separate your recyclables.'

Davies rolled his eyes. But he knew better than to argue with her, especially on topics like that. He had once seen Cole berate a fire-arms officer almost to tears because he had accidentally placed an empty Coke bottle in the can for regular trash, rather than recyclables.

Davies grabbed the trash ball and started unpicking it.

The car radio crackled to life.

Report of a possible 187 on Mulholland, the radio announced.

Cole heard the numbers but couldn't quite believe it. She always hoped they would be close by a one-eight-seven, but had never actually managed to be in the right place at the right time. But today was different. Today they were right around the corner.

This was what she'd signed up for, and at the start of every shift she wished she would be the first on the scene for one of them. Not that she would necessarily admit that to anyone; they would think her ghoulish. But here it was, practically in their lap.

A possible one-eight-seven on Mulholland.

Murder.

Cole lunged forward and grabbed the radio, knocking

Davies and tipping over his expertly crafted dual piles of trash as she did so.

'Hey!' he moaned.

'We've got ourselves a goddamn homicide,' Cole declared, her sudden exclamation startling Davies - he'd never heard her curse before, or even become remotely excited by anything (other than saving the dolphins; that had been a weird one).

Unlike Cole, Davies was in the job for as quiet a life as possible. Do his required time on the streets and then settle into a cosy job behind a desk, waiting out the years until he could collect his pension. Sure, it was good to help people, serve and protect, blah blah blah. But whatever: out of the few career options available to him, the police had the most attractive sounding pension plan when he first signed up, even if it did look like even that was slowly going down the pan.

Cole spoke into the radio, trying to contain the excitement in her voice.

'This is Cole. We're nearby. Have you got an exact location for us?'

It's Francis Romanelli's house. I'm sure you know the one.

Of course she did. Cole had made it her business to know the locations of the most wealthy, famous people on her beat. It would help somehow, she had told herself. Having an intimate knowledge of your location could never be a bad thing. And here it was, her hard work and late nights of investigative research that came close to being stalking (though, technically, legally speaking it *wasn't* stalking; she had checked that out enough with the force lawyers that even they had started to become suspicious) was all paying off.

Even Davies looked impressed. They'd never had a chance to make a call at the house of any of the Hollywood elite before; the lower classes of stars, like the one they had visited the previous evening, were a dime a dozen around there. He wiped his mouth with the back of his hand and sat up a little straighter.

'We'll take a look,' Cole informed the radio.

Please be advised suspect may still be in the area.

'Copy that,' Cole slammed the radio down, started the engine. She grinned at Davies. 'Let's do this.'

Davies switched on the lights and siren and the vehicle screeched out of its hiding place.

23

Alice stormed across the lobby towards the front door, a refilled glass of white wine in her hand, her face dark as clouds warning of an incoming storm.

'Whoever is doing all of the shouting, could you please stop,' she demanded. 'I've got a raging headache.'

She took another glug from her glass and marched towards Zach.

He was sitting beside the front door, his back against the wall, the head of the Furball animatronic cradled in his arms, safe and protected, a father caring for his new-born baby; except in this case the 'baby' was a robot head which had been forcefully removed from its body. Alice stood in front of Zach, tapping her foot in an otherwise silent demand for an explanation.

'He's dead,' Zach eventually told her.

'Who's dead?'

'He came here to see me,' Zach explained. 'He came to tell me something, but he never got a chance. He's dead and I didn't do anything to stop it.'

Alice took a step back as Zach got to his feet. Tears streamed down his face as he advanced towards her.

He had seen his best friend brutally slain in front of him

and he did nothing to stop it. He watched it happen and shut the door on him; he hadn't even gone outside to make sure that he was definitely, actually, completely dead. He could be out there, laying on the ground, drenched in blood, gasping for breath, but still in a fixable way if only someone would get him to the hospital. But Zach was too afraid to even open the front door. Who knew what terrors and evil lurked out there? He had never seen someone die before, and he doubted too many people had actually seen someone die in that particular fashion right in front of their eyes. Not in normal, everyday circumstances anyway; sure, if he had been in a war somewhere, that would have been different, perhaps, but for that to happen right in the middle of an affluent Hollywood neighbourhood, on the doorstep of a house filled with some powerful people... It didn't bare thinking about.

Perhaps, he wondered, he had led a sheltered existence.

Or, perhaps this was not one of those things people should ever have to witness.

'I did nothing,' he told Alice, continuing to step towards her. 'I was frozen. I didn't know what to do.'

He had started talking and now the words wouldn't stop tumbling out; a dam broken, the waters set free.

'Now he's dead. I could have prevented it, but I didn't, and now I've lost the only true friend I ever had.'

He stopped speaking and stared at Alice, his eyes pleading with her. Pleading for what, he didn't know, he just hoped somehow she would be able to help him. Somehow she would know what to do, what to say. Somehow, it was all make believe and Alice Blake - actress extraordinaire - was about to pull back the curtain on the whole production. He took another step forward. He needed comfort of some kind.

Alice looked at him. She lowered her wine glass to the floor beside her, reached out to Zach and held his shoulders with her hands. She stared into his eyes as if seeing him for the very first time.

'Amazing,' she whispered.

Zach's look of desperation turned to a frown.

'What is?'

'Your performance. Why couldn't you do it like that earlier?'

'My performance?'

'I never knew you had it in you.'

'I'm not - ' he began trying to explain, but once again found himself at a loss for words.

Romanelli entered the lobby from one of the hallways off to the side of the room. He noticed the two of them standing together near the front door and headed in their direction.

'There you are,' he said. 'We need to get on.'

Zach brushed tears from his eyes, but it wasn't enough to hide the evidence that he had been crying. His eyeballs were bloodshot and puffy, his face white with streaks where the tears had run down.

If Alice Blake couldn't do anything about the situation, Francis Romanelli surely could. But at the same time, Zach didn't want Romanelli to see him that way. He didn't want him to think he would break down and cry over every little thing that happened. Not that a violent murder was 'a little thing', of course, but when you're in shock, logic doesn't quite work the way it should, and Zach found himself wanting to put on a brave face, somehow.

He dabbed at his eye, trying to stop a solitary stray tear from emerging.

Too late, though: Romanelli noticed.

'What's going on?' he asked.

'You need to see this,' Alice told Romanelli, weirdly excited about something which Zach couldn't quite fathom.

Had his despair over Spengler's slaying somehow brought out this childish glee in her? Based on the albeit brief time he had spent with her so far, it wouldn't have surprised Zach if it had.

'Do it again,' she instructed Zach. 'Exactly like you did it before.'

Zach opened his mouth to query exactly what it was she wanted him to repeat, and exactly why she wanted him to repeat *any* of what he had been through in the previous few minutes. But before he had a chance to ask anything Romanelli noticed the Furball head Zach was still clinging onto.

'What have you done?' the director asked.

At first confused by the accusatory tone in Romanelli's voice, it took a moment for Zach to realise he was talking about the animatronic. He looked down at the head, the plastic eyes staring up at him from where they resided within the metal exoskeleton, covered in thick fur. He noticed what he was holding and threw it to the ground, shocked by the sight of it there in his hands, perhaps the same way he would have reacted if he had suddenly realised that it was Spengler's own head he was clutching, dripping with blood, eyes wide and lifeless. Not that that was how Spengler had gone, but still.

He realised then that he still hadn't told anyone exactly what had happened: Alice was in her own little world about something, and no one else knew Spengler had even been there.

'You don't understand,' he told Romanelli, hoping to stop the disapproving look the director was giving him. 'It's Spengler.'

Romanelli looked from Zach to the Furball head he had thrown to the ground, back to Zach again, trying to decipher what Zach was talking about.

'No,' Romanelli said in a slow voice usually reserved for a young child you were trying to help understand what should be a simple concept, but they were failing to grasp it. 'No, that's not Spengler. That is - *was* - a very expensive original prop from a movie.'

'That's not - that's not what I mean - no, I mean - I mean Spengler was here. But now he's dead.'

'Richard was here?' Romanelli asked, looking around as if the man was hiding from them somewhere and might make a sudden appearance from around a corner. He looked disappointed when he couldn't find him. 'Why didn't he come and say hello?'

'Because he was killed!' Zach gasped.

He wasn't sure how to make it any clearer to them that Spengler had been killed *right there in front of him, while he was watching*. In fact, they were having so much trouble understanding, Zach wondered if he was even really saying the words he believed he was, or if perhaps he was doing no more than opening and closing his mouth and nothing was coming out.

'I didn't see him,' Alice declared, making it clear that if *she* didn't believe something, it couldn't possibly be true. 'Where is he now?'

Zach waved a shaking hand towards the front door, pointing them in the direction of where he had last seen Spengler. On the other side of the door was his body, or at least a pool of blood, some innards: any sort of evidence that what Zach was saying had been real and Spengler really was dead. Zach had worried about them believing him, but now he was more worried that he was hoping Spengler *was* dead, and they would find his body on the other side of the door, exonerating himself from the notion everybody had in their minds that he was plain crazy.

'He's over there, is he?' Alice asked him.

Zach nodded his head, yes.

Alice pouted, gave him child-like eyes and spoke to him in

a baby voice; again with the condescending tone this particular group took with him a lot.

'Can you see Richard right now?' Alice asked. 'Is he here with us? In this room?'

Zach sighed. He took a deep breath. He could feel himself getting angry, and the last thing he needed right now was for everyone to be on edge because he couldn't control himself and started shouting at them. They already had enough ammunition to use against him should they decide they wanted him off the project. Spengler would be mad if he got himself fired, after all - he was counting on this project to help pay for the bills for at least the next six months. But then: no, he wasn't. Not any more. He *had* been counting on it, but all those plans he had for his retirement had been cruelly, suddenly and viciously snatched away from him.

Yet Zach felt he should do everything he could to respect the man by ensuring that, whatever happens, he somehow kept his cool and didn't get himself fired. He took another long breath in and let it out as calmly as he could manage.

'Outside,' he told Alice, through gritted teeth. 'Spengler was outside.'

'And you didn't even let him in?'

She sounded appalled by the very prospect that someone should be left lurking outside the property. She picked up her wine glass from where she had left it on the floor, took a long drink and trod towards the front door, wobbling slightly on her feet. Zach wasn't sure how many bottles of wine Alice had got through while he had been there, never mind before he had even turned up, but the side effects of all of that alcohol were starting to show.

She put her hand on the front door handle.

Zach had a feeling she was going to be very quickly sobered up by what she saw out there.

If she actually survived.

The killer could still be right outside the front door.

Ready to strike again.

Zach hated her, but he couldn't let someone else die. Even Alice.

'Wait, don't - ' he called to her.

But too late.

She turned the handle and pulled the door open, exposing them to the outside world.

Zach flinched, closing his eyes as the sunlight flooded through the doorway and hit him in the face. At least, that's what he would have told anyone had they asked why he closed his eyes at that exact moment. It could well have been more because he was terrified of what he might see on the other side.

'Well?' Alice asked.

Zach peeled his eyes open again.

When they adjusted to the brightness of the natural light, he realised the doorway was empty, except for Alice standing to the side, arms folded, glaring at him.

No one else was there.

No killer.

No body.

Nothing.

Zach joined her by the door. He inspected the ground outside. There was nothing on the door frame. Not even a splash of blood on the floor.

Perhaps everyone else had been right and he'd imagined the whole thing after all. But that couldn't be.

'Do you see Richard now, too, Zach?' Alice asked, sarcasm dripping from her mouth.

'But I swear...'

He examined the area once more, hoping there was something he had missed - like a great big crimson puddle in the middle of the floor.

But there was no trace.
It was as though nothing had ever happened.

24

The kids were next to arrive in the lobby to witness Zach's complete and total humiliation. Jennifer and Tim sauntered through, tapping at their cellphone screens and barely paying any attention to their surroundings, yet somehow aware of exactly where they were.

'What's going on, guys?' Jennifer asked without lifting her eyes from the screen.

'Why don't you tell them, Zach?' Alice mocked. 'What *is* going on?'

Zach glared at her. He couldn't take any more. This morning had been one embarrassment after another. From the very moment he had arrived things had got worse and worse and worse. His best friend and manager was dead, but there was no proof and no one believed him; and why would they? Now these two kids were there and ready to Tweet anything and everything that was happening. Zach would be forced out of town - probably out of state - by the morning. A laughing stock, little more than a byline in a newspaper and the occasional appearance in a 'Whatever Happened To' article where they mock celebrities who have become recluses to escape from whatever madness had been going in their lives.

Alice rolled her eyes at his lack of response to her question. She did that a lot.

'We're looking for a non-existent murder victim,' she told Jennifer.

'Cool.'

Jennifer was barely listening, still on her phone. She jabbed the screen with her finger once with a gesture of finality and slipped the phone into her pocket.

'Listen,' she said, looking up and seeing everyone properly for the first time, 'we're heading out for coffee, since nothing's happening here, and, no offence, but your coffee is beyond disgusting.'

Romanelli's face darkened. People could insult him, bash his films, mock his screenplays, or his voice, or his appearance. But the one thing he would not tolerate was people insulting his coffee. He had spent literally years of his life searching for the perfect blend of beans that produced the thickest, most luxurious body, flavour and aroma. Coffee was every bit as worthy of study as wine, yet it was taken nowhere near as seriously. People didn't have coffee cellars. Restaurants didn't have a 'coffee list' or employ a sommelier to recommend the perfect coffee to complement the fish. They didn't have a 'dessert coffee' the same way they had a dessert wine; if you were lucky a restaurant would simply offer 'coffee' once you were done. No choice, other than with cream or without. Yes, he had searched long and hard for the perfect coffee, and he had found it. People were entitled to their opinions, of course, but to flat out say his coffee was disgusting only to straight away head out to some global coffee conglomerate where the drink was made in all of thirty seconds and think that *that* was delicious coffee? Intolerable behaviour.

'That coffee,' Romanelli announced, 'has been pooped by Asian monkeys.'

Jennifer's face screwed up in disgust.

'Eww. Gross. And you drink that?'

She pulled out her cellphone and began tapping on the screen again. No doubt tweeting or messaging everyone she knew that the director she was working with (who made films that, like, *nobody* watched, so she didn't even know *why* she was doing the job) made coffee out of monkey crap. At least it had momentarily distracted her from Zach. Not that she had been paying enough attention to even take in what was happening within the scene she had stumbled upon.

'Starbucks?' Tim asked.

'Natch.'

Romanelli's face reddened again at the sound of the S-word. Alice noticed him step forward, ready to launch into a tirade about coffee, probably the same one she herself had been on the receiving end of several years ago. She took hold of Romanelli's arm and held him back, stopping him before he had a chance to even begin.

'Fine,' she told Jennifer and Tim. 'But don't be long. We've had too many interruptions already.'

'Sure. Whatever.'

'No, wait!' Zach cried out.

'Sorry, you'll have to get your own coffee. Only one free hand,' Jennifer said, holding up her hands, one of which contained her cellphone, as proof of what she had just said.

'Don't go out there.'

'Why not?'

'Because you're going to die.'

Jennifer and Tim looked at each other. They burst out laughing.

Tap-tap-tap on their screens. That one was *definitely* about Zach.

'We're *all* going to die sooner or later,' Tim said.

'And we're like, young,' Jennifer reminded him. 'It's you

guys who are all old.'

The pair headed to the front door.

'Please, don't,' Zach begged.

Tim turned the handle.

He hesitated for a moment, looked back at Zach, mouth wide in mock suspense.

He pulled the door open.

A gun fired from outside, a bullet heading straight into the lobby. Everyone inside screamed in panic and fell to the ground to escape being in the line of fire.

Outside the front door stood Officers Cole and Davies, guns drawn, pointed directly at them. Cole placed her hand on a surprised Davies' arm, shoving his weapon downwards so it was pointed at the ground.

'What the hell, Davies?!' Cole screamed at her partner.

Davies looked at his gun as if unsure exactly what had happened.

'It wasn't my fault - this thing must be faulty or something.'

The man wasn't trigger happy, but he was jumpy. Which wasn't a good trait in a police officer who was allowed to carry a loaded weapon. And *definitely* wasn't a good trait in a police officer with a loaded weapon pointed in someone's direction who was also easily surprised by a door being flung open.

Inside, Romanelli inspected the stair bannister where the bullet had lodged, driving a hole through the woodwork and lodging itself firmly in place. All things considered, they were lucky that it was the bannister it ended up inside, rather than any of the people gathered there, but that was still some expensive repair work that would need doing.

'Yeah, what the hell, man?!' Tim repeated.

'You could have killed us!' Jennifer screeched.

'Well, I didn't, did I?'

'Oh, and that's supposed to make us feel better? What's your badge number? I'm suing you for emotional distress.'

'Young lady, I - '

Tim turned his head to hide the fact that he was trying not to laugh. He knew exactly what was coming next.

'*Young lady*? Did you really *young lady* me?'

'I - ' Davies stammered, realising he was fighting a losing battle.

'All right, everybody calm down,' Cole told them, trying to diffuse the situation.

She holstered her weapon, and indicated to Davies to do the same before he ended up actually shooting anyone. He reluctantly agreed, but his hand hovered in place over the holster, ready to pounce if required.

'Can someone tell us exactly what's going on here?' Cole asked.

Zach stepped forward to talk to them.

'Thank God you're here,' he said. He glanced at the stray bullet in the bannister. 'I think.'

Having previously been blocked from the officers' line of sight by the others in the lobby, Cole and Davies saw Zach for the first time.

'You again?' Davies said.

It was Zach's luck that the two idiots who had attended his house the previous evening were back on shift again this morning and happened to be the two who would turn up when he needed them again: a second apparent crime scene with no evidence, no proof, no witnesses, no nothing. He was going to be headline news again the next morning, he was sure of it. This would definitely be the end of his career. Unless... he had to get them to believe him. Somehow.

'You called the police?' Alice demanded of him.

Zach ignored her and spoke directly to Cole, realising she was perhaps the least foolhardy of the two, and perhaps therefore also more inclined to be able to be reasoned with.

'Doesn't this prove that what happened at my house last night actually happened?'

'You've met?' Alice demanded again.

'Someone broke in to my house,' Zach reminded her. 'You saw it in the paper, remember?'

'Allegedly,' Davies interjected. 'Someone *allegedly* broke into his house.'

'Someone was there when I got home.'

'Sir, we found no evidence that ever happened,' Cole told him. 'Did you call us out here on false pretences to talk about your raccoon invasion again?'

'No, that's not… wait - look!'

Zach rushed across the lobby and picked up the Furball head from where he had dropped it on the floor. Davies became nervous again, his fingers twitching around his holster. He wanted one reason to take this guy down. *Just one reason.*

'Look,' Zach said again, passing the animatronic head to Cole.

She turned it over in her hands, inspecting it.

'Same thing exactly,' Zach announced, proud to have handed over the evidence they needed to see that the incident in his house wasn't a one off random occurrence, but in fact a targeted, purposeful attack.

'Is this yours, sir?' Cole asked him.

'No, it's mine,' Romanelli piped up from behind and stepped forward.

Cole's eyes lit up at the sight of the director. She had bumped into a number of celebrities during her time in the area, but most of them were dull and highly uninteresting. To meet someone like Romanelli, though, was a completely different matter.

She caught herself smiling, coughed and expertly

rearranged her face back to being more professional. She turned to look at Zach.

'So you're breaking someone else's toys now?' she asked him, before turning back to Romanelli. 'Did you want to press charges, Mr Romanelli?'

Mr Romanelli. She actually got to speak to the man. The legend. She would have loved to have the opportunity to sit down and talk to him. He was the sort of man who you could listen to for hours and bathe in the wisdom that spilled out of him; soak up whatever incredible insights he had about life; emerging at the end of your encounter a more enlightened being, full of new hopes, new dreams, and a new purpose you were aching to fulfil.

Perhaps he would even read the screenplay she had been working on.

Cole waited with bated breath for Romanelli to reply, to speak some words that would be forever etched in her memory: her first encounter with the legendary Francis Romanelli.

'I didn't break it!' Zach yelled, destroying any hope Cole had of a transcendent experience with the master director. 'Someone broke in here and killed Richard Spengler.'

'Where exactly did they kill him, sir?'

'*Allegedly* kill him,' Davies reminded her.

'Right outside the front door.'

'I didn't see anything out there,' Davies said. He asked Cole: 'Did you see anything out there?'

Cole shrugged. The two officers stepped back outside the front door. The examined the door frame, the front of the door itself, the ground upon which they stood before entering the house. They looked at the lawn in front of the house, poked in some shrubbery, looked high, looked low. Davies crouched down, picked something up from the ground. He held it up between two fingers for everyone to see: a smoked joint. He looked over at Tim, still standing in the doorway. Tim looked away, casting his eyes to the sky as if he hadn't noticed the officer looking his way. Jennifer back-handed him in the side, scowled at him. He shrugged, mouthed the word *sorry*.

There was nothing there. A tiny bit of weed, but certainly no sign of anyone having been murdered. A complete waste of time, once again.

Davies pulled Cole to the side, gripping her arm and turning around so they couldn't be seen or heard by those standing in the front door.

'Let me take him down,' Davies said. 'Two counts of wasting police time. Let me take him. Rough him up a bit. He'll learn his lesson. We can say he was resisting arrest.'

Cole shrugged out of his grip and glared at him.

'That's not how we do things,' she reminded him.

'It should be.'

Cole shot him a warning look before turning back to address the group.

'There's nothing out here. No evidence of foul play. No body, no blood, not even signs of a minor scuffle.'

Davies headed back over to the front door, staring at Zach and talking directly at him as he went:

'So not only did someone *allegedly* kill Richard Spengler on this very doorstep - right outside this very house - they also *allegedly* decapitated a cuddly toy - *inside* the house - *and then* they somehow cleaned up after themselves?'

'Allegedly,' Cole interjected.

'And this very same person who *allegedly* did all of this, also *allegedly* broke into your house last night and decapitated one of *your* cuddly toys. Sounds more like a Furball massacre than a killing spree to me.'

He grinned and turned to Cole, looking for validation of his joke. None forthcoming he turned back to Zach.

'Is that what you're trying to tell us happened here?'

Zach thought about it for a long moment. It didn't make much sense that one second there was a Furball head rolling down the staircase - presumably dropped down there by his attacker - and a short moment later that very same attacker was at the front door, directly behind Spengler, ready to kill him. The guy moved fast. Unless...

'Maybe there are two of them,' Zach wondered out loud.

Davies sighed and turned to Cole.

'Let's get out of here,' he told her.

'You're not going to do anything?' Zach asked.

'About what?'

'My manager was murdered. Right on this doorstep.'

'There's no crime without a victim.'

'Fine! Go to his house. Go to his office. Try and find him. *Then* you'll have to believe me.'

'I don't *have* to do anything, sir. But I'll tell you what - you want me to do something? How about I arrest you for wasting police time with this BS you keep spouting? Huh? How about I do that?'

Davies was right up in Zach's face. Cole pulled him away before he could do any real damage.

'Let's go,' she told him, directing him back down the path towards the front of the property.

Davies strode away, muttering to himself about the injustice of the whole situation, casting occasional glares back at the group standing in the doorway. Cole hung back for a moment.

'So that's it?' Zach asked her. 'You're really not going to do anything?'

'I'm sorry, sir. There is no evidence of a crime. If anything turns up, you get in touch.'

'If anything turns up? Like what? A body?'

'Sir...'

'Cole!' Davies called to her, arms outstretched waiting for her to catch him up. She held up a finger: one minute.

She peered around the group to see Francis Romanelli standing behind them all.

'Mr Romanelli - I'm sorry, sir, this is highly unprofessional of me, but: could I please get your autograph?'

'Cole!!' Davies yelled again.

Cole sighed.

'Maybe next time.'

She gave him a small wave, and gave the rest of the group a stiff, more professional nod of the head and turned to join her partner.

25

The officers ventured back down the long pathway towards the road at the front of Romanelli's property. The whole situation hadn't played out exactly as Cole had hoped. Not that she would ever admit to having 'hoped' to find a bloody corpse, but when the call out was for a possible homicide, the one thing you would normally expect to discover on the scene was, indeed, a corpse. She couldn't help but feel disappointed that they didn't find anything. Not even probable cause to search the property. There was no way anyone could have been brutally murdered at Romanelli's house without leaving behind any trace of it having happened, and only one witness to speak of; a witness who also happened to have called them out to another non-event the previous evening at that.

She would have to file that fact in the report, and it was likely that if Mr Keary were to call them again only for nothing of note to have happened, that would be three strikes for the fading movie star; he would more than likely find himself in court, facing a hefty fine, or perhaps even jail time.

That thought helped brighten Cole's mood a little.

She looked back over her shoulder towards the house.

Zach was the only one still watching them from the

doorway as they left.

Even from there, Cole could see he looked worried.

Maybe he wasn't making it up.

Or maybe he was.

Or maybe he imagined the whole thing. Both times.

If he had imagined both events, he was more in need of medical intervention than having criminal charges filed against him.

Davies noticed his partner looking back behind them, and turned to look himself.

'Goddamn actors,' he grumbled, seeing Zach watching them.

'They seemed nice to me,' Cole admitted.

26

Jennifer gave Tim a nudge, urging him with her eyes to make a move.

What? he mouthed at her.

She mimed drinking from a cup.

Realisation dawned.

'So, uh, we're gonna head out too,' he told the room. Everyone turned to look at him. 'You know, for coffee? Like we were about to do before everything went totally crazy just now.'

'After that, I need, like, triple caffeine,' Jennifer confirmed.

They stepped up to the front door, where Zach was still watching the outside world.

'Excuse us.'

Lost in the view, his thoughts, some other place - whatever, he didn't hear them and remained standing right in the doorway.

Jennifer sighed and brushed past him, rolling her eyes.

Tim followed close behind.

'Thanks,' he said sarcastically.

Zach hadn't totally zoned out. He saw the young actors head away from the building, down the path. He watched intently, hoping and praying they would be okay, that maybe, just maybe, he had imagined everything he believed had gone before. Sure, the kids were annoying, but nobody deserved to die the way (he believed) Spengler died.

He was vaguely aware that Romanelli and Alice had stalked away from him, engaged in whispered conversation on the other side of the lobby. More than likely discussing whether they should fire him there and then, or wait for a full-blown mental breakdown, where the reasoning behind his sudden departure could never be contested. But there were more important things to worry about right now; and he never thought there would be something he considered more important than his career.

His career, for what it was worth, was more often than not at the forefront of his mind. The whole reason he had no friends. No wife. No children. After today, that was probably over as well, leaving him with nothing. He may as well do something useful in the meantime, like looking out for the kids he was supposed to be working with.

He watched as they continued walking.

Still safe.

Still alive.

Tim took something out of his pocket, put it in his mouth.

A plume of white smoke emerged from his face, drifting across to Jennifer.

The girl waved a hand in front of her, attempting to brush the smoke away.

'I wish you wouldn't do that,' Zach could hear her complaining to Tim, even across the distance that now separated them.

Tim turned his head and blew the smoke straight into her face with a laugh.

Jennifer stormed up the path, away from him.

Tim picked up the pace to join her.

They went through the front gate of the property.

Turned a corner.
And were out of sight.

27

Tim glanced back towards Romanelli's house as they rounded the corner. From where they stood, the vast majority of the property was hidden, including the front entrance. Only the top floor could be seen from behind the hedgerow.

'They're all so weird,' Tim told Jennifer.

She shrugged.

'That's what happens when you get old.'

'If I live long enough to be thirty-five, kill me.'

'Totally.'

'What do you think happened?'

'About what?'

'That one guy said that some other guy had been killed.'

'He did?'

'Weren't you listening at all?'

'Hold on.'

She pulled out her cellphone and fired up Twitter. Navigating to her account, she tapped to view her own tweets. Scrolling through the list of those she had composed that morning, she came across one that read:

Are horror movie stars totally obsessed with death? Working with this wacko who imagined his best friend was killed just now! #lame #wackjob #hollyweirdo

'Oh yeah!' she sounded surprised at seeing her own words explaining the situation she had been in.

Living life through Twitter, removed from reality, the only real truth being those little nuggets of information she poured out from her soul to her army of followers.

'That's hilarious,' she laughed.

Unfazed by both having been at the scene of a potential murder and also not remembering any what had transpired, she and Tim continued on their way.

From inside a police car parked at the side of the street, Officers Cole and Davies watched the young actors pass by.

28

Zach lifted a tentative foot and stuck the ends of his toes outside the front door. Two cops and two young actors had ventured outside and nothing had happened. There wasn't any sign of anyone lurking nearby, ready to pounce.

It looked to be safe.

He placed his raised foot on the ground outside. Once that one was securely in place, he lifted the other, transferring it from the interior scene to the exterior.

Both feet were planted firm and safe outside and he was still alive.

He looked back inside, to the security of the building. There was nothing but an empty lobby, Alice and Romanelli having disappeared somewhere together. Possibly to consult with a lawyer, Zach guessed, making sure everything was done as close to legally as possible to get rid of him.

Zach turned to look to the right, scanning the length of the building as far as he could see. No one there. Nothing but the unnaturally green lawn, various potted plants and shrubberies, the bricks of the house, the windows with their shutters wide open. Absolutely nothing to worry about. Everything was perfectly fine and perfectly normal and perfectly safe.

He turned his head to the left.

A knife swung towards him.

Straight towards his face.

Zach stumbled backwards. His heel caught on the doorstep. He tumbled back inside through the open doorway and landed painfully on his backside.

Scurrying backwards, he edged away from the front door, slamming it shut with his foot as soon as he was able. He scuttled back to the door and locked it.

He scurried backwards again, creating a safe distance between himself and the door, just in case.

A loud CRACK of splintering wood jolted at Zach from the door.

The tip of a knife pierced through the wooden door from outside, emerging on the other side, plainly visible to Zach.

This was real.

All too, terrifyingly, horrifically, real.

He stared at the blade protruding from the door, shining, sharp, lethal. Who could be doing this, and why? It was like they had waited specifically for him to go outside. They had ignored the cops. They had ignored Tim and Jennifer. They had waited for him to be alone. No witnesses. But this time, Zach had proof. The evidence was right there: a knife jammed in the door.

He pulled himself to his feet and tiptoed over to the door.

He placed a fingertip on the blade.

It nicked his finger, drawing a drop a blood.

Sharp.

Ridiculously sharp.

He pressed his face closer to the door, his nose practically touching, examining the blade, examining the clean slice it had made through the door.

It disappeared again, pulled back through the door from outside. Nothing left but the tear in the door, which, now the knife was no longer there, was barely visible. Possibly even something that anyone could say had been there forever and no one had ever noticed.

'What is all this banging around?' Alice demanded as she returned to the lobby. 'Would you *please* keep the noise down!'

Romanelli joined her close behind. He looked Zach over, running his eyes from the top of Zach's head down to his feet, back up again, as if scanning him for anything they should be worried about.

'Come on,' he said eventually. 'Let's get to work. I'm sure there's something we can make a start on before the others get back.'

29

Zach trailed after Alice and Romanelli back through to the dining room. He didn't know what else to do: his brain was simultaneously working overtime to solve the problem and numb from shock. The killer was still out there, but apparently only after him. In stereotypical Hollywood star fashion, that made it far easier for Alice to not believe there was a problem: if it didn't affect her directly, it wasn't a real problem.

Zach scanned the dining room as they entered, on edge that anyone could be in there, waiting for him. It was empty. Alice headed straight for the wine. Romanelli sat himself back at the far end of the table, in front of his ashtray. In a swift, well-practised manoeuvre he single-handedly flipped open a cigarette packet, pulled one from inside and balanced it between his lips. By the time the cigarette was in place, his other hand already had his lighter in front of his face, and the cigarette was lit within less than a second of reaching his mouth.

Poetry in motion.

The director closed his eyes and took a long drag on the cigarette, a state of bliss as if it was the first one he had had in weeks. He tipped back his head and blew a steady stream of smoke from his lips up to the ceiling.

Alice carried her wine glass across to the table and took up her position beside Romanelli while Zach opted to maintain his distance, sitting across the other side of the room. Regardless of whether they believed him or not, Zach felt as though his presence alone might be enough to put them in danger.

A long moment of silence filled the room as they each settled into their own spaces.

Alice jerked alive, her whole body stiffening, a meerkat sensing danger.

'Where's Dave?' she asked.

Zach thought back to the events of the morning (was it still only the morning?). He couldn't recall having seen Dave since the game of Truth or Dare. There was only one logical explanation for his disappearance.

'He's probably already dead,' Zach told Alice, his voice filled with bitter inevitability.

Alice shrugged.

'He didn't seem that good an actor anyway, by all accounts,' she sniffed, and turned to look at Romanelli: 'I've no idea where you dug him up from.'

'Zach knows him,' Romanelli replied.

This was news to Zach.

There was a vague sense of familiarity about his face, but he didn't recognise the name, and he couldn't place where the two of them could have met. He certainly wouldn't go so far as to say that he *knew* the man.

'I do?' Zach asked.

He got up from where he was sitting and ventured closer to the other two; still maintaining what he hoped would be a safe distance, but close enough that he could feel more a part of the conversation without having to yell across the room.

'Sure you do.'

'He looked familiar,' Zach pondered, thinking out loud, 'but I can't for the life of me place him.'

'He built Fuzz!'

'I'm sorry?'

'He's the visual effects genius who brought your Furballs to life.'

'Oh, right! Sure!'

Zach still wasn't one-hundred percent at the point of remembering Dave, but if Romanelli said that was true, it must be. Based on the contents of the movie museum room in that very house, it was possible Romanelli knew as much - if not more - about *Furballs* than Zach himself. It made sense, in a way: Zach must have had contact with those guys when he was making the movies; he must have at least seen them around the set even if he hadn't interacted with them directly. On movies like that, the practical effects were integral to the whole thing and were more often than not the cause of any problems or delays in shooting, if the rig wasn't quite working as it should, or if a pyrotechnic failed to go off at the right time. Zach could certainly remember a few frustrating days like that from making the movies. And it was thirty years ago already; he couldn't possibly remember everyone he had worked with over time, plus Dave probably looked very different back all those years ago to how he did now.

Alice turned and glared at Romanelli after this revelation.

'You've got me playing alongside a special effects geek?' she asked.

Romanelli shrugged.

'He reached out to me saying that he wanted to move in to acting. I told him I'd help him out. What could I say?'

'How about "no"?'

'That wouldn't have been very fair, would it. The guy could use a break, and I wanted to give it to him. Sue me.'

'Careful; she probably would,' Zach muttered, drawing

further glares from Alice.

'Couldn't you have put together a short or something, instead of casting him in a major movie? You could have written something for the Internet and got it out of the way in a couple of days, instead of dragging all of us through this.'

'No one else seems to have a problem.'

'No one else has a reputation to uphold.'

Romanelli stubbed out the last remnants of his current cigarette. He pulled out another, lit it, and enjoyed the first inhalation.

'The way you're talking perfectly demonstrates your so-called reputation,' he told Alice.

She looked as though she was going to come back at him, her eyes wide and wild, her lips pursed together so hard they had turned white. But the hypnotic effect of watching Romanelli smoking calmed her. She took a deep breath and rubbed her temples.

'I'll let you men geek out over your toys together,' she told them as she got up from her seat.

'Where are you going?' Zach asked.

'The bathroom. If you really must know.'

'We should probably stick together.'

'What is *wrong* with you?'

'It's not safe.'

She rolled her eyes and sighed.

'Give it a rest,' she told him.

As she drifted around the table to leave the room, Zach rose to go after her.

'Don't,' Romanelli warned him. 'It's best to let her go.'

'She could be in danger.'

'If anyone can look after herself, it's Alice Blake.'

He had a point. If anyone tried attacking her, Alice could stop them in their tracks with one of her stares. She wouldn't even have to engage in any physical confrontation: the Alice-glare was powerful enough to turn most fully grown men into gibbering wrecks. Not Romanelli, though; it was like he lived on a different plane of existence to everyone else, watching from the side as if it was all an amusing show put on for his benefit.

'I should probably go with her, though, just in case.'

'You want to go with her to the bathroom?'

'Just in case.'

'What *is* wrong with you?'

30

Alice could hear the pair of them still talking as she left the dining room. They could well have been talking about her. Let them. What did she care if a less than C-grade movie "star" had problems with her? She knew enough people in that town already, people who were actually important. People who could do things for you, or at least people who knew the people who could do things for you. It made no difference to her if a horror movie actor past his sell-by date didn't like her.

What truly bugged her was how much Romanelli liked him. He had desperately wanted Zach on this picture for some reason, and no matter what she said or did to convince him otherwise, he paid her no attention. And with this latest revelation about Dave not being an actor at all, but a visual effects technician, for God's sake... Yes, Romanelli was getting on in years, but there hadn't been any previous signs of him losing his mind. She would have to keep a careful eye on the situation, and if he got any worse she might have to try and help the situation, one way or another.

She turned down the hallway and through into the lobby.

Heading towards the staircase, she noticed the animatronic Furball head, still laying there, right in the middle of the floor.

She hated that thing. More than the thing itself, she hated everything it represented.

She looked around, making sure she hadn't been followed out, raised her foot high above the ground and stamped down on the head.

The impact with her foot gave a satisfying crunch.

Who was to say it hadn't been damaged before? That shoe-shaped dent could have easily happened when it had rolled down the stairs.

Alice ran her hands through her hair, straightening it, gave a small smile, and headed up the stairs.

31

The soft glow from Romanelli's cigarette reflected in his eyes as he took a contemplative draw from it, eyeing Zach with a mixture of suspicion, worry and thoughtfulness. Zach had decided that, with Alice out of the room, now would be a good time to try and express his fears about the situation more clearly to Romanelli, without running the risk of being eye-rolled to death before the mysterious killer could get there first. He wasn't sure which way he'd prefer to go: a bloody, violent death by the hands of a psychopath wielding a particularly sharp, long, knife; or a slow, painful death through withering looks and psychological torment at the hands of one of Hollywood's most powerful stars.

Based on events so far, he thought the quick but brutal slaying was potentially more preferable than any sort of torture Alice Blake might inflict upon him.

'All I'm saying is there's no way that it's a coincidence,' Zach told Romanelli, laying out his case in its barest essentials.

The director shrugged.

'Things break. That's what they do; nothing lasts forever.'

'But for the head to come off of my Fuzz *and* yours, all in the space of - what? - fifteen hours? That's not how these things work.'

'So do you think that police officer was right? It really is a Furball massacre?'

Zach thought Romanelli of all people would be on his side, that he would see the bigger picture playing out there, and not focus on the smaller issues of a broken prop and plush toy. Yet because no one except Zach saw Spengler on the premises, everyone - even Romanelli - was quick to brush it off as something that did not, and could not, have happened.

Zach decided he needed to put things in a context that Romanelli could relate to. And , finding the revelations in the mysterious room, he thought he knew exactly how to do that.

'Do you remember the movie *Atomic Ants*?' Zach asked.

'A classic.'

'Hmm. Sure. Anyway. All this stuff was going on and Joe - my character in the movie - he's the only one who guesses what's happening. He's the only one who puts the clues together. No one else believes him until it's too late and half the city are dead.'

'Sure,' Romanelli replied. 'But this is real life. The President of the United States is not an ant that's been blasted by the effects of an experimental weapon. God only knows, that would explain a lot, though.'

'Yes - you're right. This *is* real life. And Spengler's dead,' Zach insisted. 'Believe me or don't: I saw it happen. And there *was* someone in my house last night. I'm sure of it. It was probably the same person who killed Spengler. And most likely the same person who attacked me in the bathroom of a bar.'

'Attacked?'

Zach realised he hadn't mentioned the bar attack to anyone. Not even the officers who came to his house the following evening. Somehow he had failed to think of the two events as somehow being linked until he subconsciously made the connection right at that moment.

'Someone grabbed my ankle while I was trying to get through a window,' he told Romanelli.

'Why?'

'Based on events that have since occurred, I think they were probably trying to kill me!'

'No, I mean: why were you trying to get through a window in the bathroom of a bar?'

Zach paused.

He didn't especially want to admit he was trying to escape being drawn into a social situation by fleeing a bar through a bathroom window. He didn't want to admit he would rather do that than have a pleasant conversation with a group of fans, to interact with people other than those who might in some way or another help to advance his career. He didn't want to admit he had become something of a recluse, only emerging from his house for work purposes, avoiding small-talk as much as he possibly could. Romanelli already had the wrong idea about him - that he was a fruitcake who imagined people being murdered, and dreamed up conspiracy theories about madmen breaking into houses and destroying their items; Zach couldn't afford for Romanelli to think any worse of him than he already did.

'That's not important,' Zach told him, realising he had already taken a suspiciously long time to answer the question. 'We're being deliberately targeted. I'm sure of it. None of us are safe.'

32

The face staring back at Alice Blake in the bathroom mirror wasn't hers. It couldn't possibly be. The lines and crevices that were visible in the reflection's skin when looking closely, the flecks of grey speckled within the hair, the sagging flesh underneath the eyes... That couldn't be her. She wasn't as old as that, surely? She had tried to take care of herself as best as she possibly could, but there was an inevitability to what was happening to her, and time was finally catching up. Of course there were nights like the previous evening when she had drunk more than she technically probably should have, and indeed had carried on through to this morning; but there were some occasions when the drink was necessary to ease other pains in her life. Like losing out on awards. Thinking about it, she had been doing that more frequently these days than she had used to. The younger version of her had received many plaudits, despite being in arguably inferior films. The voters for these awards perhaps didn't do everything entirely on merit; they liked to have a pretty young face on screen to "enhance the performance".

That still didn't explain Meryl goddamn Streep, of course; she was winning more as she advanced in years. And, of course, she still looked stunning.

Alice had decided many years ago she wouldn't go down the plastic surgery route as many fo her previous co-stars had chosen to do. She had seen so many beautiful actresses destroy their faces by going under the knife, or through injecting God only knows what into themselves. Trying to remain young and beautiful, they turned their faces into something mask-like, nightmarish: by attempting to remain in the acting profession by looking "young", they had ruined all chances of actually being able to act by freezing their expressions into a permanent state of bafflement.

And yet… Alice pulled at the wrinkles in the corner of her eyes, stretched them flat. Maybe a little would help.

She closed her eyes. After a moment she re-opened them, as if disappearing into her own head briefly would be enough to change the reflection she saw when she looked again.

It didn't work.

She washed her hands and dried them on a towel beside the sink.

A lock of hair fell out of place, brushing against her forehead. She stepped back in front of the mirror to put it right.

The bathroom door creaked open.

Not much, and Alice wouldn't have noticed, except for the small sound that it made.

And the fact that she was sure she had locked the door when she first went into the bathroom.

She turned to face the door, listening for any further sound.

'Hello?' she called out. The only reply was silence. 'That had better not be you, Zach.'

She waited again.

'Pervert,' she muttered under her breath.

She turned back to the mirror, pulled out some lipstick from her purse and set to re-applying it.

The bathroom door creaked again, opening inward some

more.

Alice whirled around and marched to the bathroom doorway. If Zach was out there watching her like a weirdo, there was no way she was going to let him get away with it. Romanelli would put up with all sorts of things, but there's no way he would tolerate that kind of behaviour on any of his films; it would be the perfect opportunity to get rid of him.

She poked her head through the doorway and looked out to the right, across towards the staircase.

Nothing.

She whipped her head around to the left, where the hallway continued on past other rooms.

She screamed.

There was a body on the floor: bloody, mangled, limbs twisted at impossible angles - arms and legs splayed in directions they should never be able to. Despite the state of the body, it was immediately obvious who it belonged to: Dave. She hated to admit it, and she wouldn't say the exact words out loud, but it looked like Zach was right after all. There *was* a killer on the loose, and Dave *was* already dead.

She ran along the hallway towards the staircase, away from the bloody corpse.

Drawn by Alice's screams, Zach and Romanelli rushed to the bottom of the stairs.

'Was that you screaming?' Romanelli called up to her.

'It's Dave,' Alice shouted back down. 'He's - '

She cut herself off with another scream as she waved a finger, pointing in their direction at the bottom of the stairs.

Zach spun around.

He was there.

The killer.

Standing right behind them.

Knife raised and ready to strike.

33

Running from the figure as fast as they were able, desperate to escape the radius of the swinging knife, Zach and Romanelli headed towards the stairs. It was the only safe direction is which they could go, and that was where Alice remained, watching them. Perhaps there could be safety in numbers.

But the attacker was right behind them, gaining ground: Romanelli wasn't young, and Zach wasn't in the best shape; between them, they weren't the greatest combination for out-running a knife-wielding maniac. Zach tripped on his own feet, tumbled, barely stopped himself from hitting the ground. Falling out of step with Romanelli, the attacker was right upon him, a lion spotting an injured antelope.

Romanelli noticed the misstep from the corner of his eye and risked a look back in Zach's direction.

Seeing the mysterious figure right behind Zach, he took offensive action:

Romanelli launched himself straight at their attacker.

Despite his age, he still had some strength in him, and the surprise element of the director running as fast as he could directly at the killer must have helped some. But it wasn't enough - despite his speed, he didn't have the force behind him to make much of a difference.

The attacker easily broke away from Romanelli's shove.

He angled himself towards the now flailing Romanelli. He struck out with his knife, waving it through the air, lashing out in the hope of making sort of contact.

It worked. The blade landed against Romanelli's arm, making easy work of his shirt and the flesh underneath. Blood sprang to the surface, dripping from the wound and staining the shirt crimson. Romanelli stumbled backwards, clutching his arm. It wasn't deep, but it was enough of an injury to hurt like hell, and the amount of blood pouring out of the wound was surprising, since Romanelli was pretty sure the masked menace had thankfully missed any of the major arteries, as far as he could tell.

Zach watched one of his all-time heroes being hurt and took it as a personal offence against himself. That, combined with feeling guilty about the entire situation (although if they had actually listened to him earlier, and if the police had believed him, they may not have been in this current mess anyway) led him to feel it was necessary to do something. *Actually* do something. Not just think something should be done but freeze in the moment when action was required.

The time had come to make a stand.

As the attacker lurched towards Romanelli, ready to finish him off, he made the mistake of turning his back turned to Zach.

Now was the time.

Zach stepped forward as quietly as he could while still moving swiftly.

Immediately behind the attacker, he slammed himself straight into the figure's turned body, sending him to the ground, the knife tumbling from his hand and clattering to the floor, just out of arm's reach.

Zach waved towards Alice, who had been watching the

whole scene play out from a safe viewing point halfway up the stairs, indicating for her to join them at the bottom.

'Come on, come on, come on!' Zach insisted.

Zach anxiously watched as the attacker slid himself forward on his stomach, reaching out to the fallen knife. It was just beyond the reach of his fingertips. Alice tripped down the stairs towards Zach, her path taking her straight past the fallen attacker. He lurched his body forward with a grunt and grasped the knife handle. As Alice passed by, he slashed at the air in a blind rage, hoping for a hit. It had worked with Romanelli, perhaps it would work again.

But Alice managed to get past him without any trouble; the position their attacker found himself in made it virtually impossible to do any real, targeted damage.

The three of them back together, Alice inspected Romanelli's arm. Peeling blood-soaked fabric away from the wound, she winced at the sight of the damage below and popped the shirt piece back in place.

'We need to get out of here,' Zach told them, keeping a watchful eye on the figure on the floor, who was sure to be back on his feet at any moment.

Romanelli nodded in agreement and marched towards the front door.

Using his undamaged arm, he turned the handle and flung the door open.

An axe swung towards him from outside.

He ducked.

The air displaced above his head as the axe passed by. Millimetres away from scalping him in his own home.

He slammed the door shut and locked it.

'There's two of them!' he announced.

'Where do we go now?' Zach asked.

'Come on.'

Romanelli led them to the side of the lobby, and down a

hallway. They passed by the door to the dining room, where even the bizarre nature of the supposed rehearsal now felt like something to which Zach felt like he wanted to return, past more closed doors, right up to the end of the hallway.

The director opened the final door in the hallway and ushered them all inside. He closed the door behind them and headed to the back of the room.

Zach looked around.

Romanelli had led them to his office. The room was minimally furnished, to match the rest of the house, but in a more comfortable way. This room actually felt lived in, used. There was a desk with a computer on top, a comfortable chair in front of it. Posters from each of Romanelli's films framed and mounted on the walls. A coffee machine, with plenty of supplies beside it. A wall made entirely of cork board, notes, index cards, take-out menus all pinned across the entirety of the board. Zach wished he had the opportunity to study that board, to take in Romanelli's thought processes, inspirations and ideas. To sit at the feet of the master and learn from him. As he looked around, Zach spotted the entire reason Romanelli had brought them into this room rather than any other he could have chosen.

There was a door that led outside.

Romanelli unlocked it. Standing to the side of the door, he slowly pushed it open.

Alice stepped forward and moved to go through the doorway.

'Wait,' Zach warned her. 'Be careful.'

For the first time that day, she listened to Zach.

She crouched down and edged to the side of the doorframe, making herself as small as possible, trying to avoid being detected.

Putting a foot outside, Alice could feel the fresh air tingling against her skin.

It was so refreshing.

It was funny how the experience of the past few minutes made something so basic as fresh air feel like something you would never take for granted again.

Alice smiled at the sensation.

They were going to be fine.

A gun fired through the door from somewhere outside.

Romanelli's computer screen exploded in an eruption of metal and glass.

Alice screamed, scrambled away from the door. The three of them grouped together on the ground, and ducked for cover. Romanelli swung a leg towards the door and slammed it shut.

'Why is everybody shooting at us today?' Romanelli asked.

'There might be *more* than two of them,' Zach said.

'What are we going to do now?' Alice spoke aloud the thoughts of the other members of their group.

34

The hallway outside was empty when they emerged from the office. Zach was sure he hadn't hurt their knife-wielding attacker badly, so he was surprised not to find him on their tail. He could be hiding somewhere, waiting to strike with the element of surprise. Or maybe he had regrouped with the other members of his gang to work out the next phase of their plan.

Regardless, they needed to get out of the house, or at least find somewhere safe to hide.

Romanelli led them through another door and into a darkened room. No lights were on, but there was enough light in there to make out that Romanelli had brought them into the kitchen.

They stood inside the doorway, listening to the silence for a moment, the only sounds the electrical hum and occasional *clink-clank* of the refrigerator. They were the only ones there.

'Can we get some lights on?' Zach whispered.

Ignoring him, Romanelli grabbed a chair from the side of the room and wedged it under the door handle, in an effort to secure the entrance as much as possible.

'Come on,' he told them.

They dashed across the floor towards the back of the room.

As they moved, much to Zach's relief lights flickered on in the ceiling, activated by their motion. As far as kitchens went, it was the largest one that Zach had ever found himself in. A touch smaller than a restaurant kitchen, but certainly bigger than anything he had seen in a 'regular' residence before. The refrigerator alone was practically the size of Zach's bathroom. Every possible cooking utility, utensil, machine, appliance you could think of was there, ready for use. By Romanelli himself? Zach wondered. Perhaps this was another hidden side to the great director that Zach wasn't aware of.

Romanelli continued to lead them until they were behind a large working surface. He crouched down behind it, hidden from view of anyone who might look through the kitchen door. The others followed suit.

'What do we do now?' Zach asked.

'I don't know.'

'You don't know?' Alice whined. 'Why did you bring us here?'

Romanelli shrugged.

'It's as good a place as any. Plus there's food. And coffee.'

A banging sounded throughout the room, stopping Alice from answering him back.

Someone bashing against the kitchen door, trying to get in.

The attacker knew they were in there.

The door rattled on its hinges as it was attacked from the outside.

The chair under the handle was holding fast, stopping the door from being opened.

Another bash.

The door was holding, for now.

The three of them waited, listening for another attempt to get in. Perhaps the mystery figure, or figures, didn't know they were in there after all; perhaps they were going around trying all of the doors and had decided that this one was actually locked.

BANG-BANG-BANG!

More intense bashing began at the door.

Whoever it was definitely knew the group was hiding in there.

They were throwing everything they had at the door to try to open it.

The chair shifted slightly in front of the door, causing it to open an inch or two.

A gloved hand reached through the doorway, grasping at the obstructing furniture.

He shoved the backrest down towards the floor, and the chair fell with a clatter, unblocking his access to the room. He pushed the door further open, the chair squeaking as it was forced out of the way.

The attacker stepped into the kitchen.

He took a couple of steps into the room and stopped, looking around; seeking his prey.

A moment of indecision was enough that his lack of motion caused the kitchen lights to switch back off again.

A strange sound emerged from the attacker: something like a whimper.

Surprised at the noise, Zach peered out from behind the counter to watch the mystery figure. Zach saw him take a step backwards, feeling behind himself for the apparent safety of the kitchen walls.

The movement triggered the lights nearest the door to reactivate.

Zach ducked back down, hiding behind the worktop again.

The attacker took another step forward. And another.

More lights illuminated as he trod further into the kitchen.

Emboldened by the new brightness in the room, the figure strode across the kitchen, full of confidence now.

Behind the counter, Zach pondered this chain of events,

thinking it through until there was only one logical conclusion he could reach.

'I wonder…' he whispered.

'What is it?' Romanelli asked.

'I can't believe I'm going to say this, but I think we need to get somewhere dark.'

'You're out of your mind,' Alice told him.

'Trust me.'

Romanelli thought for a moment. He decided they didn't have many options available to them, so any plan was better than no plan. He nodded his head in agreement with Zach.

'Follow me,' he told them. 'Quickly.'

The group burst out from their hiding place behind the counter. The attacker had been practically upon them, but their sudden emergence took him by surprise. Before he had time to react, they were sprinting past him, heading for the kitchen door, trying to make their escape.

Out of the kitchen, Zach slammed the door behind them, and they continued their sprint down the hallway, following Romanelli to wherever it was that he was taking them this time.

The figure tore through the kitchen doorway at speed, desperate to catch back up with them.

'Hurry!' Zach cried, seeing their attacker making ground.

Reaching yet another closed door along the hallway, Romanelli pushed it open, holding it for the other two to go in before him.

'Inside. Hurry.'

Always the gentleman, Zach let Alice go before him.

But as soon as she entered that dark space behind the door, she lost her footing and began to tumble forward.

Zach reached out and grabbed her, pulled her back to him.

Right in front of them was a dark staircase, the steps heading steeply down into a dark cellar below.

'Thanks,' Alice muttered in forced appreciation.

She put one careful foot in front of the other and slowly stepped down the stairs.

Romanelli followed close behind.

Zach looked at the darkness below. How he longed to be back at home with his lights blazing all through the day and night. Safe and secure in the constant illumination. He even found himself wishing he had taken that part in *Vampire Grannies* 3: those geriatric blood-suckers were no problem compared with where he found himself now. As he stared in to the darkness it stared straight back, until there was nothing left but black. He had to go down there and join them; it was the only way. It *was* his idea to go somewhere dark, after all.

'Come on. Quickly!' he heard Romanelli calling from somewhere within the void.

Zach took a deep breath.

He placed a foot on to the dark staircase and pulled the cellar door shut behind himself.

35

With the door shut, the darkness felt thicker to Zach. Suffocating him, wrapping around him not like a warm, thick, blanket, but like a roll of Saran Wrap around his face, stopping him from breathing. He could feel the black swirling through his open mouth, down his throat, filling his lungs, somehow spreading through his body, perhaps travelling along his veins, infecting every inch of his being.

'Give me some light for a second.'

The voice sounded in the blackness, familiar but strange without seeing who it belonged to.

'Zach,' the voice snapped.

He realised it was Romanelli speaking to him.

And he could suddenly breathe a little better: not perfectly, it was still taking some effort, but he wasn't quite suffocating the way he was before.

'What?' he whispered, but the whisper sounded loud in that vast cavern of black.

'Give me some light, will you?'

The combination of words being spoken by Romanelli shifted in his brain and he was able to comprehend what was being said to him.

Zach pulled his cellphone from his pocket and switched on

the flashlight.

'You've got your cellphone with you?' Alice realised. 'Why don't we just call the police?'

'You heard them - they don't believe a word that I say. If I try ringing again, they're just going to ignore me.'

'Then I'll ring them.'

Alice held out her hand for Zach's cellphone.

'They know you're here with me,' Zach reminded her. 'They won't buy it for a second.'

'I can try.'

'Quiet!' Romanelli snapped. 'I need that light.'

Zach aimed the light towards Romanelli. Realising he was shaking, he grasped the phone with both hands, trying to steady it, illuminating whatever it was Romanelli was doing.

The director reached up towards a lightbulb dangling from the ceiling.

He's going to switch it on, Zach's brain told him, *and the darkness will disappear and everything will be fine.*

But instead of switching it on, Romanelli unscrewed the lightbulb. He put it on the ground and stamped on it. A sprinkling of sharp shards of broken glass scattered across the top of the cellar steps.

'Go,' Romanelli commanded.

They worked their way to the bottom of the steps, Zach's cellphone guiding the way. Thick shadows cast by the phone's beam danced across the steps, confusing their minds into thinking the steps were juddering, twisting and turning, making it hard to progress with any speed.

They made it, planting their feet on the firm, solid floor of Francis Romanelli's deep, dark wine cellar.

Zach inspected the battery icon on his phone: thirty-five percent. Even if he couldn't call the police, for now he was glad that he had the cellphone with him and the security the flashlight provided. He just hoped that would last for long enough.

36

'Switch that light off,' Romanelli ordered Zach.

The three of them had ventured as far into the depths of the cellar as they were able to go and hid, crouched behind some large crates of wine. Every time that Zach shifted even the smallest amount, giant shadowy wings leapt out of hiding, flickering to existence for the briefest of moments before disappearing again, as the beam of the light shuddered with each of his movements. The walls of the cellar were lined with bottles, some coated in a thick layer of dust, others more recent acquisitions. On the floor were several crates, unopened and waiting for a space to be cleared in the racks for the bottles to take up residency. There must have been hundreds of bottles down there. Knowing nothing about wine, Zach had no idea how much it was all worth - even if it was the cheapest wine available, there would be a lot of money's worth down there - but he was pretty sure a man like Romanelli wouldn't settle for the cheap stuff. There was sure to be bottles worth hundreds or even thousands of dollars; probably those covered in dust, more a status symbol or investment than something to enjoy with a nice meal.

Zach placed his hand across the flashlight beam, stopping the full illumination but allowing some light to seep through the gaps between his fingers, making them glow as if they were on fire. He looked over at Romanelli and even in the faint light he could tell the director was glaring at him.

'It's fine,' Zach told him. 'No one will see it.'

A *crunch* came from the top of the stairs. Someone had stepped on the broken glass Romanelli had scattered there.

'*Off*,' Romanelli hissed.

Zach did as he was told, plunging the cellar once more into total, absolute darkness.

They listened, straining their ears to get an indication of what was happening across the other side of the dark void.

Click-click-click-click-click-click.

The intruder was pulling the cord for the light switch hanging from the ceiling: *on-off-on-off-on-off* - but of course there was no bulb, so it made no difference.

A long moment of silence.

They imagined the figure standing in the darkness, listening for movements from below the same way the three of them were listening for movements from him. What was he doing up there? Was he standing perfectly still, or had he found some way of navigating around the smashed glass to get to them, and the first thing they would know about it, being unable to see anything, would be the feel of the cold metal of his knife sliding between their ribs?

Another crunch of glass.

Zach stiffened. He closed his eyes. Not that there was any difference in having his eyes open and closed down there; it was more of an involuntary reaction, trying to block out the sight of anything that scared you. This was the end. He was sure of it. The killer was going to come across the cellar and pick them off, slicing his way through them, one by one.

But instead of coming to get them, the attacker turned and left, closing the cellar door behind himself.

Zach waited for as long as he could force himself to,

making sure the killer had definitely left and it wasn't part of some ruse to lure them out of hiding.

He switched the cellphone light back on.

'Thank God,' he exhaled.

He ran the back of his hand across his forehead, wiping away a waterfall of sweat that had sprung up during their time down there.

Romanelli couldn't help but notice.

'You okay?' he asked.

'Sure,' Zach laughed. 'There's a pack of killers after us and I'm trapped in a cellar in the dark. Everything's great.'

'You don't like the dark?' Alice piped up.

'*That's* what you're focusing on?'

She shrugged as if it wasn't important and turned her attention to the racks of wine. She ran a finger along the bottles, leaving a path through the dust. She rotated a bottle or two, turning them so that the labels were visible, looking for something specific.

'Sorry the wine list isn't available to peruse this evening, madam,' Romanelli told her.

She smiled half-heartedly, showing she heard but didn't feel that the comment warranted any real response on her part.

A particular bottle caught her eye. She pulled it from the rack, brushed the dust away and examined the label. With a slight sneer, she put it back where she'd got it from. Alice wasn't usually fussy about which wine to drink, but she knew Romanelli had better bottles than that hidden away in the cellar somewhere, and now was as good a time as any to try to find them.

'So. What's the plan, boys?' she asked the room as she continued browsing the selection.

'Plan?' Romanelli scoffed. 'There's no plan.'

'Hmm.'

Romanelli detected something in her *hmm*, and he was sure that it was aimed directly at him for some reason.

'What?' he prodded, though he wasn't sure he wanted to hear whatever it was she had to say. Not now.

'I was just thinking: that should make you happy,' Alice told him.

'Why?'

'Improvisation! That's your thing, isn't it? Got to have your improvisation going on so that you've got something to say in those interviews about how you brought out the best in your actors by allowing them to "speak their truths" and "craft their own characters".'

Romanelli watched her, knowing she wasn't done yet. Zach stared, open mouthed, at the way Alice was talking to this legendary director. He couldn't help but flinch every time she emphasised the air-quotes in her speech. And Romanelli was taking it, letting her go on at him.

'And then - *then* - they praise your exceptional writing skills! They give you awards for Best Original Screenplay when you *didn't write a single damn word of it*. Those actors, those poor actors, you exploit on every single one of your films, making them write the script for you, and you just sit there and take credit for it.'

'Are you done?'

'Not even close.'

'You're done.'

They exchanged another glare. Alice spun around and turned her attention back to the wine rack. She grabbed a bottle at random, picked up a cloth that was laying on top of one of the crates and wrapped the bottle in it.

'What are you doing?' Romanelli asked her.

Zach and Romanelli watched as Alice smacked the bottom of the bottle against the cellar wall; once, twice, a third time. The cork came partially loose. Alice put the end of the cork between her teeth, yanked hard, pulled it out completely, and spat it on to the floor.

'Improvising,' she told them and took a drink from the bottle.

'Ah, crap,' Zach suddenly said, remembering something they should have thought of before hiding themselves away down there.

'What is it?'

'Jennifer and Tim. They must be on their way back by now. We need to warn them about what's going on.'

37

Starbucks was busy, as it always was. The tables were mostly filled with those who wanted to be screenwriters, sitting there for the majority of the day leeching the free electricity and nursing a single cup of coffee for hours at a time to save paying for another; endlessly scrolling through their social media feeds as they waited for inspiration to strike, only to head home later, disappointed with themselves for not making any progress before getting changed and heading out to work in the bars in the evenings, serving drinks and watching out for anyone who might enter their establishment who was in a position to hear their pitch and bring their vision to life on the silver screen.

Tim and Jennifer waited at the counter for their drinks to be made by the barista, scanning the room and hoping to be recognised so they could do the whole routine of being surprised at having been recognised.

'Here you go,' the girl behind the counter said, handing them their drinks, her mouth smiling but her eyes lost in her own thoughts about how to solve a major plot point that would send her story hurtling full force into the third act.

Tim took the cups from her.

The labels read *Tym* and *Giniffer*.

'Close enough,' he smiled.

In LA it was rare to find people who spelled their names the "proper" way; the barista was probably so used to getting yelled at for spelling things the "wrong" way that they took a wild guess at the most ridiculous spelling possible.

Tim went to pass Jennifer her coffee when her cellphone rang.

She pulled it from her pocket and looked at the screen. It showed "unknown caller".

She pressed the call reject button and grabbed her cup from Tim.

'No one interrupts my 'bucks break,' she announced.

'Damn right.'

They took their cups and wound their way through the store towards the sole empty table that remained, pushing past people and cutting off another guy with a MacBook under his arm who was heading in that direction. They sat down, pretending to have not seen him.

Jennifer's cellphone rang again.

She jabbed her finger hard against the call reject button again.

'Go. A. Way.'

She went to put the phone in her pocket, but changed her mind.

'In fact…' she said and switched it off completely.

A triumphant look on her face, she put it away and smiled at Tim.

38

Romanelli sat on the cellar floor with an unlit cigarette dangling from his mouth. Somehow he had managed to leave his lighter in the dining room, but his face felt uncomfortable without a cigarette between his lips. It hadn't been long since his last smoke but it was already starting to feel like forever, what with everything that had happened. How he already missed the taste of the smoke in his mouth, the feel of the exhalation. Also: coffee. Damn, he could kill for a nice hot cup of his coffee right about now.

Alice had already guzzled down half a bottle of red, and had reached the point where she no longer cared if she was sitting on a floor covered in dust, so she had made herself as comfortable as possible leaning against a rack, next to Romanelli. She glared at the cellphone in her hand.

'Little bitch hung up on me,' she snapped. 'Twice.'

'Keep trying,' Zach urged.

Alice jabbed at the screen with frustration and put the phone to her ear.

It went straight through to voicemail.

'She's switched it off,' Alice told them.

She waited for the voicemail greeting to end. At the sound of the beep, she left her message for Jennifer in a disturbingly sweet voice:

'Hey, Jennifer, it's Alice. But you already know that because you keep hanging up on me. Anyway, I'm calling to let you know that if you don't want to be killed by a masked maniac, it's probably safest if you and Tim stay away for the time being. Okay? Oh, and if you ever hang up on me again, it's probably safest if you stay away from me forever. Okay? Okay.'

She hung up and tossed Zach's phone back to him.

She noticed Romanelli giving her a look.

'What?' she snapped.

'Nothing.'

While Alice and Romanelli seemed comfortable enough to be seated on the floor, Zach couldn't bring himself to be so relaxed. He paced back and forth, chewing his fingernails and trying to work out a solution to their current predicament. Up above, they were being pursued by a crazed person with a knife, and one or two other accomplices, armed with axes and even guns. Before they came down to the cellar they at least had possible routes of escape, different paths they could follow and places to try out if it became unsafe in the place in which they were hiding at the given time. Down there in the cellar, though, was a different story entirely. They were trapped. There were no alternative exits. Only one way in and one way out, and for all they knew the killer could be standing right outside that door, waiting for them to make their move. They were as likely to die down there in the cellar from starvation as they were back upstairs by the blade of a knife.

Zach paced in front of Alice one too many times.

'Would you *please* sit down,' she demanded.

'I'm fine.'

'Well at least have a drink. Your apparent lack of vices is distressing.'

She grabbed a bottle from the rack beside her and launched it through the air towards Zach. He turned and saw it hurtling towards him, ducked his head just in time as it sailed over the top of his head. It crashed against the wall behind him, landing on the floor in a puddle of broken glass and spilled wine.

'What are you doing?!' he cried.

Alice shrugged.

'I thought you'd catch it.'

She laughed slightly, a drunken, childish laugh, and turned to Romanelli, expecting him to join in with her joke. He stared at her, a look of disbelief on his face.

'You two need to lighten up,' Alice told them.

'We need to get out of here,' Zach declared.

'You know where the door is,' Alice told him. 'Best of luck to you. Let us know if you get out safely.'

At that moment, Zach was sorely tempted to take her advice and go, take a chance, get out of there and not look back. What was the worst that could happen? Painful, violent, bloody death. Was that so bad compared with spending his last living moments on the planet with an increasingly intoxicated actress who hated him for no apparent reason? He thought about it for longer than was necessarily sensible, and slouched to the ground with a sigh, keeping a safe distance away from Alice and hoping she wouldn't throw another bottle at him.

Alice put her half-empty bottle to her lips and drank a couple of mouthfuls.

She turned to look at Zach and smiled.

Zach didn't like the look of that smile. He was sure it could only mean something bad was about to come his way.

He waited for it.

Any second now.

'Truth or dare?' Alice asked him.

Zach was glad he hadn't been drinking anything at that point, because he was sure he would have performed an enormous spit-take. Of all of the things Alice Blake could have said to him in that moment, that was certainly not what he expected.

'What are you talking about?' he asked.

'We were playing it earlier, before all of this... interruption. You never finished your turn.'

'I really don't think now is the time for games.'

'It doesn't look like we're going anywhere, so we might as well play a game.'

'Alice...' Romanelli half-heartedly tried stopping her.

'No, come on. We've got to pass the time somehow. Tell us your most embarrassing secret. It's not like we're going to live long enough for anyone to find out anyway, so you might as well.'

Zach sighed. She had a point. And even if they *did* somehow make it out of there alive, he could always threaten her that he would write a tell-all exposé of their time spent in a wine cellar, hiding from an attacker. He would keep track of the amount of booze she consumed during that period and write in intimate detail every little thing she said or did. She would be too drunk to know what was real and what wasn't. He could make up all sorts of incredible things about what happened down there, and who was to say if it had actually happened or not? Not that he would do anything like that. Not really. That wasn't the sort of person he was, and he knew it deep down; it was but a pleasant fantasy to indulge in for the moment.

Plus, he didn't have the patience to sit down and write a book, whether real or imagined.

'Fine,' he accepted defeat. 'Alright.'

'Go on, then. Most embarrassing secret.'

Zach took a moment, as if he was trying to think of

something, as if there was nothing already on the surface he was embarrassed about, no one thing he didn't want anyone to know. But as soon as she had asked the question, he already knew the only possible answer he could give.

'I'm afraid of the dark, okay? I always have been, for as long as I can remember.'

Alice looked disappointed. She had wanted something juicy, something gossip-worthy, but instead all she got from him was an incredibly common, albeit childish, phobia.

'That's not so embarrassing,' she told him.

Zach mistook her words for ones of comfort, rather than disappointment, as though she were telling him it was okay to be afraid of the dark; nothing to be embarrassed about. Before he realised what was happening, Zach found himself offering up further details to expand on his original answer.

'I have to have the lights on all the time.'

'*All* the time?'

Zach nodded and looked down at his feet. That extra morsel of information had clearly whet Alice's appetite for gossip more than the original confession. She looked him over, head tilted to one side as though examining a fascinating specimen.

'Wow,' she said. 'Is that why you're still single?'

Partly, maybe, but Zach didn't feel the need to justify the question with an answer.

'Wait,' Romanelli joined the conversation. 'Wasn't it your idea to go somewhere dark? Why would you suggest that if you're so afraid?'

Zach realised he hadn't had the chance to spell out his theory for them yet. They had been so busy going from place to place and drinking and playing stupid games that he had almost forgotten the whole reason for going somewhere dark in the first place.

'There was something about the killer,' he told them. 'He

stopped when it went dark in the kitchen, as if he couldn't go in there. Only when the lights started to come back on again was he able to move forward and come after us.'

'So now *he's* afraid of the dark, too?' Alice scoffed. 'You really think someone with a knife like that would be scared of the dark?'

'Not necessarily scared. But he can't go in to the dark for some reason.'

'What are you talking about?'

He hadn't yet processed all of the information, or thought things through completely, so speaking it out loud was giving Zach the opportunity to work out his theory. The more he spoke out, the more it started to make sense to him, and the more he thought perhaps he was right. He may have found the chink in their attacker's armour. At least, one of the attackers anyway; he couldn't be sure if the others had the same affliction. It sounded unlikely, so whatever plan they came up with based on his theory - otherwise known as assumptions - they would have to proceed with caution, in the highly likely situation that it didn't apply to the others.

'It was the same when he trapped me in your collection room,' Zach continued.

'Collection room?' Alice chimed in.

Romanelli shot him a look that he couldn't quite make out in the dark, but Zach was pretty sure it meant Alice knew nothing about that particular room in the house, and Zach shouldn't have said anything about it. But now, trapped in a cellar, avoiding possible decapitation, that should be the least of anyone's worries.

'It was dark in there, and he couldn't find a light. So he left.'

'So you're saying if we stay in the dark, we should be safe?' Alice asked.

'Yes. Maybe. I don't know. Possibly safe from one of them,

anyway.'

'Good,' Alice said in such an upbeat tone that it sounded like she believed they had found the answer to all of their problems and there was nothing left to worry about. 'We'll stay here until nightfall, and then sneak out in the dark.'

She twisted around to look through the wine rack beside her, pulled a bottle out and examined the label. She nodded slightly, satisfied with her wine selection and settled back against the rack, ready to wait it out.

'You're forgetting something,' Romanelli told them.

'What?'

'The lights. They're on a timer and they'll switch on automatically.'

'I told you not to get that stupid system installed - and now look what happens!'

'There's a psychotic killer after us because I installed smart lights?'

Romanelli and Alice began to argue over the merits or otherwise of having smart technology of any sort installed in the home, Romanelli with the view that it was practical, more secure, easier to control, and Alice countering his arguments with talk of lack of privacy, hack-ability, and the worry that some day machines would take over and there would be no work left for humans, and everyone would become slaves to robot overlords. Zach wasn't sure whether she was drunk, or had actually seen too many science fiction movies, despite what she thought of his own movies, or if that was indeed her genuine perspective of the whole situation. Whichever it was, the arguing was getting to Zach and making the whole situation all the worse.

'Don't forget the party,' he told them, speaking loudly to be heard over their argumentative voices.

'Who told you about that?' Alice snapped.

She spun her head to glare at Romanelli, but the director

looked blankly at her, shrugging his shoulders, knowing full well it wasn't him. It wasn't even his idea to have the party at his own home; it wasn't his sort of thing. It was all Alice.

It was *always* Alice.

'That doesn't matter,' Zach said quickly before any further arguing could begin. 'What matters is: we can't have the crème de la crème of Hollywood turning up to a house where a killer's on the loose.'

His words looked to be sinking in, but Zach added: 'that wouldn't look too good now, would it,' just to make sure he was getting through on Alice's wavelength.

Alice clumsily got to her feet, wobbling slightly from excessive alcohol consumption.

'Then let's get out of here,' she said. 'Sneak past him, go outside and make a run for it.'

'You're assuming there's only one of them - it looked like there were more. You saw what happened both times we tried leaving before. They'll be expecting us to do something like that now. Even if we somehow got past the first of them, the odds are slim that we'd get past them all.'

Zach slumped back to the floor, dejected. He had thought he was on to something: he'd talked himself in to believing they had an escape route, thanks to the idea of being in the dark, but, coming full circle, he managed to talk himself out of believing it could work. Classic over-thinker. That's what Spengler had always called him. If something good was happening (which was rare), Zach would think about it for so long, think about the different permutations of events that could happen as a chain reaction to this good thing going forward, and manage to somehow, somewhere along the line, decide it wasn't a good idea after all.

That was when something *good* happened: when something *bad* happened, he over-thought it until he had essentially brought forth the apocalypse due to the poor decision he had made, be it taking a role in a movie, *not* taking a role in a movie, making a large investment, or even changing energy suppliers. Thinking too hard more often than not brought about inaction on his part, which inevitably led to him missing out on things - roles, events, meeting people - which further led to him thinking about what would have happened if he *hadn't* thought too hard about it, and on and on his brain went in an ever spiralling descent into madness.

Seeing Zach back on the floor, Alice realised that nothing was about to happen any time soon, so she returned to her own spot in the corner and bashed open her new wine bottle.

Noticing that Romanelli had distanced himself from the group, staring into space and actually working his cigarette as though it was lit - putting it in his mouth, taking it out, exhaling - Zach thought it time to try to get him more involved again.

'How about you?' he asked the director.

It took a second for Romanelli to realise he was being spoken to.

'What?' he asked.

'Truth or dare.'

Romanelli smiled slightly.

'There's not much I haven't done that you could dare me to do. So: truth, I guess.'

Zach knew what he wanted to ask, but was still a little afraid to ask it. Yet he would be annoyed with himself if he or Romanelli got killed, or if this whole situation ended and they went their separate ways, and he didn't take the opportunity to ask. Don't over-think it, he told himself. Spit it out.

He took a deep breath.

'You didn't speak to me once in Spengler's office.'

Romanelli waited for him to continue, but nothing more

was forthcoming.

'That doesn't sound like a question.'

'Okay, so, truth: *why* didn't you speak to me when we first met?'

Romanelli gave him a long look, meeting his eyes and staring at him as though the answer was so obvious any idiot could have worked it out. Zach was first to break eye contact; feeling the pressure of the director's gaze upon him in that way was making him feel nervous.

'I wanted to find out if you knew,' Romanelli told him.

'If I knew what?'

He smiled again and pretended to stub his cigarette out on the floor. He took his pack out of his pocket, pulled a fresh stick out and popped it between his lips.

'You don't notice anything much outside of yourself, do you?'

He was sure this must be going somewhere, but Zach was starting to feel like the question had turned on him, and it was once again *his* turn to answer the Truth or Dare question. Romanelli's question sounded vaguely accusatory.

'Excuse me?'

'Who produced *Furballs*?' Romanelli asked him.

That was an easy one, and Zach still couldn't connect the dots as to how this all worked into Romanelli's truth being revealed.

'Sid Cosgrove, of course,' he answered.

'And…?'

Zach sat there, stumped. Cosgrove was the name everyone knew from the movie, the name that flashed up on screen at the beginning: PRODUCED BY SID COSGROVE. A name synonymous with *Furballs* throughout the entirety of the franchise. A name that more people knew than Zach's own, last time he checked. Zach couldn't think of a single other individual who was involved in the production.

'I give up,' he admitted.

'Roman Productions.'

Romanelli accentuated each syllable, making sure they were heard individually, clearly, obviously.

'So?'

The director gave him that look again, the one that told him he was being stupid and should know exactly what he was talking about without it having to be spelled out. But Zach's blank face made it clear that perhaps it *did* need spelling out to him, and perhaps he *was* stupid after all. Slowly, very slowly, enlightenment dawned, his whole face changing to one of realisation. Romanelli smiled when he saw the change, knowing Zach had *finally* twigged as to what he was getting at.

'Roman, as in Romanelli,' Zach told him.

'Bingo. My name wasn't directly on the credits, but my production company was.'

'I still don't get what that's got to do with not talking to me.'

'I was only able to watch you working from afar at the time,' Romanelli explained. 'I wanted to keep my anonymity, knowing having my name front and centre on a production of something like *Furballs* would stop my directorial work from being taken so seriously. I'm embarrassed by it now - not the movie, rather the fact I was scared to have my name on it - but I know it was the right thing to do for my career. People are judgemental about movies like that. As you know.'

Zach couldn't help but feel his own embarrassment at his thoughts on those movies he had helped bring to life. He promised himself there and then that, if they made it out alive, he would re-watch every single one of his movies and try to look for any redeeming qualities they might have.

'Anyway,' Romanelli continued, 'what I'm getting at is that yesterday in Spengler's office was the first time I ever met you properly.'

'So?'

'Have you never been star-struck?'

Zach stared open-mouthed at the director.

This man he had looked up to for the entirety of his career, this man he held on a pedestal so high it was impossible to see the top, this man who he had dreamt of working with forever, watching past interviews, archival footage, documentaries, commentaries, trying to get an insight into how his brain worked should he have any opportunity - *any* opportunity - to speak with him even for thirty seconds: this man he had idolised for so many years had just told him *he* was star-struck when he met *Zach*.

It was too much for him to take in.

No one had ever been star-struck by Zach before.

Sure, he'd had fans gushing over him at conventions, but none of them were *important*, not like Francis Romanelli. No one he had met before in his entire life had meant so much to him as this one man, and *he* was the one who was star-struck, unable to speak due merely being in Zach's presence?

Out of all of the crazy things to have happened on that day, this was surely the craziest.

Zach felt like now he could face anything.

Now he could go out there and stand up to the attacker. And if he died? Well, that would be fine.

Francis Romanelli was star-struck by Zach Keary.

Nothing life threw at him going forward could even come close to that moment.

Romanelli got to his feet and looked up at the cellar door.

'We need to get to the garage,' he announced.

While Zach had reached the defining point of his career - his life, even - he thought perhaps Romanelli was so embarrassed by what he had said that he was ready to get out of there, whatever the cost; Zach thought the director wanted to get away from him so desperately that he'd risk death rather than look at him again.

'We can't leave,' Zach told him. 'Not even in a car. Who knows how many of them are out there?'

Romanelli turned and looked at him. He smiled.

He had a plan.

'I'm not suggesting leaving,' he said.

39

The trip to Starbucks was a bust and now Jennifer was in a foul mood.

'How can you not know the difference between soy milk and almond milk?' she complained. 'They taste completely different.'

For the first time since he had known her, Tim had been embarrassed to be seen with Jennifer: their barista got it in the neck for that one, with Jennifer creating a whole "do you know who I am?" scene in the coffee shop. Sadly for her, most people there *didn't* know who she was, and the one guy who *did* only knew her from a project she would rather be lost to the mists of time than have anyone remember her for. Tim had to listen to her moan about the milk mix up all the way back to Romanelli's house, but he did make a mental note of the specific movie that triggered her, trying to remember to look it up when he got back home.

'I mean, if I'd had a nut allergy, I could have died.'

'But you don't, so you didn't.'

'That's not the point, Timothy.'

They headed up the path from the road towards Romanelli's front door.

'I'm going to sue them,' she declared.

'No you're not.'

'Watch me.'

'It takes a lot of time, money and effort to sue someone.'

Jennifer thought about it for a moment.

'Fine. Then I'll boycott Starbucks.'

'No you won't.'

They reached the front door.

'What is that thing?' Jennifer asked.

Attached to the handle of the door was a length of wire. Tim followed the taut wire across to a hinged contraption mounted to the wall. An axe was in turn attached to the contraption, its blade roughly the same height as a grown man's neck.

'I don't know,' Tim admitted.

He plucked on the wire with a single finger.

The hinge sprang to life, closing with one swift motion, swinging the axe straight towards the front door - and Tim's hand. He yanked his hand out of the axe's trajectory, narrowing avoiding having it severed at the wrist. The axe landed in the door, splintering the wood and embedding itself a few inches deep.

Jennifer screamed.

'What the hell?!' Tim yelled.

He tugged on the front door, but it was locked.

'Guys? Is anyone here?' Jennifer cried out as she banged on the door.

She took a step back, looked across the front of the building, left, right, up, down. Nothing - no movement, no open windows, no sound coming from inside.

No signs of life.

40

The cellar door creaked opened a fraction, almost imperceptibly slowly. The squeak of the hinges was far too loud for Romanelli's liking - on a similar level to someone scraping their fingernails down a chalkboard - but realistically it couldn't have been that loud: their attacker stood nearby and didn't turn to look towards the door. Romanelli watched the figure as he paced back and forth a short distance from them down the hallway. Pacing as though he was worried or anxious about something. A nervous person with an arsenal of weapons wasn't the best combination.

He turned around, ready to head back down into the cellar, but Zach and Alice were already standing right behind him, waiting for the go-ahead to get out of there. He decided that perhaps it *was* best that they take their chances, rather than hiding out for the rest of their lives.

They needed some way to make sure that the figure was distracted.

Alice had a wine bottle clutched in her hands, fresh from the cellar and unopened.

Romanelli grabbed it from her.

She was about to complain when Romanelli glared and put

his finger to his lips: noise could equal death.

He focused his attention back out on the hallway and their assailant.

He waited until the figure's back was fully turned away from them and stepped fully out of the cellar door.

Romanelli launched the wine bottle through the air as hard as he could.

It sailed over the top of the intruder's head and smashed against a wall, a firework of red wine and glass bursting to life and raining to the ground.

With the attacker temporarily distracted, Romanelli waved Zach and Alice out of the cellar door into the hall. He pulled the door shut behind them, and the three of them ran as fast as they could away from there.

A growl came from behind him. Zach looked over his shoulder and saw that they had been noticed.

The attacker was giving chase. They had a reasonable head start, but it wouldn't be long before he gained ground.

The group rounded a corner, hidden from sight.

Romanelli stopped in front of a closed door. He took a key from his pocket, unlocked the door, pushed it open a fraction. Eager to escape, Zach went to go through the door when Romanelli stopped him.

'Wait,' he told Zach.

He proceeded to the next door in the hallway, unlocked that one as well and ushered the other two inside, following after. He eased the door shut and locked it behind them.

Romanelli placed his ear to the inside of the door, listening.

He heard the footsteps of their attacker running in their direction.

They stopped suddenly, close by.

A door creaked: the door next to theirs, left open as a trap.

Muffled footsteps of their attacker stepping inside that room.

'Let's go. Quickly,' Romanelli told them.

He unlocked and opened the door to their own room and ushered everyone back out again.

In the hallway, he looked towards the door the attacker had gone through.

'Go,' he told Alice and Zach. 'I'll catch you up.'

The two of them ran down the hallway a short distance, but Zach stopped, guilt and fear taking over. He turned and watched Romanelli, wanting to make sure that he was okay. Alice stopped beside him.

'What are you doing? Come on,' she insisted.

'I'm not leaving him,' Zach told her. 'Besides, I don't know where we're going.'

They watched Romanelli creep up to the partially open door their attacker went through. He reached for the door handle and slowly, carefully, pulled the door shut. Almost immediately, the door started to rattle, being tugged from the inside. Romanelli held on to the handle, keeping it shut and pulled his key from his pocket once again. He turned the key in the lock and released the handle.

Despite the tugging from inside, the door stayed shut, their attacker trapped inside.

Zach couldn't help but be impressed with the man's survival skills. Sure, it wasn't anything that would necessarily keep him alive if his plane came down in the middle of a jungle, but it was Romanelli who was coming up with all of the ideas for getting them out of this particular time of trouble: a broken lightbulb at the top of the cellar stairs, the whole wrong-door-left-open routine, followed by locking their stalker inside the trap... It suddenly dawned on him that those weren't Romanelli's ideas. They were all things that had happened in movies Zach had been in. The broken lightbulb was something he put to good use to alert him to the presence of the demonic toy in *Play Time's Over*.

His movie *Sleight of Hand* used the switch-and-bait routine of the fake open door as a major part of the plan for trapping the possessed stage magician antagonist. Zach was seriously impressed; not just with Romanelli for making use of these ruses, or the screenwriters for writing something that actually worked in real life, but also with himself for remembering those particular scenes in those specific movies. Perhaps he held on to the memories of them more fondly than he had realised.

Romanelli caught up with them.

'Let's get going,' he told them. 'That door won't hold forever.'

He winked at Zach, and Zach realised that was one of his own lines being quoted back at him.

41

All of the downstairs rooms at the front of the house were empty, as far as Jennifer and Tim could make out from peering through the windows. The whole place looked as though it was deserted. It was weird, like everyone had disappeared while they were gone for coffee. Or maybe they went somewhere else, all of them together, out for a meal, or a few drinks, or…

Jennifer could feel her fear of missing out kicking in.

She switched her cellphone back on and swiped away all of the missed call and voicemail notifications from the home screen and fired up Twitter.

Scrolling through the hundreds of posts she had missed during the past hour or so, she looked for any sign of anything happening that might have included those who were supposed to be there with them now. After all, if it wasn't on Twitter, it couldn't be real.

Nothing much was going on, but she did RSVP to a party the following weekend.

'Let's try going around the side,' Tim suggested. 'They might be in the back.'

As they wandered to the corner of the house, Tim glanced back at the axe embedded in the front door. He was sure it hadn't been there when they'd left the house earlier. It was plain weird.

Even for Hollywood.

42

Romanelli, Zach and Alice poured through the interior door to the garage, panting and out of breath. They caught no sign of any of their attackers all the way there, but there was no guarantee that the one they had trapped was still safely locked away inside the room; interior door locks weren't made to be particularly strong, so it was more than likely that he was able to bash his way out sooner or later. Where the others were was anybody's guess.

The lights in the garage worked in the same way to the kitchen, with more bulbs springing to life the further they ventured into the space.

The garage was almost as large as the entirety of the downstairs of Zach's house.

Inside were two vintage cars: an all-American red and white Chevy, so well polished that your reflection gleamed straight back at you, and a 1957 Eldorado Brougham Cadillac, deep black and glimmering chrome. Zach looked at the cars and wondered for a moment whether they should jump in one and go for it: drive straight through the garage doors, don't look back, keep driving until they were miles away from their troubles.

'They don't run,' Romanelli told him as if picking up on his thoughts. 'I just like the look of them. Can you imagine being stuck in LA traffic in one of these?'

Zach ran the tips of his fingers over the chrome finish on the Cadillac and imagined that scenario, how blissful that would actually be, compared with the mess they were currently in.

'So what are we doing here?' Zach asked.

Romanelli grinned at him and stepped over to a control panel mounted to the garage wall.

'You think we'll be safer in the dark?' he asked.

'Maybe,' Zach replied, worried about where Romanelli was going with this.

'Well then.'

Romanelli pressed a large, round button on the control panel.

A strange clanking sound came from outside the garage, emanating from all around them, coming from all over the building.

'What did you do?' Zach asked.

43

Officers Cole and Davies sat in the front of their patrol car sipping on fresh, hot coffees. Seeing the two young actors heading out for their own drinks had given Davies a craving, with which he somehow managed to infect Cole, who eventually agreed they could quickly pop to a coffee place to grab a drink, so long as it was considered their allocated break time.

Deciding it would be best not to go to the same place as Jennifer and Tim, they headed to another coffee shop, which turned out to be twice the price of Starbucks for half the amount of coffee. But, damn, it was good coffee.

'Treasure every sip,' Cole had said once she'd gotten over the price. 'Each mouthful is about two dollars of liquid gold.'

After getting coffee they had returned to outside Romanelli's house, parked so that they could see any comings and goings along the street. The hedgerow around the property meant they could only see the top floor of the building from where they sat, but it was better than nothing. Davies had not wanted to go back, and declared them all kooks and "up themselves so-called celebrities". But something hadn't felt right about the whole situation to Cole. She wasn't sure she believed the story about a killer being on the rampage, but it was a weird thing to make up, what with the decapitated robot / plush toy and all. Stars were odd in their own ways, but to invite the kind of negative publicity a wacky tale like that could generate - it went against everything a self-respecting actor would stand for. Could be that they were all high; it wouldn't be the first time she had to deal with people imagining crimes due to having smoked a bit too much weed. But even that didn't seem to fit in this particular situation. In the end, she reached a compromise with Davies that they could watch the house so long as he could enjoy a leisurely cup of coffee in the car as well as having another break later.

They had been back in their surveillance spot way before Tim and Jennifer had returned, just a couple of minutes ago.

A strange metallic *clank-clank-clank* drew Cole's attention back towards the house.

She wiped away the condensation from the coffee cup steam and peered out of the car window.

Large metal shutters were sliding shut across all of the windows on the top floor of the house.

'What's going on there?' she asked, more to herself.

Davies leaned across her, massively invading her personal space and forcing her to clutch her coffee way too close to herself to pass any sort of risk assessment, so he could see through her window.

'Damned if I know,' he shrugged, and sank back into his own seat.

'Should we check it out?'

Davies reclined his seat and closed his eyes.

'That's a negative,' he told Cole.

44

Jennifer and Tim were still struggling to find any signs of life in the house, based on what they could see through the windows. At the back of the building Tim spotted the door that led into Romanelli's office.

'Maybe that's unlocked,' he suggested.

They peered through the window that was set into the door.

The exploded computer was visible on Romanelli's desk.

'That's weird,' Jennifer said.

'Maybe he's in to fixing things.'

Jennifer pressed her face against the glass, trying to see better. Everything else about the office looked neat and tidy. The computer looked strangely out of place: a pile of broken bits, shards of glass. It didn't look like something that had been taken apart deliberately; it didn't even look like something that it was possible to fix, more like something that had been dropped from a great height.

A *clank* came from right beside her and a metal shutter slid into place across the window, blocking her view.

'What the hell?' she shrieked. 'That nearly took my nose off!'

'You'd only get another new one,' Tim teased.

'Screw you.'

'That's another one to add to today's list of people to sue.'

She took a step back and surveyed the whole outside of the house: every window was now covered with similar shutters. There was no way of looking inside the building any more.

'Now *that's* weird,' Jennifer repeated.

Tim shrugged.

'Security system, probably,' he ventured. 'A camera caught us snooping around and shuttered the place against intruders.'

'Could be.'

Tim always had an answer for everything. Not that Jennifer would admit it, but he was usually right, with his common-sense attitude to things. But one of these days, Jennifer was going to be right, and there actually *was* going to be some sort of major conspiracy, or something deeply troubling going on that they were witness to. She looked forward to the day when they actually *were* in trouble, and she could rub it in his face. Jennifer turned away from him and looked across at the manicured hedges. Something about the shape of one of them looked peculiar. She wandered over to inspect it as Tim reached out and took hold of the office door handle.

He turned it.

A wire attached to the door pulled taut as he cautiously pushed the door open.

He continued to push the door, oblivious.

The wire pulled tighter.

Tim poked his head around the doorway and looked inside.

'Hello?' he called into the empty room.

No reply.

'There's no one here,' he called out to Jennifer.

'Well, duh,' she replied, frowning at the misshapen hedge

as she edged towards it.

'At least we can get inside.'

Jennifer screamed.

Spengler's body had been dumped unceremoniously within the hedgerow, his legs sticking up at awkward angles. His face was buried further with the branches, twisted in a distorted expression of pain. Jennifer ran back towards Tim.

'What is it?' he asked.

'Get inside, quickly!' Jennifer yelled, running towards to him.

Tim pushed the door open completely and took a step forward.

The wire pulled tight.

Something fell to the ground just in front of Tim.

He looked down to see what had landed at his feet.

A grenade lay there, its pin removed.

'Oh, sh—' Tim began.

His whole body exploded as the grenade detonated.

Jennifer screamed, again, as blood and flesh rained down on her from her exploding friend.

The final parts of Tim that were still standing collapsed to the ground, landing in a pool of bits of himself, splashing Jennifer further, speckling her with red.

Jennifer screamed once more.

She had been right after all. But, surprisingly, she didn't much feel like rubbing this one in Tim's face.

45

'Did you hear something?' Zach asked.

He was sure that a loud *bang* had sounded somewhere outside the building. It sounded vaguely like an explosion, but the walls were too thick for him to make out much more than a muffled noise. Alice and Romanelli shrugged; it was clearly something else he had imagined, as he had a habit of doing.

Unlit cigarette dangling from between his lips, Romanelli stood beside a large metal fuse box. He opened it up. Inside were a couple of dozen fuses for controlling the power throughout the whole house and beyond. He scanned them and landed on the one he wanted.

'Hold on to your butts,' he told them, quoting one movie for which, sadly, Zach didn't even get the opportunity to audition.

Zach pulled his cellphone from his pocket and readied his finger on the flashlight icon. He noticed that his battery was already down to nineteen percent. It wasn't looking good. That was likely less than an hour's worth of flashlight usage left in there, at a push.

Romanelli pulled the fuse.

The lights immediately died, plunging the whole of the

garage back into absolute darkness.

Zach switched on his flashlight.

'Nicely done,' he said.

A mechanical chugging, whirring sound filled the garage. Something electrical springing into life.

'What's that?' Alice asked.

'Uh oh,' Romanelli muttered.

The lights in the garage flickered back into life, staggering up to half-illumination, and gradually easing up to slightly less than their usual full brightness. Romanelli stared across at the machine in the corner of the garage from which the sounds were emanating.

'The emergency generator,' Romanelli told them. 'I completely forgot about that. Never had to use it. It just needs - '

'Look out!' Alice screamed.

The attacker appeared right behind Romanelli, knife poised for attack.

Alice's warning came too late.

The long knife found its way into Romanelli's back, startling the cigarette from his mouth. The weapon was jerked back out of his body, then plunged straight back in, one quick, fluid motion. Romanelli crumpled to the ground.

The attacker turned his sights on Alice and Zach.

For the first time in his life, Zach found an improvised plan hatching in his brain. Romanelli's survival skills must have been rubbing off on him, though in the end they had failed the director himself.

Zach rushed to the containers, drawers and boxes scattered around the walls of the garage and rummaged through them, looking for something. All the while the attacker stalked towards him, knife at his side, itching to be used again.

Zach found what he was looking for.

Thanking God for the garage having a low ceiling, Zach

darted around the room, striking the lights with a hammer, ducking away from each explosion of broken glass falling from the ceiling, every smash of a bulb creating another small area of darkness within the garage.

The figure lunged towards Zach.

Zach lifted the hammer and struck out at the final bulb.

The garage once again fell into absolute darkness. Zach remained still, staring out into the black, trying to get some sense of location, for himself, Alice and their attacker. But it was impossible to even make out outlines, the darkness was so deep. Zach felt his throat closing up, beads of sweat breaking out on his forehead. Just because he was trapped in the pitch black with a knife-wielding maniac, there was no need to panic, he tried telling himself. But he kept imaging that knife swinging through the darkness, edging towards him, ready to slice him into pieces at any second. He could feel his legs weakening, his knees ready to give way.

Stay strong, he told himself. *Don't give up now.*

In the darkness, he heard footsteps. They sounded as if they were going away, backing out towards the door through which they had come into the garage. It wasn't Romanelli, obviously, and Zach very much doubted it was Alice; the tread was heavy, uncertain. It could only be their attacker, moving away from them. As the imagined space between himself and the figure increased, so too Zach felt himself regain control of his breathing. He was still terrified, of course, but the thoughts of the blade being within inches of spilling his intestines to the ground started to dissipate.

The door to the garage opened a fraction, a sliver of light from within the house oozing its way through the crack and into the garage. Enough for Zach to see the outline of their attacker standing in the doorway. Enough to see him sidle out of the door, back out of the garage and into the main house and close the door behind himself.

As soon as the door was closed, Zach switched his flashlight back on. He headed to the emergency generator and pressed the large, red button labelled *STOP*. The chugging and whirring slowed down, slower and slower, grinding and whirring, until it was more of a gentle purr, and, then it stopped. The silence felt as thick as the darkness had done, oppressive and overwhelming, their heartbeats pounding in their ears loud as the percussion section of an orchestra.

Alice went over to be with Zach.

'Are we safe?'

'I think so. For now.'

'Why wouldn't he leave the door open to let some light in so he could attack us without being in the dark?'

It was a fair question to which Zach didn't have an answer.

'Fear makes us act irrationally, I guess,' he replied with a shrug.

A moan came from across the garage. Zach aimed his flashlight in the direction of the sound.

Romanelli.

He was still alive, but barely.

Alice and Zach rushed over to him.

A dark pool of blood surrounded him, spreading further even as they watched. Romanelli tried to pull himself up on his elbows and get at his pockets, but to no avail. The knife wound in his back was too much, the pain too great. He collapsed back down again, exhausted from the effort.

'Keep still,' Zach advised him. 'Tell us what you need.'

'Cigarette,' Romanelli replied, his voice barely a whisper.

Zach rifled through Romanelli's pockets until he found the cigarette packet. He placed it between the director's lips.

'Sorry I don't have a light.'

Romanelli waved an unsteady hand towards one of the drawers at the side of the garage.

Zach stood and headed over to where Romanelli was pointing.

'Here?' he asked, indicating a particular drawer.

Romanelli nodded.

Zach opened the drawer and looked inside. He couldn't help but smile. Always the improviser.

Inside the drawer was a miniature blow-torch. Perfect for the smaller home projects, or for caramelising a dessert. Or for lighting a cigarette. He took the torch back to Romanelli and, careful not to burn the man, lit his cigarette. The ferocious blaze of the torch looking like it would burn straight through. Romanelli closed his eyes and took a long, satisfied inhalation. He blew the smoke back out through the corner of his mouth.

He had been told it would be his excessive smoking that would kill him.

Look how wrong they had been.

'Thank you,' he whispered.

'Can I get you anything else?' Zach asked. 'Coffee? Anything?'

Romanelli laughed, but the laugh turned to a cough, and the cough turned to excruciating pain wracking throughout his body.

Alice took his hand in hers.

'You're going to be okay,' she told him. 'We'll get out of here and straight to a hospital. You'll see.'

Romanelli's eyes began to close, the life flowing out of him along with the blood.

'Stay with me,' Alice said.

'Truth or dare,' Romanelli croaked, eyes still closed.

'Truth,' Alice whispered.

'Did you ever love me? Really?'

Alice took a moment. It would be so easy to lie and let this poor, dear man go in peace. But she owed it to him to be truthful, as he always had been with her. She couldn't let her last words to this great man, great director, great friend, be an untruth.

'I was starting to,' she admitted.

Romanelli lifted a bloody hand to Alice's cheek and stroked her skin with his fingertips.

'Be happy,' he told her.

He turned to look at Zach, removed his hand from Alice's grip and indicated for Zach to move closer to him.

Zach did as instructed. Romanelli drew on what little strength he had left in his body to lift himself up and pull Zach close to him, right in his face.

'Do one thing for me,' he told Zach.

'Anything.'

'Give 'em hell, little guy.'

He released Zach and lay back down.

Romanelli closed his eyes.

His breathing stuttered, coming in jagged gasps, until finally, finally it stopped.

The cigarette fell from his lips and landed on the floor, floating on top of the pooled blood.

He was gone.

Zach bowed his head, feeling the tears prickling at his eyes, desperately trying to be free. Alice lay over Romanelli, resting her cheek on his chest, sobbing as she let the tears flow, feeling truly emotional for someone else for perhaps the first time in her life. No ulterior motive, no hidden agenda; pure, unselfish despair.

Zach lifted his head and looked at the two of them there together, Romanelli dead, Alice broken.

He got to his feet, his jaw set, his face determined.

'We need to finish this,' he announced.

46

Even with the emergency generator disabled and all of the window shutters in place, small emergency lights set in to the ceilings at regular intervals provided an ambient glow. Enough light to be able to see where you were going, but not enough to read a book by.

Holding the hammer he picked up in the garage with one hand, Zach led Alice with his other, out of the garage and down the hallway. Zach hadn't taken hold of her hand; rather, she had slid hers into his as they left the garage. Based on how his day had begun, Zach never imagined he would end it holding hands with Alice Blake. Not that there was anything more to the hand-holding than a sense of security in a time of crisis. She had just lost someone she almost loved and she needed the comfort and safety of human contact.

Nothing more.

The hallway was clear. No sign of any of their attackers at that moment, but they had learnt from experience that didn't necessarily mean they weren't nearby.

Despite the relative darkness of the place, the two of them kept to the sides of the hallway, creeping along the wall, trying to remain out of even the dimmest of light and keep their presence hidden for as long as possible.

The house must have taken some getting used to for Romanelli when he first moved in there: all of the hallways and doorways looked near enough identical, with nothing to distinguish between each individual room. Zach was sure Romanelli must have spent much of the first few weeks living there wandering into the wrong rooms.

As they reached the end of the hallway, Zach indicated with his hand for Alice to stay where she was. He peered around the corner and into the entrance lobby. It was deserted. The stairs, too, were empty. He cast his eyes up the staircase to the level above. Everywhere he could see from that viewpoint was empty.

He took hold of Alice's hand again and led her across the lobby, onto the red carpet and towards the staircase.

'Where are we going?' Alice whispered.

'I have a plan,' he told her.

Leaning against the bannister for support, they trod up the staircase, careful to take it one step at a time, testing their weight with each footfall to make sure the step wasn't going to creak.

At the top of the stairs, Zach looked in both directions, down the two identical hallways that branched off from the landing, trying to remember which way he needed to go. He decided to turn left, fairly certain that was indeed the correct direction, and led Alice past several more nondescript doors.

They reached a door Zach was one-hundred percent certain could only be the correct one.

A door that had been forced open at some point, the wooden frame splintered where the lock had been bashed until it gave way.

He pushed the door open, ushered Alice inside, stepped in with her and shut the door again.

Zach switched on his cellphone flashlight. Twelve percent battery remaining.

'What is this place?' Alice murmured as the light shone against the memorabilia that filled the room.

Ignoring the question, Zach strode across the room straight over to the *Furballs* display.

He peered in the glass cabinet that had contained the Fuzz animatronic. It was still there, minus the head. But that wasn't what he had come looking for.

'Can you hold this, please?' he asked Alice, handing her his cellphone.

He reached up and took down the fire axe from where it was hanging. The wooden handle felt solid in his hands, and reassuringly heavy. He let it swing against a nearby wooden table. The blade embedded itself in the surface without any effort. Definitely still sharp enough to do some damage. Something still didn't feel right, though. He wasn't quite ready.

Zach looked up at the *Furballs* leather jacket.

'You can't be serious,' Alice said, reading his mind.

He gave her a half-smile and grabbed the jacket. The sheen had faded on it over time, but holding it in his hands and smelling the scent of the material brought the memories flooding back.

Attempting to put it on, it was clear that he had put on a few pounds since he had made that movie - it was thirty years ago, so no one could blame him for that. But it still fit. Sort of. There was no way he would be able to fasten the zipper over his now less than flat stomach, and the sleeves barely reached his wrists. But there was enough give in the arms to be able to move - swiftly if necessary.

'Really?' Alice snorted.

'No doubt.'

He took the cellphone back from Alice and shone it around the room, looking for any sort of inspiration he might be able to find. The beam fell upon some night vision goggles, displayed beside the poster for a movie called *Obadiah's Owls*. Zach picked up the goggles and turned them over, inspecting them.

Please work, please work, please work... he said to himself over and over.

He found the power switch for the goggles and flicked it.

Nothing happened.

Damn it.

He gave them a gentle bash, the same as he always did with his TV or laptop when they stopped working.

The device whirred to life.

Zach smiled.

'What's the plan?' Alice asked.

Zach put the goggles on his head. Everything turned green and white, the whole room visible in a strangely spectral image, Alice standing in front of him, her face ghostly and eyes white glowing dots.

He lifted the axe to his shoulder and tugged the sleeves of the jacket back down.

'We're gonna find those sons of bitches,' he told Alice. 'And we're going to kill them.'

47

The emergency lights were easily disabled, either through simply unscrewing them from the ceiling or with a swift bash of the end of the fire axe. Their destruction was easy, certainly, but reaching up to do it in the leather jacket was more of a struggle. Zach tried to hide his discomfort from Alice, but it was obvious when he spent the majority of the time he wasn't destroying light bulbs tugging at the sleeves, or the bottom of the jacket. Eventually he declared that he was starting to get too warm, removed the jacket and tied it around his waist by the arms.

A relief both to himself and Alice.

The two of them wandered throughout the house, removing the emergency illumination wherever they went, leaving a trail of darkness behind them. Zach never thought he would reach a point in his life where he would be deliberately making somewhere darker, but in the context of the day's events, his nyctophobia found itself taking a backseat to the fear of being stabbed to death. It's not that fear of the dark was anything to be ashamed of - the last study Zach had read on the issue found that nearly twenty million American adults had the same condition - it was just that this new fear was very visible, and he had seen the effects first hand. If he had had the opportunity to stop and think about it, Zach probably would have even realised that the dark no longer bothered him. Survival instinct had taken over. Of course, the night vision goggles meant it wasn't *completely* dark wherever he went, but they didn't exactly present the world in the gleaming technicolour splendour he was used to.

With Romanelli gone, he felt a responsibility to the late director to work with Alice to try and get both of them out of there in one piece.

The house felt even larger in the darkness.

So many places for someone to be hiding, waiting, watching.

After trekking across the entirety of the house - as far as Zach could tell anyway, in the dark, in a location he did not know especially well - he and Alice reached the final upstairs room: the master bedroom. A huge room, but, like the rest of the house, decorated in a minimalist style. There was a vast bed in the middle, piles of pillows at one end, a thick comforter draped across the bottom. A desk in the corner of the room with a chair in front of it, notebooks, pens and pencils on top. Along one of the walls there were a few closets, and very little else. Thick drapes flowed from the ceiling to the floor, open at the moment, but the shutters on the outside of the large, arched windows prevented any light from entering the room anyway.

Zach peered under the bed, the night-vision goggles making things that would have been invisible visible. He opened the closet doors, checked behind where the drawn drapes hung... Everywhere he could think to look, as if he was playing a particularly deadly game of hide and seek.

Coming, ready or not...

But there was nothing. No one to be found.

Zach pulled the goggles off of his head. Sure, it left him in the dark, but the things were heavy, and starting to press against his temples. They were going to leave a permanent mark if he left them on for much longer. He switched the flashlight back on anyway, just in case.

Nine percent battery.

'Where are they?' Alice asked.

Zach frowned.

'I don't know,' he admitted.

It didn't make sense that they hadn't stumbled across one of their attackers during their tour of the house. They should have at least seen signs of them somewhere, surely. Why chase them down only to hide out without making any further appearances? It was starting to feel like a very elaborate game, to which the pair of them had no knowledge of the rules. Or perhaps a game in which the rules were being made up as they went along.

'Maybe they've gone,' Alice suggested.

She laid down on the bed, resting her head on a stack of deep pillows, sinking into them and closing her eyes. Alice didn't realised how exhausted she felt until she did that. She opened her eyes again straight away, worried that, if she didn't, she would likely fall fast asleep right there and then. Sleep sounded nice. Blissful. The one place she wanted to be right now. But she couldn't allow herself to be seduced by the sweet siren song of dreamland. She had to remain as alert as possible, in case they needed to make a run for it; they needed to keep their wits about them, otherwise they would both be dead before they knew it.

'Maybe they *have* gone,' Zach replied doubtfully. 'Probably not. But maybe.'

'We should leave. Take our chances and get out.'

'I don't know…'

Sure, the kids had made it out okay, as far as Zach and

Alice knew - but there was also no sign of them having made it back. They could have been killed when they returned, outside of the house, away from anyone's line of sight, oblivious to the situation going on in the house, despite Alice's attempts to warn them. There were at least three dead bodies that Zach knew of, and on no less than three separate occasions when he had been near a door into the outside world he had come close to being killed. He felt like somehow their chances were better inside.

'We can't stay in here forever,' Alice reminded him, as if reading his exact thoughts.

'I know, but - '

'But nothing. We need to get out of here. Call the cops. Get *them* to track these people down.'

'We've been through this already. They won't believe anything we say. They won't come out here again.'

If they did come out, it would probably be to arrest them for wasting police time, and the last thing they needed was a bunch of police officers showing up at the doorstep. Admittedly, if they were taken into custody they would probably be in one of the safest places on earth, as far as knife-wielding attackers went. But that situation could play out one of two ways. First, the police could show up and immediately be killed by the mysterious figures lurking somewhere on the property. If that happened, Alice and Zach would have police officers' blood on their hands. Second, the police *could* successfully arrest them, put them in a cell for the night, but with the headlines that followed their lives would essentially be over anyway. Not physically, maybe, but work-wise. They would have no chance of ever making another movie, or living their lives in peace, again. The best they would be able to hope for would be appearances on late-night talk shows where the host would encourage them to share their "wacky" story with the audience for the millionth time.

That wasn't a life Zach wanted, or was willing, to lead.

Their only chance was to try and survive on their own terms.

'I think we can make it if we leave,' Alice told him, a firmness in her voice telling Zach it wasn't necessarily a suggestion, but rather something she was about to try.

He couldn't let that happen. For both of their sakes.

'There's a party happening here later, right?' Zach asked.

'Yes. Why?'

'That means lots of people will be coming. Completely unaware of any danger.'

'Yes, but…'

'It would be a blood bath. We have to find whoever is doing this. *We* are the only ones who can make this stop without anyone else losing their life.'

Zach carefully put the goggles back on his head, disabling the flashlight on his cellphone. He felt bad for Alice, being in complete darkness while he could more-or-less see their surroundings. She would have to trust him to keep her safe.

Alice climbed off the bed to join him, heading towards the spot where she had last seen him in the hope he hadn't yet moved away from there. He hadn't.

'Fine,' she sighed. 'So what do we do?'

'I don't know,' Zach admitted. 'But they have to be around here somewhere.'

CLANK-CLANK-CLANK.

Loud mechanical noises filled the room, coming from the windows.

The shutters were starting to re-open.

Light streamed through the windows. The brightness rammed straight into Zach's eyes through the goggles. He yanked them from his head, pained by the sudden piercing light, feeling like it was scorching his retinas. He threw the goggles onto the table near the window, flinging them as though they were suddenly hot in his hands. If the shutters were opening in that one room, chances were they were doing it throughout the whole house. It didn't make sense that they should start opening by themselves, though. Unless…

Zach turned to face Alice.

The attacker was there. Right behind her.

'Look out!' Zach yelled.

Alice turned. She screamed.

The figure lunged forward with the knife.

48

The police car was steaming up again, with the hot coffees and Officer Cole's constant jabbering about some cause or other that she was currently supporting, or had supported, or was telling Davies he *shouldn't* support.

Davies cranked down the window on his side of the car to let some air in, hoping that would sort out the misting.

It started to work, but not quickly enough for his liking.

'Open yours, too, would you?' he instructed Cole.

Cole pressed the button to open hers a fraction.

She frowned as she looked through the gap and opened the window further to give herself a better view.

'You always take things too far,' Davies growled.

'No - look.'

She indicated for Davies to take a look at the house they had been watching, before the windows became too fogged up to see.

Davies leaned across her again, so he could see what she was looking at.

The shutters were re-opening all across the top floor of the house.

'What the hell are they doing?' Davies asked.

'Shall we check it out now?'

Davies settled back in his seat and thought for a second. He picked up his coffee cup and rolled it from side to side, feeling how much was left in there.

'Give it a minute,' he told his partner.

49

The knife scratched Alice's side. She felt it snag on her clothes, but thankfully it was fabric that it ripped, rather than flesh, as she managed to side-step out of the way in time. With her temporarily out of reach, the attacker launched himself towards Zach.

As the attacker rushed at Zach, Zach grabbed hold of his arm. He pushed with all his strength, aiming the vicious blade away from his body, wrestling with the attacker to keep him at bay. Neither making much progress against the other, Zach kept the knife-wielding arm away, but was unable to push it any further, while the attacker was not quite strong enough to push back against Zach.

They turned together; a violent potentially fatal ballet, pirouetting across the room in small movements. Gradually heading towards the bedroom window.

The attacker gave a sudden, swift shove. It caught Zach off-guard.

Zach lost his grip, his palms slick with sweat, unable to keep hold of the attacker's arm.

The figure took his opportunity.

He stepped closer to Zach, lifting the knife.

Zach reached out and grabbed the night-vision goggles

from the table.

Grunting with effort, he swung them at the attacker's head. They made contact with a solid *crack*, the blow making a clear impact.

Stunned by the force, the attacker lost his balance. He stumbled, his feet heavy, thumping around the room with little awareness of where he was or what he was doing. But he couldn't stop the momentum. He continued to fall. He grasped around, trying to grip something, anything, to stabilise himself.

His hand made contact with Zach's leather jacket.

He gripped hard, clinging on to it.

Zach tried to peel the fingers off, attempting to release himself from the tight hold they had on him.

But it was no good.

The dazed attacker continued to stumble.

He floundered towards the bedroom window, dragging Zach along with him.

'Zach!' Alice screamed, seeing what was about to happen.

'Help me!' Zach screamed back.

But there was nothing Alice could do.

The attacker tripped backwards against the window, the glass shattering at the heavy impact. Shards sliced the air outside, cascading down to the ground.

Zach gave Alice one last panicked look before he, too, was pulled through the window.

Latched on to each other, Zach and the attacker fell.

The two police officers watched through their open car window, surprised at the sudden sight of a rain of glass, followed immediately by two people launching through the window and tumbling to the ground.

Cole turned to Davies, an accusatory look in her eyes. If they'd moved when she'd said to, when the shutters had re-opened, or even the time before, when they'd first closed, this would likely have been something they could have prevented.

Davies threw back the final dregs from his coffee cup, making sure he got every last drop. He sighed.

'Perhaps we'd better take a look,' he admitted.

Zach and his attacker landed heavily on their backs on the ground. Both lay still, unmoving. The knife had fallen from the attacker's hand mid-fall, and Zach's night-vision goggles had also made their way out with them. Both objects rested close beside them.

From the bedroom window, Alice stared down at the scene below. She saw the two of them laying there, watching carefully for movement, for any signs of life. Nothing. She had no way of knowing if they were alive or dead, wounded or just winded.

No way of knowing from up there in the house anyway.

50

Slowly, painfully, reality started to seep back into focus. Zach tried to move from the spot in which he had landed, but his arms and legs refused to give in to his demands. Pain shot through his body. The brightness of the sky hurt his eyes, causing big black spots to float around in his vision. He wondered if he had concussion. He had fallen from a first storey window, so it was more than likely. He was lucky to even be alive, he realised.

Inch by inch, he gradually managed to move an arm, and reached up to touch his face.

He winced at the touch as something sharp dug into his skin. He carefully used his fingers to inspect the area. A piece of glass embedded in his face; nothing too big, but enough to draw blood. He pulled it out, his hand shaking and making the job more difficult than it should have been. Once it emerged completely, he dropped it on the ground beside him.

Even that motion was enough to wipe him out again.

Zach let his head drop to the side.

The attacker was right there beside him.

His masked face looking straight at Zach.

If his body had been working, Zach would have jumped.

He realised his companion on the ground also wasn't

moving.

It looked like he, too, was winded from the fall - or, maybe, if Zach was lucky, the drop could have killed him. It hadn't been that great a fall, but if he had landed awkwardly, or if he'd fallen on a carelessly placed spike or something... You never know.

With huge effort, Zach lifted himself up on to his elbows and began the painful process of nudging himself towards the fallen form of his attacker.

The sprint from the hallway outside the bedroom to the top of the staircase seemed to go on forever, taking Alice longer than it should have done. She hoped more than anything that Zach was okay, and he hadn't been killed in the fall; but on the other hand, she also hoped the fall had been enough to kill their attacker. If one of them had survived, the odds were likely that both of them had.

All or nothing.

Part of her didn't know which particular scenario to wish for, but deep down she knew she wanted Zach to have survived, even if that meant they had to continue fighting for their lives. With any luck, the attacker was at least now impaired somehow and would be less of a match for them.

Lost in her thoughts, seeing the top of the staircase getting nearer and nearer, Alice stumbled over something laying on the ground and fell to the floor.

She looked up from where she had landed and almost gagged at the sight.

She had tripped over Dave's corpse.

Something about it caught her eye.

Something puzzling. Something disturbing.

'What the...?' she asked herself as she crawled towards the body.

* * *

With trembling hands, Zach reached towards his attacker's face. He needed to know who was behind the mask. Remove the anonymity, and half of their power was gone with it. He also knew from experience that in *any* horror movie ever made, the moment at which the killer is supposedly dead, or at least unconscious, and someone goes to remove their mask to reveal their true identity is the exact moment that said killer would miraculously spring back to life and attack the person doing the de-masking.

Hence the hesitant, trembling, hands.

Zach grasped the black fabric covering the face. Surprisingly soft in his hand. It felt like it would have been a very warm fabric to be wearing for any great length of time. The attacker was likely sweating under there. Zach realised his thoughts about the softness of the material the mask was made out of were nothing but delay tactics on his part, stopping him from revealing the true identity of one of the people behind this endless pursuit.

He closed his eyes and took a deep breath.

He opened his eyes again. He was ready.

With one swift movement he whisked off the mask.

'Dave?!' he exclaimed, caught by surprise by that revelation more than if the "surprise" attack had happened.

Dave's eyes flickered open.

Zach jumped back. This was it. His attacker was about to roar back to life, spring into action and hack his way through Zach. It was over.

But Dave just laid there.

For a brief moment immediately after the mask was removed, he had looked panicked. But now he looked strangely relaxed. It was over - for him. His identity revealed, it was too late to worry about it.

'It was you all along?' Zach asked. 'Who else was helping you? Where are they?'

Zach spun around as fast as his aching body would allow, imagining swarms of others dressed in black flocking towards him behind his back.

A small smile crept across Dave's face.

'There never was anyone else,' Dave told him. 'It was all me. Carefully planned, and brilliantly executed, if I do say so myself.'

'Just you?'

'You still don't remember me, do you?'

Dave was right, and Zach couldn't deny it. Dave had looked familiar to him when they had first met at the house that morning (which now felt like forever ago), but he couldn't place him at the time, and he hadn't had much opportunity to think about since that meeting; he had been somewhat busy, one way or another. Romanelli had told Zach that Dave had worked on the visual effects for *Furballs*, but that was it. There had to be something more - something important - Zach had forgotten. He racked his brain, mentally trying to scan through the faces of everyone he had ever known. Suddenly, remembering Dave felt like the single most important piece of information he should have been concentrating on all day. But Zach realised he didn't actually know that many people, and the faces of those he had worked with in the past were now little more than just that - faces. Blurred, unnamed faces relegated to the depths of his memory banks, unlikely to ever be accessed in any meaningful way again.

'*Should* I remember you?' Zach asked, trying to play it cool.

'I gave you everything you've got,' Dave growled, his eyes darkening, anger seeping back into his face. 'But did I get anything in return?'

'I'm guessing… no?'

'No. Instead, I had everything taken away from me. Everything.'

51

Guns drawn and pointed in front of them, Officers Cole and Davies edged their way up the main path towards the front of Romanelli's property. It was a long path, and it was taking them far longer to get there than Cole would have liked, but she had been taught to exercise caution, and the slow advance was giving her time to assess the situation.

Though she was struggling to make much sense of any of it, it boiled down to five main points:

1. A crazy once famous actor suggested that another person had been brutally slain on the property, but when they attended, there were no signs of violence, or struggle; no blood, no corpse.

2. Said crazy actor person claimed to have had an intruder in their own home the previous evening. Again, no signs of any wrong-doing on attendance at the scene.

3. They, the police officers, witnessed for themselves window shutters closed across the entire house in the middle of the day. In and of itself not necessarily suspicious, and certainly not illegal, but when added to everything else going on, it was kind of odd.

4. The aforementioned window shutters they had previously seen closing subsequently re-opened across the

entire house.

5. Two people (indistinguishable from the distance of the car away from the house) fell together from a first floor window.

It had been a crazy day, and Cole had no idea what to expect when they reached the house.

All she knew was, there must be *something* going on.

52

Zach cranked himself into a kneeling position beside Dave, who continued to lay on the floor without any indication that he was planning on getting up any time soon. He hoped Dave was going to stay there and not launch a surprise attack. If he *did* try anything, Zach hoped his knees would allow him to get to his feet in good time. In hindsight, he wondered if kneeling was such a good idea; his joints were more than likely to seize up if he spent any great amount of time that way. But he couldn't think of another position that would be any more beneficial anyway, so decided to stay there. There wasn't much else he could do at that point. Running was pointless, both due to his current physical condition, and also because he had promised Alice they would end this, so he couldn't risk Dave getting away again. And physically attacking Dave while he was laid, disabled, on the ground felt like it would be incredibly unfair, despite everything he had gone through.

Instead, Zach opted to hear him out.

'What are you talking about?' Zach prompted.

'I invented Furballs,' Dave told him.

'You did the visual effects for it. Yes, I know that much.'

'Not just that. They were my creation.'

'You wrote it?'

'No. Someone else did that part. The easy bit.'

'What, then?'

'I came up with the design. That iconic look that sold millions of t-shirts, posters, action figures, cuddly toys. That cute, furry face that you brandish about for profit at every convention you can get yourself invited to, that the fans go ga-ga over and desperately want to have a photo taken with.'

'You must be very proud,' Zach said, not knowing what else to say.

'I created the animatronics,' Dave continued. 'I made them move. I made them seem real. I gave them life.'

At the risk of encouraging a *Frankenstein* like tale from his attacker, Zach nevertheless couldn't think of anything much to say other than:

'You did a great job. I mean, I - '

Laying there on the ground, Dave interrupted Zach and told his story.

53

1986.

Pre-production of Furballs *is in full swing; has been for several weeks now. Dave's staff are working solidly to get everything ready for the cameras to roll.*

This particular morning, Dave arrives at the visual effects workshop and the producers are there - all of them. Dave immediately knows something's up. They're like harbingers of doom, only appearing to him when there's bad news to be shared. It's clear there's going to be some sort of change happening that he's not going to like.

They tell him straight away that they're over budget and over schedule. They're having to slash three weeks prep time, and forty percent of the visual effects budget. But it's all got to be done in time for principal photography, to the same standard they would have expected from the original budget and schedule. The Furballs creatures have to look goddamn realistic, otherwise there's no hope in hell of them even coming close to making their money back, never mind having any profits to distribute to those in the profit sharing scheme (which Dave isn't actually a part of, but that was none of the producers' concern; they were looking out for their own investment).

Dave tells them there's no way that's going to happen, not under these new terms. They're not even close to getting it right; those kind of robotics take time and money.

The producers tell him if he can't do it they'll find someone else who can.

There is no one else, Dave tries to tell them: he's the best of the best. But they're convinced he's easily replaceable, an expendable commodity, so Dave has no choice but to agree, and tells them he'll get it done.

He looks through everything they need to get the project finished.

Some electrical parts haven't arrived yet, and it doesn't look like they'll come through anywhere near in time for the newly imposed deadline.

He asks around, seeing if he can get the parts from anywhere else. There is one supplier, and they're offering the parts considerably cheaper than Dave's outstanding order. Despite seeming like a less than reputable company, Dave has no choice. He's got to get the job done, otherwise he's out of work. With a young family to support, he can't afford to lose this job; they've been counting on it more than they probably should have. And if he lost this job because he had a disagreement with the producers, he knew his name would be mud. Regardless of the quality of his work (and he always prided himself on his exceptional quality), those producers would make it clear to anyone else in the industry that Dave was not someone who could, or should, be worked with. He would, essentially, be black-listed.

He orders the parts.

They arrive two days later.

The quality definitely isn't up to the standard he would have liked, but at the price he paid for them, they're about what he expected.

He clamps pieces in place, takes out his soldering iron, ready to stitch everything together.

He's under real pressure to get this animatronic in front of the producers and the investors. He's been left under no illusion that today is make or break for the production - and for him. They need a successful demonstration, and they need it today. Time is ticking away.

He fires up the soldering iron.

It barely even touches the electrical piece when it explodes.

Tiny shards of metal spray into his face.

Into his eyes.

He screams.

Co-workers rush over to help. They run cold water into his eyes, but it stings so badly. They try to pluck splinters from his eyeballs, but it's too risky. They don't know what damage they'll do in trying to help.

He ends up in hospital.

The doctors examine him and declare that the retinas in both of his eyes have become detached from the trauma he experienced. It leaves him with night blindness. If it's dark (not even pitch black, just not light), he can't see anything. Not a shadow, not a flicker of movement, nothing but an empty black void in front of his eyes, as though there is nothing there. The doctors tell him it might improve, but the chances are so slim, he certainly shouldn't count on it. Gradually, his daytime vision starts deteriorating, too, and he thinks some day he will likely be completely blind. But that comes later in the story…

After his discharge from the hospital, the studio refuses to accept responsibility. They say Dave cut corners, buying cheap parts from an unapproved supplier. They say he ignored policies and procedures. They say he was one hundred percent to blame for what happened. Dave wants to sue, but, after much legal arguing, the studio eventually offers to pay him off if he doesn't speak about what happened. Dave's wife says they don't need the hassle of going through the courts; the giant studios would crush them, and they'd end up with a mountain of legal bills. Dave should take the money. So he does.

He takes the hush money and the studio sends him on his way.

But the money doesn't last long. It wasn't a huge sum by

anyone's standards, and with no job, little hope of getting *a job, his family to support, mortgage payments to make… It soon runs out, and he's left with nothing.*

He watches from the background as Furballs *mania sweeps the country, then the world. The creature's face* he *designed. The animatronic* he *created. All plastered over every lunchbox, mug, cereal box, t-shirt, poster as far as the eye could see (no pun intended). He can't escape this creature he's created, and the creature has become a vast, unstoppable monster that's killing him inside bit by bit.*

His wife can't deal with the angry yet withdrawn man he has become. She takes the kids and leaves him. He's left with nothing but his bitter resentment to keep him company.

Furballs *becomes the most profitable movie of all time for the studio, mostly due to the merchandise. And the merchandise is successful entirely due to Dave's design.*

And what does Dave get for it? Not a single dime.

All because he took the hush money.

54

'At least I had one more opportunity to put my practical effects skills to good use. I fooled you all, didn't I?' Dave said.

'I'm so sorry,' Zach told Dave when he was sure the story was finished.

'You took everything from me,' Dave replied, his face seething with anger once again.

That seemed like a particularly unfair statement to be aimed at Zach: he had nothing to do with what had happened to Dave, as far as he was aware, and for Dave to make out that it was his fault was plain wrong. It didn't seem wise to argue with someone who had been trying to kill him for the past few hours, but if all of this was down to a misunderstanding, Zach felt he had to put the record straight.

'Wait a minute,' he began. 'I had nothing to do with - '

'Not only you,' Dave interrupted. 'It was mostly Cosgrove - he was the one who told them to get rid of me. And Romanelli - he never knew exactly what happened with me. But that money went through him, whether he knew about it or not.'

Cosgrove and Romanelli. Two of Dave's victims from the day. He was picking off everyone he had a grievance with - whether it was a justified grievance or not. Zach could understand being angry at Cosgrove if he was in fact directly responsible for Dave's firing. But there were so many people involved with making movies, and Romanelli probably never saw anything going on during the production short of budget sheets and the occasional set visit. He wouldn't have been privy to every single day to day decision being made. He didn't deserve to die simply for helping to bankroll the movie.

'What about Spengler?' Zach asked, feeling himself, too, become angry. 'He had nothing to do with any of this.'

Dave shrugged, and that nonchalant dismissal of Zach's friend's death made him all the more angry.

'Not directly, I guess,' Dave admitted. 'But he got a percentage of what should have been mine. What *would* have been mine if I hadn't been forced to cut corners. Which brings me to you.'

'I had no idea - ' Zach admitted.

'Why would you?'

Zach suddenly realised that Dave hadn't remained on the ground because he couldn't move. It was because he was slowly, almost imperceptibly, reaching out towards the knife that had fallen a short distance away from him. So slowly that Zach had failed to notice any motion whatsoever.

But now that knife was in Dave's hand.

And Dave was suddenly on his feet.

Zach scurried backwards as fast as his knees would allow, tripping, stumbling, until he managed to lift himself to his feet. Dave advanced towards him, knife held up, ready to strike.

'Why would you care about anyone but yourself?' Dave asked him. 'You got *everything* from the movies. Fame. Money. Success.'

Zach almost laughed. Money? Sure. Fame? Maybe. Success? That depended upon your definition of the word. At that point, Zach hardly considered himself to be a success. A high number of credits in your filmography does not necessarily equate to being a success. It's more of a state of mind than anything truly measurable, Zach had realised quite some time ago.

'It's not all that, honestly…' Zach tried to placate the advancing Dave.

'And you're so *ungrateful* about it all. I saw you. I was watching you at the convention the other day. You said you'd be happy to do another *Furballs* movie and get killed off in it, so long as you got your pay check.'

'I - ' Zach began, but couldn't counter-argue the point.

'You would whore yourself out to those movies. To *my* creation. You even took the *name*! Calling yourself Furball all this time'.

Zach shook his head, vigorously objecting to that last part in particular.

'That wasn't - ' he stammered, but the time seemed wrong to argue specifics.

Dave took another step forward, Zach another back. 'Then you and Romanelli get together. Making money for each other once again. And here I am as well. It's like a little reunion. Thirty years too late.'

'Dave. Please.'

'I have nothing,' Dave exclaimed. '*Nothing.*'

Zach took another step back but found there was something blocking him from going any further. Something large and covered in prickles. A hedge. He was trapped.

Dave's knife arm lifted up high. He swung it down towards Zach with a cry. Before Zach had a chance to get out of the way, the knife found his flesh, burying itself in his chest. He crumpled to the ground, fallen before he could even cry out in pain.

A scream rang out somewhere behind Dave.

He whirled around to find Alice standing there, watching him. She held something in her hand that it took Dave a moment to recognise. When he did, he smiled. It was his own head. A near perfect replica and some of his best work, if he did say so himself. Alice must have taken it from the "corpse" he left laying at the top of the stairs to draw suspicion away from himself.

Alice was temporarily frozen at the sight of Zach's fallen body. Now she was on her own. She had to survive. She had to make it out, for the sake of everyone who had died, if not for herself.

She threw the head at Dave, who ducked with ease out of the way of its flight path, and ran back towards the house.

Dave headed towards her, his long strides making easy work of closing the gap.

Passing by where the night-vision goggles had landed on the ground during their fall from the window, and without breaking his stride, Dave reached down and scooped them up. He placed them on his head, but not yet positioning them over his eyes. Ready for when they were needed.

He broke into a run and headed after Alice.

55

From down the path, the officers saw Alice being chased by someone wielding a knife, wearing some sort of contraption over the top of their head. They watched the two of them run into the house, the maniac chasing the actress. Cole felt her heart sinking. It looked as though what they had been told was true. But they had ignored it. They could have helped prevent whatever it was that was going on here, but they chose not to believe the statements. There was going to be a lot of explaining to do, and Cole wasn't sure she would ever get over the guilt if someone had died there because of them.

As they approached the house, they saw Zach Keary's body laying on the ground.

Cole rushed over and knelt down to examine him.

He had been stabbed, and had lost a lot of blood.

Another one they should have been able to save.

She looked across at her partner, and could see that he, too, looked to be struggling with the decisions they had made over the past few hours.

In actual fact, Davies was more worried about the amount of paperwork that was going to come out of this whole episode. They had a dead movie star on their hands. There were going to be questions raised. *Lots* of questions.

Hopefully Cole would deal with the reports; she usually enjoyed doing that sort of thing. But they were sure to both be interviewed, probed, interrogated about what went on here, no doubt separately, too, so they had to get their stories straight to make sure they didn't land the blame for the whole thing.

'So we got here and found him like this, right?' he tried convincing Cole. 'We didn't see anything prior to arriving at the scene?'

Cole got to her feet. The killer was still there, in the house.

They still had the chance to save at least one life today.

'Come on,' she told Davies and marched towards the front door.

'You're seriously going *inside*?'

'It's our job.'

'We should call for backup.'

'They would be too late.'

'That's on them.'

Cole whirled around and turned on her partner.

'Enough people have died already, Davies. I'm not going to stand back and wait for another person to be murdered. Not if I can help it.'

She turned back around and couldn't help but let out a scream.

A bloody figure drifted around the corner of the house, heading in their direction.

Eyes wide, whole body painted red, clumps of organic matter speckled here and there.

Davies pulled his gun from his holster, raised it at the figure.

'Freeze! Police!' he cried out.

The figure kept heading towards them, holding something in its hands.

This was it, Davies thought. The zombie apocalypse had

begun.

Cole quickly stepped in-between Davies and the new arrival, forcing Davies to lower his weapon.

Underneath the gore, Cole recognised the person lumbering towards them: Jennifer Hughes, her cellphone clasped tightly in her hands, her thumbs moving in a subconscious tapping motion on the blood covered screen. Cole carefully pulled the cellphone from her grasp.

'What happened?' Cole asked her.

'Tim, like, totally blew up on me,' Jennifer told her vacantly.

'Jesus,' Davies stared her up and down. In all his time as a cop that was probably the most disgusting thing he'd ever seen.

'There was nothing I could do. I think I passed out for a bit. Then I hid. I only came out again when I saw you coming.'

'Go after them,' Cole ordered Davies, indicating towards the front door. 'I'll see to her.'

'But - ' Davies began to plead.

He didn't much like the idea of going inside when it was both of them, but to go in alone was downright stupid. A suicide mission if ever he saw one.

'Go!' Cole commanded.

Davies looked towards the front door, back at Cole, back and forth, back and forth, stalling as if he thought Cole would change her mind if he waited long enough. But Cole wrapped her arms around the blood-covered Jennifer and glared in Davies' direction. His lips had become extraordinarily dry, the moisture from his mouth somehow having made its way up his head and converted itself into sweat, prickling out of his forehead. He wiped it away with the back of his hand and hitched up his belt.

'Whatever happens, I want you to remember one thing,' he told his partner.

'What's that?'

'You're the one who made me do this.'

Cole rolled her eyes.

'Go. Now.'

Davies let out a long breath and headed through the front door.

56

Alice sprinted as fast as she could through the hallways of Romanelli's house, Dave hard on her heels. When she had first visited the place, she had been impressed with the building: so clean, so modern, so big. So *expensive*. It was everything she had wanted in a house, and, if she was completely honest, part of the thinking that led her to try to start a relationship with the director. He hadn't been her type, by any stretch of the imagination. But relationships were about more than love and romance and all of that nonsense. They were about what two people could do for one another, how they could help each other. How they could open doors for their career.

Now, though, as she ran through the building, Alice wished the decor wasn't so sparse; she wished there were more places to hide; she wished there weren't so many closed doors all around her; she wished she had never agreed to this stupid project in the first place. She wished she wasn't so very, very alone.

She reached the end of a hallway and ducked around a corner.

Dave wasn't far behind, but somehow she had managed to increase the distance between them. It could be that he was wounded, or at least still winded, from the fall. Whatever it was, it had meant he hadn't caught her. Yet.

Alice pushed a door open and fell into Romanelli's office.

She slammed the door shut behind her and ran towards the open door that promised a way to the outside.

Outside.

Escape.

Inside the front door was a pile of mushy, red, gloop that had once been Tim. Alice put her hand over her mouth, gagging at the site of the exploded body, trying hard not to throw up.

The study door opened as she was about to step over the mess to freedom.

She dived for cover behind the large desk at the back of the room, hoping she hadn't been seen.

She could hear Dave's footsteps. He was inside the room. She hadn't heard the door close again behind him, so he must have left it open. Alice realised her mind was subconsciously calculating escape scenarios, and she was impressed by her new-found skill, even if it was something she wished she had never had to develop, and definitely wished she would never have to use again any time in the future.

She listened carefully.

Dave was approaching.

Slowly.

Alice had nowhere to go. She was trapped behind the desk, and Dave knew it.

He was playing with her.

Movement outside the office window caught the corner of Alice's eye, drawing her attention. Dave's footsteps had stopped. He had seen it too.

Alice followed the motion and couldn't help but smile.

Zach was alive.

Standing in the open office doorway.

Hurt, bleeding and exhausted, but most definitely alive. And he didn't look like he was going to let Dave get away this time.

Zach reached an arm behind his back. The fire axe was hiding back there, tucked uncomfortably into the waistband of his pants. He brought it out in front and held it firmly in both hands. He turned and caught Alice's eye. She could see what he was about to do, or *try* to do. He didn't look like he was in any fit state to fight Dave. Alice shook her head slightly, telling him *don't do it*. But Zach gave Alice a small, sad, tired, smile and stepped through the office doorway, making it known plainly and clearly that he wasn't going to be backing down. Not this time.

'I thought I'd done with you,' Dave told him.

'Maybe,' Zach replied. 'But I'm not done with *you*.'

Zach couldn't help but wonder where that particular line had come from: it sounded too good to be something he made up in the heat of the moment; it must have been from one of his movies. He shook his head, trying to stop his brain from going over his filmography looking for the reference, and to concentrate on the moment.

Zach rushed towards Dave, yelling as he ran.

He swung the axe, straight towards Dave's head. Dave ducked out of the way, circled his knife back around towards Zach. The blade whizzed past, narrowly missing making contact.

Zach turned back around, swung the axe back and forth, trying over and over to reach his opponent. But Dave was fast on his feet, always able to avoid the swinging blade, launching his own counter-attacks with the knife.

Both wounded from the fall, they were too evenly matched for either of them to gain the upper-hand.

The front of the house was empty. Davies couldn't see anyone around at all. He looked up at the staircase in the centre of the lobby, across at the pair of hallways that branched away from the entrance, his gun drawn and pointing in whichever direction he happened to be looking at the time.

The stairs felt like far too much effort to climb, and he didn't want to risk falling back down them again should the need to run away arise.

One of the other hallways it was, then.

Sweat ran into his eye, stinging him.

He rubbed at it with his hand, but that, too, was sweaty and wasn't helping things much.

He pulled up the corner of his jacket and used it to pat away the sweat.

Davies blinked a few times, trying to clear his vision. More-or-less able to see again, he crept towards the hallway on the left-hand side.

The axe swung heavily towards Dave, barely even at waist height, and the intended target stepped aside as effortlessly as if he were allowing an elderly person to pass by in the street.

Zach was exhausted. The wound from where Dave had stabbed him radiated pain, and Zach could feel warm, sticky blood trickling down inside his clothes. He knew if he stopped he wouldn't be able to start again, but his choice of weapon had become too heavy for him to handle. He let the head of the axe fall to the floor and leaned against the handle, trying to take a moment to catch his breath.

Dave sauntered towards him, smiling the smile of someone who knows he's won.

Zach tried to lift the axe from the floor, but his arms had become too weak to even raise it slightly, never mind swing it around for a killing blow. The blade landed back on the floor with a clank.

Dave kicked the blade away. Zach, still resting against it, stumbled as his prop disappeared from underneath him.

Dave raised his knife.

No messing about.

Time for the final strike.

Dave thrust the knife forward with all of his strength.

Zach ducked.

The knife scratched past his ear, nicking his skin, and embedded itself in the office wall.

Dave tugged on it, trying to free the blade from the brickwork, but it was stuck.

Zach saw the predicament. He knew this was likely his only chance.

He drew together all of his precious little energy reserves and, with a cry of pain and great effort, he threw himself towards Dave. Dave pulled the knife free of the wall as Zach made impact against him, but Zach had taken him by surprise, launching him backwards, practically sailing through the air.

Zach continued to yell as he drove Dave across the room, through the door and back out into the hallway.

The endless closed doors lining the hallway were giving Officer Davies the jitters. The killer could be hiding behind any one of them. It was only a matter of time before a door burst open and a knife-wielding maniac rushed out at him, and he would be dead before he even knew what happened.

He approached each door with caution.

He tried each handle in turn, pushed the door open a fraction and raised his gun.

He shoved the door, full-force and pointed his gun straight out in front of him. If the creep had been hiding behind the door, he would likely at least have a broken nose, so that would be something. If not, Davies had full view of the inside of the room from the doorway.

It was a slow process, and so far he hadn't found anything or anyone.

Part of him hoped it would stay that way.

But a sudden crashing and yelling sound from down the hallway and around the corner somewhere made him realise this was going to be anything but a quiet, easy solution.

Through his surprise attack, Zach found he had the upper hand. He continued to use his forward momentum to drive Dave ever onward. Dave had his weapon in his hand and was desperately lashing out with it, trying everything he could to get at Zach, but the grip Zach had on him made it impossible for Dave to get the angle necessary to make any contact.

They fell together through a door across the hallway, straight into the kitchen.

Zach only stopped pushing forward once Dave landed against the side of a large, walk-in pantry. The sudden impact stunned the pair of them, and Zach almost lost his grip. He quickly corrected that mistake, and took the opportunity to change position, grasping at Dave's wrists, pinning them against the pantry to stop him from lashing out.

'Can I get some help here?' Zach asked, looking over his shoulder at Alice, who had followed them into the kitchen from a safe distance.

Zach indicated towards the pantry.

Alice caught on to his idea and opened the door.

Inside, the pantry was vast. And dark.

Zach manoeuvred Dave through the pantry door and into the darkness.

'No, wait, please,' Dave panicked as he realised what was happening.

He struggled furiously against Zach, trying with all of his

might to break free of Zach's grasp. But Alice joined Zach in helping push their assailant inside. Zach gave him one final, hard, shove, sending Dave tumbling into the blackness. He backed out of the pantry, and Alice slammed the door shut. She put the lock in place. Dave was contained.

From inside, they heard Dave pounding at the walls, screaming at them to let him out of there.

But his cries fell on deaf ears.

Zach and Alice leaned against the door and let themselves slide down until they were sitting on the floor, tired beyond belief, relieved that it was, finally, done.

'Is it over?' Alice asked.

'I hope so. I really hope so.'

Drawn by the noise coming from the room, Officer Davies jumped around the kitchen doorway, gun waving straight towards Alice and Zach.

'Freeze!' Davies cried out.

The sounds coming from inside the pantry stopped.

Davies saw Zach and Alice sitting in front of the pantry. He pointed his gun straight towards Zach.

'Well, look who it is. I thought you were supposed to be dead.'

'No, I - ' Zach began.

'Get your hands above your head,' Davies demanded.

57

Zach wearily lifted his arms above his head. Even as he did so, he felt pain in his wound as it pulled further apart. He could sense, if not physically feel, more blood spill from it, down his front. With his arms raised, the leather jacket pulled open, revealing his blood-stained, ripped top.

He tilted his head to indicate towards his knife wound.

'Do you believe me now?' he asked Davies.

'You could have done it to yourself,' the officer replied after a brief moment's thought, during which time he must have stretched his mind outside the realms of possibility to come up with some sort of explanation, no matter how ridiculous.

'Seriously?' a voice questioned.

Davies jerked to look behind him, whipping his raised gun around with him.

It was Cole, standing in the doorway with a slightly less blood-caked Jennifer beside her. They had taken the opportunity to go to the bathroom and wipe some of Tim off of Jennifer's face. Her skin was still more red than it should be, but it looked like they had picked off the clumps of flesh, at least.

'Jesus, Cole, you scared me half to death.'

'Put that thing down before you end up shooting someone,' Cole instructed.

Davies lowered his gun a little, but refused to holster the weapon.

'Where's the perp?' Cole asked.

Zach pointed the thumb of one of his raised hands towards the closed pantry door.

'You can put your hands down now, sir,' Cole told him.

It was almost less effort to leave his arms where they were than to force them to move again, reigniting the flaming agony in his chest. But Zach didn't want to disobey an instruction from a police officer, especially one who was doing what she could to help them out.

He allowed his arm to drop, flinching at every slight motion, and let his hands rest in his lap. Alice, in the first sign of any sort of compassion Zach had seen from her, placed a gentle, soothing hand on his arm. The warmth of her hand against him, even through the thick leather jacket, was reassuring, comforting. Human contact that he hadn't realised he had missed for a very long time.

'If you could move aside, please, sir, ma'am,' Officer Cole asked them. 'We'll take things from here.'

Alice took her hand from Zach's arm, and Zach felt as is he had lost a part of himself straight away. It was strange how that small, insignificant to some, piece of physical contact had affected him so greatly. Perhaps he was simply exhausted, physically and emotionally, from their whole ordeal, but he felt as though he could cry. He fought back the tears, not wanting to let them out in front of Alice or the police officers.

He tried to get to his feet, but the pain in his chest sent him collapsing back to the floor. Alice took his elbow (blissful contact) and guided him upwards, keeping hold of him until he was standing firm on his feet and not about to fall again. She put her arm around his waist and led him across the room where the two of them stood with Jennifer, watching the police do their jobs.

Cole indicated to Davies to join her by the pantry door. She motioned for him to stand by the side while she stood in front of the opening. She raised three fingers. Two. One.

Davies braced himself, took a breath and unlocked the door.

He pulled it open a fraction, no more than a couple of inches.

Holding his gun up near his face, he stuck the barrel through the opening and used it to crank the door open a little more.

'This is the police,' he called through the part open door. 'Come out with your hands above your head.'

There was no response from inside. Nothing but silence emanated from the darkness within.

'I said: come out with your hands above your head.'

Still nothing.

Davies turned to give an accusatory look at Zach.

'You sure he's in there?'

'He's most definitely in there,' Alice replied on Zach's behalf.

Davies looked across at Cole, uncertainty plastered across his face. He still didn't know whether to believe everything they had been told; it was so ridiculous, and all the evidence (or lack thereof) pointed towards it being nothing more than some sort of crazy hoax. But on the other hand, if this thing *was* real, he was going to have to be careful.

Cole motioned with her gun for Davies to go inside the pantry.

He opened his eyes wider, drew his lips together and motioned for *her* to be the one to go.

Get in there, Cole mouthed at him.

No, he shook his head.

Now!

He rolled his eyes. He didn't have much option. If he refused to go in, with Cole going in his place and she got shot, *he* would be the one to get it in the neck. Even if he didn't get fired, he would be mocked and ridiculed for the rest of his working life for letting a female police officer go in harms way instead of going himself. At the precinct they already knew that he tried to avoid any sort of dangerous police work, and would much prefer to be sat behind a desk with his feet up, filling in paperwork rather than taking on anyone in a potentially violent confrontation. This would be the last straw. He wouldn't even be able to transfer to another precinct - word got around in the police community about officers who didn't fit the mould of what other officers thought they should be. His reputation would reach the new precinct before he did, with no chance of him escaping the shadow of this situation.

He would have to go inside the pantry.

He gave Cole one last glare, hoping he would have the opportunity to glare at her some more on his way back out.

Careful not to open the pantry door too wide, giving the (possible) perpetrator an easy escape route, Davies pushed himself through the opening.

The inside was dark. Only a faint sliver of light made its way through from the partially open door, but the pantry itself was so large there was no chance of the whole room being illuminated from that small slice of light. He stepped into the darkness and tried to force his eyes to adjust to the gloom, trying to make out something, anything, about his surroundings.

'Hello?' he called out, but it was only his own voice that echoed back at him.

'Dammit,' he whispered to himself, now sure the whole thing was an elaborate hoax.

He turned around, ready to get out of there. A strange sound emerged from the darkness of the pantry. A *whirring*, like something electrical coming to life. A green glow appeared, an emerald spot suddenly springing to life in the black.

'What the…?'

The glow got bigger and bigger.

No, not bigger, but closer. Coming straight towards him.

Fast.

Davies tried to move out of the way, but too late.

Dave barrelled straight into him, the night-vision goggles over his eyes, the green glow of the power indicator on the front of the device showing that they were active. Knocked off-guard, Davies fell straight to the floor. At a speed that even impressed himself, he turned where he fell and aimed his weapon blindly. He fired a shot.

He heard a grunt as the bullet made impact.

Dave pushed the door open from the inside, flooding the pantry with light. He ripped the goggles from his face as he emerged, the light too fierce through the device to make them wearable, barrelling and barging his way past everyone. Too fast for them to react in good time, he fled straight out of the kitchen. Cole picked herself up from where she had been pushed to the ground, whirled around and tried to aim her gun towards him, but he was already gone.

'Stay here,' Zach told Alice.

'What are you going to do?'

'I don't know. I guess I'm going to have to improvise.'

He turned to leave. Even that motion sent jarring pains through his body, but he knew he had no option but to follow. He thought it was all over, that containing Dave within the pantry would have been the end of it, but now he realised it had to end the way that all of his horror movies ended: with the killer as the one being hunted.

'I can't let you do that, sir,' Cole told him. 'It's completely against procedure.'

'It's me he wants,' Zach said. 'No one else. I'm the one who has to stop him.'

Cole glanced across at Davies as he emerged from the pantry, limping from his fall, though she was sure he was putting it on as much as he could; a disability brought about in the line of duty was a sure-fire way to get himself put behind a desk for the rest of his time of service. He'd likely get some sort of compensation pay-out too. Possibly even a medal for heroism. Everything he ever wanted.

'Let him go,' Davies told Cole.

Alice took Zach's hands in hers.

She looked right into his eyes, looking at him properly for probably the first time that day.

'Be careful,' she told him.

'You too.'

He gave Alice's hands a gentle squeeze and left the kitchen.

58

Zach staggered into the entrance hall, blood leaking from his wound, escaping through his top, down the sleeves of his jacket, oozing out anywhere that it possibly could, leaving a red trail behind him wherever he went.

Standing in the middle of the lobby he looked around the deserted space.

He knew Dave was there, somewhere.

He had come too far, accomplished too much of what he set out to do, to stop now. Zach knew Dave had to complete the plan, one way or another; he wouldn't give up before he or Zach was dead.

'I'm here!' Zach cried out. 'Come and get me.'

No reply.

He limped across the room, over towards the staircase.

'It's just you and me. That's what you want, isn't it?'

'Absolutely,' a voice replied from behind him.

Zach spun around.

Dave was right there, heading straight towards him, ready for the kill.

Zach limped up the stairs as fast as he could.

Pacing back and forth in the kitchen wasn't helping things,

and Alice knew it. But she couldn't help herself. She had even started biting her nails again, which was something she hadn't done since she was ten years old. She was worried about Zach. He wasn't exactly the action star type to begin with, but his wound had weakened him even more. She hated to think it, but she was convinced there was no way Zach was going to make it out of any sort of confrontation with Dave alive.

She looked across at the two police officers.

Davies was sat on a chair, slumped back, his legs raised and resting on a crate Cole had found in the pantry. He was making a scene about his supposed injuries, about how he would likely never walk properly again, how this was the end of his time on the beat. Jennifer sat beside them, leaning against the wall, rocking back and forth with her arms wrapped around her knees. She had been violently shivering, so Cole had given Jennifer her jacket to wear, though it didn't seem to be helping a great deal.

'Suck it up,' Cole told Davies having examined him. 'You're fine.'

'I'm not "fine", and even if I was, which I'm not, the emotional trauma we've been through today is enough to give me doubts about whether I'm psychologically fit for street duties anymore.'

'Uh-huh,' Cole responded, making clear her lack of conviction about his answers.

'You weren't in there,' Davies reminded her. 'You don't know what I went through.'

'Sure.'

'I thought if I'd get sympathy from anyone, it would be my partner,' he sulked.

'Should have got yourself a more sympathetic partner, then, shouldn't you?' Cole told him and slapped his leg.

It took him a moment, but Davies remembered he should

be in pain, and let out a scream in delayed reaction over Cole's slap.

'What was that for?' he exclaimed.

'Why don't you make yourself useful and call for backup and an ambulance.'

Davies glared at her, but pulled out his radio and called it in.

'I'm going to help,' Alice suddenly announced from across the room.

'We're fine,' Cole told her.

'Not you. Zach. I'm going to help Zach.'

'What? No - are you crazy?'

'No one else is doing much, are they?' Alice snapped back at her.

Serve and protect? There wasn't much of that going on at the moment, and hadn't been for the majority of the day; why change now?

'I'll come with you,' Cole said.

Jennifer looked directly at her for the first time since they had sat down in there together, her eyes wide and fearful.

'Don't leave me. Please.'

Cole turned to look at her partner. He shrugged his indifference about whether Alice went or not.

'Take care,' Cole told Alice.

Zach hobbled his way along the hallway at the top of the stairs. He knew Dave should have easily caught up with him. He was sure he was being played with now. Toying with his prey. Enjoying the thrill of the hunt. Zach risked a glance over his shoulder. Dave was still there, a short distance behind him. He was grinning at Zach. Definitely enjoying it.

His attention focused on Dave, Zach tripped on something:

Dave's "corpse", still laid there in the middle of the hallway, its head missing from where Alice had taken it.

Nothing more than a prop dummy, dressed up to look like Dave. Expertly crafted, certainly, and the amount of fake blood covering it would had stopped them from immediately recognising it for what it was. Dave had been using his visual effects tools and techniques as part of this whole elaborate setup. He had cleverly arranged everything to make it look like he wasn't the only intruder. Everything had been set up by him, traps rigged to go off should they be tripped by any one of them. He was still very much the visual effects expert.

Zach threw open the door to the prop room and stepped inside.

He took out his cellphone to fire up the flashlight. It was already dead. Somehow it didn't bother him; he was strangely starting to feel safer in the darkness than in the light.

He hobbled around the room, searching for something - anything - that might be able to help him put some sort of improvised plan into motion.

That should do it: he came across a prop display for the movie *Ninja Shark Attack*. Not one that Zach had even been asked to do, which he was glad about, because he would have flat-out refused that particular one, regardless of how desperate he was for work at the time. A samurai sword was on show, held in place by two small brackets. Zach detached the sword, lifted it down. He unsheathed the blade and ran his finger across it.

He flinched at the sharpness of the weapon.

'Again, most definitely not a prop,' he whispered to himself, starting to wonder how many times in his career he had been in real, physical danger due to financial constraints forcing the production to make use of real weapons because they couldn't afford to produce prop versions. He shuddered to think, amazed he was still standing, even in the shape in which he currently found himself.

Nevertheless, at this point, he was glad they had cut corners on this particular movie.

He put the sheath down and withdrew to a corner of the room, clutching the sword against his chest.

Dave arrived on the scene, silhouetted in the doorway.

The whirr of the night-vision goggles springing to life.

The sickly green glow from the power indicator.

'There's no hiding this time,' Dave announced as he stepped into the room.

He closed the door behind himself, plunging them both into complete darkness once again.

59

The splashes of blood on the floor made it easy for Alice to follow Zach's path across the house. They took her straight into the entrance lobby and across to the bottom of the staircase.

She stubbed her toe and barely suppressed a cry that wanted to emerge. Trying to keep herself quiet, she sucked in a sharp intake of breath, keeping a squeal at bay.

Looking down, she saw that it was the detached animatronic Furball head that she had accidentally kicked.

Without thinking about what she was doing, she reached down and picked it up.

Continuing to follow the crimson trail, Alice headed up the stairs.

There were a lot of places in the collection room where Zach could be hiding. Dave scanned the area, the green display of the night-vision goggles helping immensely, but also giving everything a flat, two-dimensional look, the reduced depth perception making it tricky to navigate the space with any ease. It was still better than being in pitch darkness, of course. Just the two of them, together in that dark room, Dave knew he had the upper-hand. He could take his time tracking down

Zach. He could enjoy this final part. He could, and he would.

He stepped up to a display and peered around the side, looking for signs of life.

Nothing there.

He tried another.

Still nothing.

He stood up straight and surveyed the landscape before him, trying to come up with a plan. Looking behind each and every display in turn was going to take too long, and also give Zach the chance to move from behind one place to another, probably circling around, back to places where Dave had already looked. They could be at it for hours.

He somehow needed to bring Zach out into the open…

It was like the actor had read his mind.

Dave spun around at a sudden sound from behind him.

Through blurry green-lit images he saw Zach rushing straight towards him, a long Samurai sword raised high above his head. The sword swung in his direction, slicing through the air, ready to dissect anything in its path. Dave ducked. He felt the air move close to his ear, displaced by the sharp metal blade piercing the atmosphere close by.

He swung his knife to the side. It scratched Zach's arm as he passed by.

Dave turned to see where Zach was heading, but he had already disappeared from sight.

A trail of blood ran across the floor.

Maybe it had been there before. Maybe it was fresh.

Either way, Zach shouldn't be hard to find.

'You're hurt,' Dave called out in to the dark room. 'There's no way you're making it out of here.'

He tip-toed forward, treading along the line of blood.

It stopped beside the display for *Alligator Attack 3: Fresh Meat*.

Bingo. Zach must be hiding behind that display.

Dave snuck up to the side of the unit. He leaned his back against it, waiting in silence for the right moment, making sure he was ready and no sound was coming from anywhere else in the room.

He grabbed his chance:

He whirled around to the back of the display, thrashing and thrusting with his knife, slicing and dicing in front of him.

But Zach wasn't there.

He was slicing and dicing empty space.

'No,' Dave whispered.

Too late.

He turned as Zach lunged towards him with the sword.

It pierced straight into Dave's shoulder. He cried out in pain and lashed out with his foot to get Zach away from him. His shoe made a solid connection with Zach's stomach.

The blow winded Zach. He found himself tumbling backwards. The hilt of the sword still in his hand, the blade slid back out from Dave's body with ease, causing Dave to cry out with pain as it came loose. The air knocked out of him, Zach couldn't stand upright. He continued to flail backwards, knocking into things as he went, heading towards the windows.

All the time that Zach was falling, Dave advanced towards him. The surprise attack had only enraged Dave further. Zach could hear it in his breathing; thick, deep, dark breaths, heading in his direction. All Zach could do was back away from the oncoming assault.

He hit his back against the wall, beside the windows.

Nowhere to go.

Trapped.

He tried to lift the sword, raising it to aim in Dave's direction. But he was too weak even to do that, his hands trembling with the effort, knowing there was no way he was ever going to make meaningful contact with his attacker.

There was nothing he could do except await his fate.

'You deserved this,' Dave told him as he marched ever forward. 'You, and all those who turned their backs on me.'

'That's not true,' Zach argued. 'Sure, the studio acted terribly towards you - absolutely they did - and maybe I forgot who you were, and maybe you *are* going blind - '

'Have you got a point you're trying to make?' Dave cut him off.

'My point is, you can't just go around killing people.'

Of all the regrettable things Zach had said over the course of the day - or even over the course of his career, or indeed life - that was one that sounded ridiculous even as it left his mouth. He felt like a kindergarten teacher teaching little Johnny not to play with knives: *you can't go around killing people - that's not a very nice thing to do, now, is it? Apologise to the other children for hacking them apart, otherwise you'll have to go for a time-out.* The stupidity of the statement was lost on Dave, however, as he answered Zach in all seriousness:

'Well, I'm nearly done now,' Dave told him. 'After you, I'm finished.'

'Oh, you're definitely finished,' Zach muttered under his breath.

With an almighty shriek, Dave raised his knife high and rushed straight towards Zach.

Moving quicker than he had allowed himself to over the previous few minutes, Zach lifted the sword and slashed at the curtains covering the room's windows. Over and over again he slashed away the fabric, ripping them from top to bottom. Streaks of sunlight poured in through the windows, spilling into the room and chasing out the darkness.

The light hit the night-vision goggles Dave was wearing.

He screamed in agony as the sunbeams shone through the device and in to his eyes.

He ripped the goggles from his head and blinked furiously, helpless against the blinding whiteness that filled his eyes. The white began to shift. Shapes emerged from the snowy landscape, and the shadowy figure of Zach filled his vision, rushing straight towards him with the Samurai sword held in front.

'No!' Dave yelled.

The sword skewered his chest, through one side and straight out the back as though he were no tougher than butter.

He fell to the ground, the sword still in his body.

The door to the room burst open with a bang.

Zach couldn't help but scream.

He wasn't *alone!* Zach thought to himself. *I'm going to die after all!*

He cowered against the window, knowing he had no fight left in him. Nothing left to give. If it was going to end, he wanted it to be over quickly now. It wasn't worth the effort if he was going to die anyway.

'Are you okay?'

Zach opened his eyes at the sound of the voice.

Alice stood over him, peering down at him with a concerned expression on her face. For some reason she was holding the decapitated Furball head, but the reasoning behind that didn't matter to Zach. Nothing else mattered except the fact that maybe they were going to survive after all.

'I'm okay,' he told Alice.

She held out her hand and helped him up.

Zach staggered to his feet, unstable from injuries and exhaustion.

Alice tried to gently encourage him out of the room, but he was too tired to go very far. He made Alice stop, and sank back down to the floor. She sat beside him and placed the

Furball head in front of them both. Zach stared at it long and hard. Strange how that funny, cute, little make-believe creature was the cause of all the trouble they had been through together. It had been the start of his career, and it had almost been the end of his life. It actually *had* been the end of Romanelli, Spengler and Tim's lives. And he wasn't sure any of the rest of them would ever get over the emotional weight of what they had been through.

'Is it over this time?' he heard Alice asking him.

He drew his thoughts and eyes away from the creature's head in front of him and looked across at the woman beside him.

'Most definitely,' he told her with a smile.

Exactly on cue, Dave rose from where he had slumped to the ground. A great guttural roar came from somewhere deep within his body. He pulled the sword out of his chest. Blood sprayed from his body as the wound was further opened up. He rushed towards Alice and Zach.

Alice was frozen with fear. She had already entered a state of mind where she didn't have to fight anymore, and this sudden moment was too much for her to flick the fight or flight switch back on again. She couldn't find any way of reacting.

Zach looked around.

He reached for the only thing close by that he could use for a weapon:

The Furball head.

He grabbed it, pulled back his arm and hurled the animatronic as hard as he could, straight towards Dave.

For a small creature, the head was surprisingly solid, due to all of the robotics and mechanics inside the device. It make a satisfying crunch as it cracked against Dave's forehead.

Dave stumbled backward, immediately knocked out from the blow.

He fell straight onto the *Furballs* display case.

The glass shattered on impact. Thick shards glittering in the light and spraying in all directions.

All except for one large, vertical shard that remained in place in the corner of the case.

That was the one upon which Dave's body fell.

The shard sliced through the back of his neck before reappearing at the front, a sharp, bloody spike ripping straight through his neck and piercing his larynx. He was dead before his body stopped spasming. Blood spurted and flowed from the massive wound.

There was no way he would be returning this time.

A resurrection from that particular death would be hard to believe for even the most far-fetched of horror movies.

'*Now* it's over,' Zach declared.

60

The pictures on the cinema screen faded to black as the music swelled, the orchestral score reinforcing the full emotions of the final scene. After a few seconds, large white lettering appeared in the centre of the picture:

In loving memory of Francis Romanelli and Richard Spengler.

The editor had allowed a few respectful moments of black on the screen before the full credits began to roll, starting with the title of the movie:

FURBALLS 3: THE REVENGE.

The lights came up in the cinema amidst cheers and applause from the assembled audience.

Sat in the middle of the screening theatre, Zach and Alice smiled, shook hands, embraced and chit-chatted with the assembled throngs of fans, executives and other industry members. The premiere had been a success. The fans had been calling for the third part of the franchise for decades, and the eventual release was a nerve-wracking experience for all concerned. But the audience had laughed, cried, cheered, gasped and screamed in all the right places, much to the studio's relief. And Zach's. He had lived with that franchise - and all of the baggage that came with it - for the longest of anyone there, and now this third (and final?) instalment was out in the open, he felt an incredible weight had been lifted from his shoulders.

Now he could truly move on.

As the audience filed out, Zach turned to look at Alice in the seat beside him.

He couldn't help but smile.

He never thought he would be sat there in a cinema, having watched *Furballs 3*, with Alice Blake by his side.

He took Alice's hand in his, leaned across and kissed her.

The usual media circus awaited them as they stepped out of the cinema into the early evening light. Zach blinked away the harsh flashes of cameras going off right in front of their faces, making it hard to see where he was going.

He took Alice's hand and led her down the red carpet.

Fans waved photos, banners and posters from behind the safety of security barriers, screaming Zach and Alice's names, desperate to get that once in a lifetime selfie with their new favourite celebrities; at least until the next premiere took place and they had to switch their allegiance to whoever was treading the carpet on that particular day. Crowds still made Zach uncomfortable, and even then, a couple of years after the events that went down at Francis Romanelli's house, he still found himself scanning the faces, just in case Dave was there, somehow. Alice gave him a reassuring smile, and his hand a gentle squeeze. He smiled back.

Everything was fine.

Zach and Alice were guided towards to a journalist for *The Hollywood Reporter* standing beside the carpet, camera and microphone at the ready. Zach looked out across the red carpet, at the other bubbles of interviews being conducted. He scanned all of the familiar faces he had worked with on the movie. There was the director - a good man who seemed to have a knack for making horror with heart. Zach was sure that they would work together again, and probably quite soon at that. Officer Davies hovered uncomfortably at the side of the carpet. He had retired from the force shortly after the whole affair, somehow managing to wrangle a full pension. Even more incredibly, he had also managed to hustle his way in to being the "police advisor" for the movie, imparting his apparently valuable knowledge of the force upon the rest of the cast and crew, to give it added authenticity. Cole had remained very much an active member of the force, having received a promotion for her apparent efforts during the situation.

Zach finally found the one face he had been looking for. Not being interviewed, but surrounded by legions of screaming fans, cellphones aimed to capture the perfect selfie, Jennifer looked and acted every inch the star that she had wanted to be. Zach couldn't help but smile. She had bounced back better than most, considering the state she was in when the survivors left Romanelli's house.

Zach's view of the carpet was quickly cut short as he was physically handled to be placed in front of a camera ready for his own interview. After some brief pleasantries and introductions, the reporter launched straight into her questions.

She turned to Zach first.

This was one part of his job he hated, but he knew that - for some reason - it was a necessary evil. Why people couldn't go and watch a movie, enjoy it and move on was beyond him. They needed to know everything about the process, the people, the gossip, relationships…

He braced himself for whatever was about to be fired his way.

'Zach,' the reporter asked through a wide, forced smile. 'However did you get the mighty Alice Blake to co-star in this movie with you?'

Zach had wondered that himself every single day of the shoot. For a woman who had hated everything Zach stood for but twenty-four months ago, the events of that day had changed her perspective on things. A *lot* of things. When Zach had finished reading the script for *Furballs 3* he had asked Alice to take a look at it. When she was done, he had nervously, from a safe distance, asked her to play his co-star. She said yes almost immediately. He was so surprised, Alice told him later that he had asked her the same question over and over again, probably no less than six times, to make sure he had heard her correctly.

'Well,' Zach replied, pulling out one of the rehearsed replies to an expected question from his mental filing cabinet, 'I have to say, there was a fair amount of blackmail involved.'

He grinned, sure that the joke would hit.

The reporter, though, looked shocked. Her eyes widened, and mouth cracked open slightly, but there was something in her face that Zach recognised from countless previous interviews: the hope of a real, exciting scoop.

'Really?' she asked.

'No. Of course not.'

Zach almost felt sorry for the woman as her face fell, her entire body language conveying the deepest disappointment. The reporter turned her attention towards Alice as she tried to regain her professional composure and "you're the greatest star on the planet" smile.

'How do you feel being a part of one of the most beloved horror franchises of all time?'

A section of the crowd nearby, listening intently to what was being said during the interview, let out a massive *whoop* upon hearing their favourite movies being talked about in such a favourable light. It wasn't so long ago that Zach had been on the other side of the fence about it. But now, with the release of the newest movie, he was proud of what they had accomplished, and truly felt that the new film was a fitting tribute to all that had gone before, and hopefully a satisfying conclusion to the trilogy that almost never was.

Alice scanned the faces of the crowds that lined the carpet, their posters, photographs and Fuzz soft toys clutched in their arms, cellphones aimed in every conceivable angle to try and get a snapshotted memory of this day that was for whatever reason so important to them.

'A little bit overwhelmed, truth be told,' Alice admitted.

'I bet. And, tell me: when did you first find out that Francis Romanelli had written a *Furballs* sequel screenplay?'

That particular piece of information had taken everyone by surprise when it was first discovered. Of course, Zach was one of a select few who knew of Romanelli's obsession with all things horror, but the fact that he had written a spec script for a sequel was a secret the director had taken with him to the grave.

'Not until after… you know…' Alice tried to answer.

She felt Zach squeeze her hand a little tighter. The little extra security of physical contact that both of them needed whenever those tragic events of the past were brought up.

'After his brutal murder?' the reporter finished her sentence.

'Yes. That.'

'Who would have thought such a secretive, artistic, serious man would have taken the time to write what was essentially fan fiction for a genre he so clearly had no particular interest in?'

There were so many things Zach wanted to say to the reporter. Yes, Romanelli *had* been a secretive, artistic, serious man, but that was only one side of him. The side people didn't see was the playful, adventurous, humorous man who loved all those schlocky B-movies, serial killer sequels and giant killer mutant monster movies. The movies people watched for *fun*. The ones they went to see to feel something different. To feel excitement, adventure, and, yes, sometimes even terror. To escape from the real-world fears that plagued their every waking moment, like how they were going to survive another week in a job they hated; how they were going to patch up an apparently unresolvable argument with their wife; how they were going to manage to put food on their table that night; how they could possibly keep their kids safe in a world such as this.

Romanelli knew better than anyone the impact movies could have, and the therapy they could provide.

Romanelli —

Alice could see that Zach was about to open his mouth and likely upset the reporter with a rant about how no one truly knew Romanelli. To save Zach from making headlines for all the wrong reasons, she stepped in:

'How well do we ever know anyone?' she asked the reporter. 'Above all else, Francis Romanelli was a fan of cinema. It didn't matter to him if those films were high art or pure entertainment. To him, movies were magic. And that's all there was too it.'

She smiled at Zach, and Zach knew she had said what he wanted to say in a far shorter, more diplomatic way.

'How lovely,' the reporter replied, trying to bring the interview away from anything too heavy and swinging back around to make it light and glossy. 'One final question, please, Zach.'

Zach smiled his sweetest forced smile, fearing the worst.

'Sure!'

'When can we expect *Furballs 4*?'

Printed in Great Britain
by Amazon